DAUGHTERS AND SONS

A C.T. FERGUSON PRIVATE INVESTIGATOR MYSTERY (#5)

TOM FOWLER

Turning my rubbish visual ideas into an excellent cover: 100 Covers

Turning my mad ramblings into proper English: Chase Nottingham

Getting this book out into the world: Widening Gyre Media, LLC

For Lisa and Isabel

CHAPTER 1

A RINGING CELL PHONE IS AN OCCUPATIONAL HAZARD IN my line of work.

I ignored it. Tonight, I was off the clock. My girlfriend Gloria and I had just come from a play at a community theater. It was so memorable I forgot the name—without the assistance of adult beverages—as soon as we walked out into the night air. Gloria wanted to go to a fancy place for dinner. Had we gone to the Hippodrome, I might have agreed. A local production, however, called for Brick Oven Pizza in Fells Point.

The name of the place tells exactly what it is and how they prepare the pies. The lady who takes orders at the counter reminded me of my grandmother. Like many places in Fells Point, Brick Oven Pizza operated out of what had been a rowhouse long ago. Tables had little space between them and a large group could clog the whole floor.

Despite these apparent shortcomings, the place possessed a ton of charm. The wall featured articles testifying about the quality of the pies, and even a signed picture of some celebrity chef I felt glad not to recognize. Also on the walls, and covering the tabletops, were pictures of Baltimore as it existed decades ago. Gloria and I placed our order, walked past the arcade machine in the corner, and snagged a cozy spot for two. The people in line would need to fight for the sole remaining open table.

"I can't believe the business this place does," said Gloria. She'd barely unwrinkled her nose since we entered.

"A combination of quality and location," I said. "It's easy to get to when you stagger out of a bar."

"Speaking from experience?"

"Not much. We usually stayed near Towson."

A few minutes later, a short man served us our pizza. It came on a pan with a wedge-shaped spatula for lifting and paper plates for eating. Gloria looked at the single-use platters as if the man plopped a dead rat atop the table. "Paper plates?" she said.

"Only the finest for my best girl," I said. Gloria still bristled when eating at places she thought beneath her. She'd gotten a lot better about this minor snobbery in the time I'd known her. I used to find her entitled nature annoying—and I knew it made me a hypocrite—but it grew on me, and I've long thought it part of her considerable charm. To Gloria, tales of how the middle class lives are found in books.

I served us each a slice, then refreshed both our teas. True to form, Gloria cut hers with a knife and fork. I let mine cool for a minute, then picked it up and ate it. A group of six college-aged kids left, and a group of hipsters seized the table as soon as it became available. I considered this a downgrade. The two girls with them looked unimpressed, both with the hipsters and the restaurant. I sympathized with the former.

"What did you think of the play?" Gloria said as we ate.

"I think I would never have gone to see it if you hadn't sponsored the theater group," I said.

She smiled. "They're friends of a friend, and they needed the help."

I bit off a reply heavy with suggestion of some other help they needed. Instead, I opted to say, "Your career as a matron of the arts is off to a good start."

"Baby steps. I think what you do for people is great. If I could find some work with a charity, I'd do it." The idea of working used to be anathema to Gloria. She'd softened her stance when she saw how my *pro bono* PI service helped people. Somewhere beneath the entitled exterior, flawless skin, and bewitching curves beat an altruistic heart.

Gloria ate one more piece and stopped; I devoured another three. She made delicate oinking noises at me. This almost spurred me to a fifth slice, but I abstained. I got a box and put the remaining slices in it. Gloria and I walked out onto Broadway and headed toward Thames Street, where I had parked in a garage a few blocks down. As we turned onto Thames, my cell phone rang. I looked at the caller ID, prepared to ignore the phone. It was Rollins. I took the call. "C.T., how's it going?" he said.

"I just finished a late dinner," I said, "and now I'm going to drive home and ravish my lovely girlfriend." It still felt strange thinking of Gloria as my girlfriend. We'd formalized our formerly fun and casual relationship about six weeks ago.

"Before you do, I think we need to talk. I need your help."

Rollins didn't ask for help often. Ravishing Gloria would have to wait a while. "Come by my house in fifteen minutes," I said.

"I'll be there," he said.

* * *

A FEW MINUTES after Gloria and I got home, we heard a knock at the door. Gloria said she would leave us to our business and headed upstairs. I opened to find Rollins on the doorstep. He wore a salmon button-down shirt with the sleeves rolled up over his well-muscled forearms, dark blue skinny jeans, and dark brown loafers (with pennies). I beckoned him inside. His black head was still shaved as smooth as a bowling ball, but I noticed traces of blond in his beard stubble. "This must be serious," I said. "You put coins in your shoes."

"How could I not?" he replied.

Rather than offend Rollins' fashion sense further, we went to my office. I'd rented a proper office in the CareFirst building but still maintained the remnants of one here. My small desk held only a single computer and monitor, but I still rocked the leather executive chair. Some things cannot be sacrificed, satellite location or no. Rollins sat in a guest chair. "Thanks for seeing me on short notice," he said.

"Of course. What's going on?"

"You were right . . . it's pretty serious. It's work I'm not really cut out to do."

"I can't imagine there are many jobs you can't handle."

He grinned briefly. "A few."

"What's so hard about this one?"

Rollins crossed his legs. The skinny jeans hugged his calves. He didn't have socks on under the loafers. "A hooker hired me to look after her."

"Isn't that what her pimp is for?"

"Theoretically. She felt someone was stalking her."

"Eager john?"

"I don't know." He shrugged. "I haven't seen a stalker. I haven't seen anything to alarm me."

"How can I help you, then?"

"The hooker is convinced she's being followed. I can't watch her all the time. I can handle a stalker as long as he shows up, but finding people is more up your alley than mine."

"True. Have you talked to the hooker about this?"

"I told her I might have to refer her case to an expert."

"Are you talking to an expert after you leave here?" I said.

He chuckled. "You're the best I could find this late."

"I guess it'll have to do. What's the hooker's name?"

"She goes by Ruby."

I rolled my eyes. "Not, I presume, the name I'd find on her birth certificate."

"It's the only name she provided," said Rollins. "I asked her for her real name. She wouldn't give it up."

"I guess I'll see if I can get it from her."

"Female hookers are a lot more your speed than mine."

"I'll go along to get along there," I said. "Do you know who her pimp is?"

"I don't know. Some guy."

"Some *guy*?"

"What?" he said.

"Here I figured you'd be more progressive. This is the twenty-first century." Rollins rolled his eyes. I continued undaunted. "How long have you been helping Ruby?"

"She hired me three nights ago. I haven't seen a stalker yet, but it hasn't made her change her tune."

"Who have you seen around her?"

"A lot of guys who wanted to fuck her."

"She didn't seem scared of any of them?"

"No. She'd go off, and . . . they'd do their business. I didn't follow them for those parts, of course."

"Where would they go?" I said.

"A hotel, usually. The kind probably renting rooms by the hour, if you know what I mean."

"So she's not working in a great part of town."

"Route Forty," Rollins said, "from Monument up to around Moravia."

I pictured the stretch of road in my head. I didn't get to the seedy part of town he described too often. "Definitely not a very good area," I said.

Rollins smirked. "Good areas tend not to have a lot of hookers," he said.

"If they do, they have the class to refer to them as 'call girls.'"

"Touché."

"Big area, though. She cover it on foot every night?"

"Moves around. She told me she sticks around Erdman on weekends because a lot of guys come out of the strip clubs horny. During the week, she's closer to Moravia. More truckers and more no-tell motels."

"Sounds like she has a business plan all figured out."

"She's no dummy, I'll give her that."

"Surprised?" I said.

"I didn't figure too many smart girls got into hooking," Rollins said. "Being a call girl or a madam, maybe, but not this. This girl's putting in her time on the streets."

"If I look into this situation for her, are you still going to be around?"

"Not as much. She doesn't have to pay you. I feel sorry for the girl, so I'm giving her a good rate, but I don't think she can pay me forever. Plus, I don't want her working overtime to try, you know?"

"I hear you. OK, I'll see what I can find out." I looked at my watch. "Should be prime working hours for her."

"No doubt."

"What's this girl look like?"

Rollins pulled up a picture on his phone. Ruby had red hair —kind of a light, fiery auburn. It looked bottled, but she could have won the genetic lottery with respect to awesome hair colors. Her face was pretty with a delicate nose and soft lips. In the picture, she wore a short denim skirt to show off long, smooth legs, and a tight top to hug her curves. She looked a little thin for her frame but was certainly an attractive woman. I zoomed in on the picture. Her blue eyes looked clear. No bruising or signs of a beating marred her features.

"She looks a lot better than the average Baltimore hooker," I said.

"I know," said Rollins. "I don't see any signs she's a druggie or someone is forcing her into this work."

"Has she talked about why she does it?" I asked. "Or maybe what she's trying to do with her life?"

"I didn't ask her where she saw herself in five years. Figured I'd save that question for her next job interview."

"What I mean is does she intend to take over from her pimp, or open her own . . . business, so to speak? You said she's smart, and she obviously has enough money to pay you for a few nights. Maybe she's trying to work her way up to being a madam somewhere."

Rollins shrugged. "Could be. I didn't ask her. You can, though."

"I guess I'll have to," I said.

GLORIA WASN'T PLEASED with me leaving late at night but accepted it as a part of the job. I even told her I was going to look for a hooker, which made the conversation more interesting than it otherwise would have been. Such are the pitfalls of being me. On the whole, it's worth it.

I drove the Caprice to the Route 40 corridor where Rollins said Ruby worked. U.S. 40 goes by a few different names as it weaves its way through Baltimore; past Ellwood Park, it changes from Orleans Street to Pulaski Highway. It retains the name through Baltimore County, then goes back to being

Route 40 as it heads farther north. I drove through the city and picked it up when it was Orleans Street.

The area Ruby frequented might have been more vibrant in my youth, but the remains were not the kind of neighborhood to get lost in. The big draw was the Gentlemen's Gold Club with the rest of the area littered by shabby housing, check-cashing joints, convenience stores, and the detritus of bygone industry. The Caprice with its irregular blue paint let me fit right in. The Audi would have drawn too much attention.

I did a few circuits of the area from Monument Street up to Moravia Park Drive and didn't see Ruby prowling the streets. I saw a few other working girls with hard faces belying their skimpy attire. They looked more beaten down by the world and their profession than Ruby did. Maybe I would need to talk to one of them if I couldn't find her.

From across the street, I saw a girl who looked like Ruby cross a motel parking lot with a man in tow. Her hair proved easy to spot. I turned around the next chance I got and parked the Caprice a few spots away from the other cars. I didn't know which room Ruby and her john had gone into, and I wasn't about to knock on the doors to find out. I could have waited for them, but the idea struck me as unsavory, not to mention a good way to draw attention to myself. I got out of the Caprice and walked into the motel office.

The differences between a hotel and a motel are legion, chief among them being the severe downgrade from lobby to office. The Deluxe Plaza Motel, which was not deluxe and had no plaza I could see, featured a sharper downgrade than most. Two people with bags would have a hard time turning around inside the office. The walls needed several days of intense disinfecting before getting a few coats of paint. In addition to selling things like aspirin and maps, the gift shop stocked a wide variety of condoms. I supposed advertising the hourly rate would have been too obvious.

"Need a room?" the fellow behind the counter said. He looked oily, the exact kind of person who would work at such an establishment. He wore a dingy unbuttoned blue shirt atop a multi-stained wife-beater whose immolation would have been a mercy. He smiled at me like he had seen a thousand guys just like me before. My sense of uniqueness cringed along with the rest of me.

"Just some information," I said, showing him my ID.

His insincere smile vanished. "You a cop?"

"Does this say I'm a cop?"

He squinted and looked at my ID. "No."

"There's your answer."

"What do you need?" He busied himself with something on his old CRT monitor. I had no interest in knowing what he looked at.

I queued up a picture of Ruby on my phone and showed it to him. When he reached for the phone, I pulled it back. Boundaries are important, doubly so with motel employees. "I'm looking for this girl."

"Never seen her."

"Odd. I saw her go into one of your rooms a few minutes ago with a man."

"Wasn't her."

"Bullshit."

He looked away from his screen long enough to glare at me. It was probably supposed to be menacing. Considering the source, I felt non-menaced. "I said I ain't seen her. What do you want?"

"The truth. I know what she does. I'm not trying to make trouble for her, and I don't care what arrangement you have with her."

"Who says I have an arrangement with her?"

"Because I don't think she's renting your room for the whole night."

He looked at me for a few seconds. I guess he'd decided he hadn't seen a thousand guys just like me before. My sense of uniqueness stopped cringing. The rest of me kept at it. "Fine. She uses a room when she needs to."

"Same one?"

"I try to, yeah."

"You get a cut?" I asked.

"I thought you didn't care?"

"I like to be thorough."

"Sure, I get a cut," he said after a sigh.

"She make the deal herself?"

"No, Johnny Cochran came in and negotiated for her."

I gave the oily man a thin smile. "Look, asshole. You just admitted you have an arrangement with a prostitute. I'm guessing you have arrangements with more than one. You can either fake-smile your way through my questions, or I can call some friends in the BPD, and you can answer theirs."

He shook his head. I hoped nothing flew off it. "No. No, someone set it up with me."

"Her pimp?"

"I didn't ask."

"What's he look like?"

"Black dude but light-skinned. Kinda tall . . . a little taller than you. Pretty slim. Doesn't dress like a pimp."

"All right. Thanks. I'm going to wait and talk to the girl."

"Try not to scare off my customers."

"It could only improve your clientele." I left to wait in my car. Before I got in, I checked my clothes to make sure none of the taint from the office rubbed off on me.

* * *

About forty minutes later, Ruby and her john came out of room six, three doors to my left. I got out of the car and walked toward them while they chatted. They both peered at me as I approached. The john gave me a look like I intruded on something. "Ruby, I need a few minutes of your time," I said.

"I charge by the hour," she said, sizing me up.

"Take a walk, Jack," the john said. "The lady and I are talking."

"Your hour is up."

He turned to face me. This fellow was an inch or two shorter and about fifty pounds heavier. His combover, tussled from his tryst, couldn't hide his large bald spot. When he snarled at me, I noticed missing teeth. This was exactly the kind of man I would expect to patronize a prostitute. "I told you to beat it."

"I only need to talk to the girl."

He threw a punch at me. I blocked it. Undeterred, he threw another. I blocked this one and countered with a sharp left to the solar plexus. He took a step back and sucked wind. "Why don't *you* beat it?" I said. "This is only going to get worse for you."

He shambled to an old pickup truck, got in, and drove off with screeching tires. Ruby, to her credit, didn't run away. I didn't know if the fact made her brave or simply foolish. The line is often thin "We need to talk," I said.

CHAPTER 2

RUBY EYED ME WARILY AS WE LEANED ON THE CAPRICE. "You a cop?" she said. "This is a cop's car."

I figured she had more expertise with police cars than I. "I'm not," I said, showing her my ID.

"Rollins send you?"

"He asked me to look into something for you, yes."

"What did he tell you about it?"

"He said you're convinced you have a stalker, but he's never seen anyone stalker-ish around."

"Yeah," Ruby said, shaking her head. "He doesn't show up in any kind of pattern."

"Why don't we go somewhere and talk about it?"

"I'm working."

"I'll pay your rate."

She walked to the passenger's side of the Caprice. "Let's go."

* * *

I DROVE a couple miles up Route 40 into the county to find a place open after midnight. We ended up at the Happy Day

Diner. Both the outside and the inside looked like they had seen happier days over a decade ago. There is a difference between retro and old. Many diners are retro, paying homage to their heyday by decorating as if it were still the 1950s. The Happy Day was simply old. The benches were patchy and in some cases, even the duct tape strained to hold them intact. The décor begged for a refresh a few years ago. The staff looked like they'd rather be working anywhere else.

Our waitress strolled to us and pretended to be interested in what we ordered. Ruby got a coffee; I opted for a decaf, not wanting the caffeine so late and hoping the pot still clung to some freshness. "Let's talk," I said.

"Money first," said Ruby.

"You're a shrewd businesswoman," I said. Her expression didn't change. She would have fit in with the diner staff. "What's the rate?"

"Eighty for a half-hour, one-fifty for the full." She had the sense to lower her voice. The diner was about half full.

I slid her the money across the table. "For an hour, just in case."

"A lot of guys say that," she said with a smirk.

"I guess you don't offer refunds for unused time?"

She showed me a smile. "Nope."

Our waitress brought the coffees. I added a pack of raw sugar—which surprised me in a place like this—and enough half-and-half to turn it a pleasing brown. Ruby added three packs of regular sugar and no creamer. I took a tentative sip. It packed a strong taste but lacked freshness. Still, it tasted better than the swill brewed by the Baltimore Police Department.

"Do you want to give me a name other than Ruby?" I said.

She shook her head. "Not yet. Maybe never."

"All right. Tell me what's going on."

"There's a guy I see around every now and then." I waited for her to elaborate, but all she did was sip her coffee.

"No offense, but I'm sure there are a lot of guys you see around every now and then."

"This is different. He's always trying to hide somewhere, you know? Like he's in the shadow of a building or a car across the street."

"You recognize him?"

"No." She shook her head again, though not as hard as before. Her hair barely moved this time.

I decided not to press her. "How long has he been around?"

"I don't know. A couple weeks, I guess."

Our waitress returned. Ruby asked for a pancake breakfast with bacon and sausage; I declined to order anything. When the waitress left, I said, "Don't you have a means of protection?"

"I can take care of myself."

"I meant your pimp."

Ruby sighed. "He's good to me. Treats all his girls well, and that's pretty rare. He doesn't follow us around and hassle us. It's kinda like he trusts us to go out and get the work done. He takes his cut. If he has to be around more to protect us, the cut is higher."

"Interesting business model."

"It works pretty well."

"You ever need him to help you deal with anyone?" I said.

"Nah. I've taken some self-defense classes. I know where to kick a guy."

"Have you told him about this stalker?"

"Not yet," she said. "If he hangs around more, I lose money."

"Saving for a rainy day?"

"I don't want to do this forever. I have plans."

"You have a steady place to live?"

"I stay at a couple places," Ruby said with a shrug.

"You're not telling me a lot about this stalker."

"You're not asking me a lot about him."

"Rollins said you were scared." I watched her for any change of expression. She would make a good poker player. "You don't seem scared to me," I said.

She eyed the people sitting near us. They hadn't taken any interest in our conversation so far. "I'm spooked, OK? I don't spook easily."

"You don't seem like you would. Is there anything you can tell me about this stalker? Any particular nights he's around. Any area you see him more than others?"

"No, it's pretty random."

Our conversation bordered on non-productive. I hadn't learned much besides Ruby's coffee preference and late-night eating habits. "You said he's sometimes in a car. Do you know what kind of car?"

"No," she said with a shake of her head. "I haven't kept up with cars, really. It looks like an expensive ride, though. Not like yours."

"My other car is an Audi," I said.

"His car might be an Audi. Maybe a Benz. I'm not sure. It looks foreign and pricey."

The waitress brought Ruby's food. She dove into it like it was her first meal in days. I'd gotten used to Gloria slathering pancakes in butter and using enough syrup to give a diabetic a contact buzz. Ruby dabbed on the butter they gave her in the small dish and only about half the syrup in the mini decanter. She cut the pancakes as she ate them, placed her napkin on her lap except when she dabbed her mouth with it, and kept her elbows off the table. This was a lady of manners. How did she end up a prostitute?

"If I'm going to see this guy, I'm going to need to hang around you."

"I know," she acknowledged.

"I won't get in the way. You'll need to let me know if you see the stalker." I gave her a business card. She added my number to her phone.

"I have your info," she said, sliding the card back to me. "I'd rather not be seen with your card. No offense."

"None taken."

Ruby finished her food and glanced at her watch. "We still have forty minutes. You wanna fuck?"

"No, thanks."

"You married?"

"No."

"Girlfriend?"

I paused. "Yes."

"You sure?" she said with a grin.

"I'm still getting used to the relationship idea."

"Sure you don't wanna fuck, then?"

"You're a nice girl, and you're very attractive, but I don't sleep with prostitutes."

"You just protect them from their stalkers."

"So it seems," I said.

"You're weird, C.T."

"Ah, now you have me at a disadvantage. You got my name, and I don't have yours."

"I don't know your name," she pointed out. "Only your initials."

She had me there. "Fair enough."

"You going to follow me around tonight?"

"Maybe. I have some people I want to talk to first. I'd like you to text me the hours you usually work, though. I'll need to know when I should be around."

"I will."

I paid the check when the waitress dropped it off. She didn't offer to refill our coffees; normally, I would consider her neglect poor service but in this case, she may have spared us further pain. Ruby and I got back into the Caprice. I dropped her off across from the Gold Club. She promised to call me if she saw her stalker, regardless of when it was.

I told her I needed to talk to some other people, and I did. Cases involving hookers made me keep odd hours.

* * *

A PREVIOUS INVESTIGATION involving gang violence brought me into contact with a pimp named Romeo who began as a gangbanger. I've had a couple occasions to consult with him since then. He came with his large and menacing shadow, Tank, who possessed the most apt nickname in all of Baltimore. Romeo occupied a chair at a table in Crazy John's. Tank dominated the seat he'd taken. Crazy John's would not have appeared near the top of the list of places I wanted to go, but when one is meeting a pimp on the wrong side of midnight, one takes what one can get.

I slid onto a chair opposite Romeo and Tank. "Gentlemen," I said.

"My girls are out there makin' money without me," Romeo said. "Let's get to talkin'." Tank, as usual, remained quiet.

"I've become acquainted with a working girl. She says she has a stalker problem."

"Does she?"

"I don't know yet. She says her pimp is really hands-off. He trusts the girls to do the work and takes his cut but isn't around a lot. If he has to be around to handle business, the rate goes up. You know anyone who fits the description?"

"No, man. I don't talk to stupid pimps." Tank chuckled at his boss' comment.

"I take it this *laissez faire* system is not a business model you would support?"

Now Romeo laughed. "No way. You can't be all hands-off. The girls need to know you'll be around. They might need you."

"Maybe geography would help," I said. "The girl works Route Forty, the corridor near the Gold Club."

"Tank, who's that guy over there? Skinny cat."

"I think it's Shade," said Tank.

"There you go. Shade. He's her pimp."

"I might need to talk to Shade."

Romeo shook his head. "I wouldn't. If he don't like to be around, the girl won't want him to be. You going to be hanging around her?"

"Some of the time. I can't be there all the time."

"She got anyone else lookin' after her?" asked Romeo.

"She hired someone. He referred her to me, but I think he's still going to check on her."

"He sweet on her?"

"Definitely not. Any of your girls get stalked?"

"Here and there. Never for long, though." Romeo and Tank bumped knuckles.

"Are they normally just johns who can't let go?" I said.

"I guess. I don't ask them too many questions. Your girl get a look at this guy?"

"No . . . she says he always finds enough darkness so she can't see him well."

"You think she's lying?"

I frowned in thought. "I think she has a suspicion who it is, but I think she's telling the truth about not seeing him."

"Sounds like you got an interesting case."

"Don't I always?"

"Me and Tank gotta get back to work. Next time you call, I'm makin' you get food from a nice place."

I spread my hands wide and looked around. "And what do you call this?"

"A shithole," said Romeo.

I couldn't argue.

* * *

Weariness hit me when I got home. In my college days, I could stay up past 2:00 AM, get up not five hours later for class, sail through the day, and woo a coed at night. As the specter of thirty stared me down, though, it wasn't the case anymore. I crawled into bed a bit before two. Gloria woke up long enough to mumble something at me, then went back to sleep. I joined her within a minute.

Someone shaking me roused me. I opened my eyes. Gloria sat on the edge of the bed, her hand on my shoulder. Sunlight peeked through the blinds behind her, illuminating her chestnut hair as it framed her face. I couldn't recall seeing her look more beautiful that she did in this moment. "Wake up, sleepyhead," she said, sporting a lopsided grin.

I looked at my phone; it was 9:45. I hadn't slept so long without the aid of Percocet in quite some time. "Do I need to?" I said, still feeling tired.

"Remember, we have that luncheon today."

"It's today? I forgot all about it."

"I thought you might have. That's why I had your gray suit dry-cleaned during the week."

"I know what I'm wearing. Even better. Did you make breakfast, too?"

Gloria raised an eyebrow and snorted delicately. "Why do you think I woke you up?"

I figured as much, and I felt relieved. Gloria could not be trusted in the kitchen. She could use the coffee maker, pour cereal, and make toast, but beyond those basics, I wanted the fire department and Gordon Ramsay on speed dial. I tried to show her how to make pancakes once. A debacle of flour clouds and spilled batter convinced me never to try again.

I trudged downstairs, opened the refrigerator, and took inventory of the contents. I found eggs, pico de gallo, and shredded mozzarella cheese in abundance. The rest of my shelves yearned for a trip to the grocery store. For today, I would make omelets. I oiled two small pans and put them on the stove to heat while I cracked the eggs into a cup, added a splash of water, and mixed them with a fork. I poured some into each skillet and let them cook. When they solidified, I sprinkled cheese onto the right half of each pan and folded the eggs into omelets. While they finished, I put wheat toast down and brewed a pot of coffee. I flipped the omelets, topped each with pico de gallo, poured two coffees, and put everything on the table in short order. Gloria, drawn by the wafting smells, sat at the kitchen table.

"Refresh my memory on this luncheon," I said when we had both eaten about a quarter of our omelets and consumed some revitalizing coffee.

"The Nightlight Foundation," she said, "for missing kids and teens."

"You're involved with them?"

"I've started doing some fundraising for them. This is the first event I've organized." Gloria sipped her coffee and offered a small, tentative smile.

"I wouldn't miss it, then," I said, giving her a bigger one in return. "I'm sure it'll be a hit." I believed it, too. Gloria, for all her talk about not wanting to work, embraced a role of fundraiser. She'd been something of a socialite before, and while she still could be, her heart was in the right place. She credited me for her change. I, of course, would not dispute it.

"The supportive boyfriend," she said.

"It's me." I supposed I was.

After breakfast, Gloria and I both showered and got dressed. I thought about Ruby and her stalker. Did she work at this hour? Had her pursuer watched her to figure out the pattern of when and where she worked? Hell, did she even have a stalker? Rollins never saw one, and he didn't miss anything. Ruby thought she did. Maybe she noted different people and overreacted.

Regardless, Gloria and I had a luncheon to attend.

* * *

"How was the hooker?" Gloria asked on the drive over. "Ruby's her name, right?"

"There are many ways to interpret your first question," I said.

"I'm hoping there's only one."

"She's . . . I'm not sure. She's convinced she has a stalker."

"Does she?"

"Rollins didn't see one. He referred her to me in the hopes I can figure it out."

"Do you think she's telling the truth?"

"Maybe. She seemed pretty sure of it, but when I asked, I didn't get the sense she was scared. Most people are frightened of stalkers."

"Does she know who it is?" Gloria asked.

"Says she doesn't." I stopped at a yellow signal. Traffic light synchronization grew much worse over my years of driving.

"You don't believe her."

"Not entirely," I said. "I think she might harbor an idea who the stalker is but hasn't recognized him yet. Kind of like a hunch she can't confirm."

"Is Rollins going to stay around?"

"In some capacity. I will, too, but even between us, we can't be there all the time. We're certainly not going with her while she earns her money."

"That's a relief," Gloria said with a grin.

"Ruby's something of a mystery," I said. "She's smart. She has manners. Why is she a prostitute?"

"Do you think only dumb girls become hookers?"

The light turned green. I made a left turn. "No, but I think the odds of ending up a hooker and intelligence are inversely proportional."

"That's probably true."

"This girl is smart," I said. "She's educated. I heard her talk. She speaks colloquially, but I can also tell she learned to speak properly, maybe in a private school. Her table manners would make my mother proud."

"That's strange." I looked over at Gloria, who frowned. "Do you know if she's from around here?"

"No. I didn't ask her, and I don't think she would have told me. Think she's an old classmate?"

"No," Gloria said. "What are you going to do if you're around when her stalker shows up?"

"Please," I said, doing my best to sound offended. "I like my odds against some asshole who follows hookers."

"Do you think it might be an obsessed . . . client?" Gloria said

"They're called johns," I said, smiling at Gloria's lack of street smarts. They probably didn't delve deeply into prostitution at Brown.

"Do you think it's a john who became too attached?"

"It's a possibility."

"It seems like there's a lot you don't know."

"Welcome to my world," I said.

Gloria patted my knee. "It's still early in the case."

We arrived at Martin's West, and I pulled into the line for the valet. "Let's not worry about detective work right now," I said. "Go raise some money."

* * *

I ATTENDED events at Martin's sporadically over the years, but only once since I returned from Hong Kong. The venue looked like a gallery from the outside, with its front full of tall windows guarded by columns plucked from a coliseum. The ballroom featured a brown marble floor, neutral walls, a high ceiling with a chandelier designed to make Warren Buffett jealous, and round tables set with fancy napkins and utensils.

Guests filed in. Gloria mingled and greeted while I worked on a glass of mediocre champagne and a small plate of tasty hors d'ouevres. She engaged in conversation easily, held people's attention, and turned a sympathetic ear when the tenor of the conversation called for it. She knew how to work a room. The fact she wore a fantastic blue ball gown helped. It wasn't as curve-hugging as some of her other gowns—she came here as a fundraiser, after all—but I still couldn't wait to get her out of it later.

The event itself started right on time. Gloria joined me at the table right before it began. I'd made small talk with the other three couples at the table, all of whom were into their middle years. The chairman of the foundation, Vincent Davenport, opened with the usual thank-yous to all involved (including Gloria) and shared some anecdotes from his own experience. He established the Nightlight Foundation when his daughter went missing. Since then, even though she remained missing, Davenport kept the foundation going, and it served as both a resource and support group for affected parents.

Lunch came out after Davenport's remarks. Whenever I go to a fundraiser or reception, I always choose a non-steak meal. I have nothing against steaks, but I realize the venue prepares hundreds in advance. This minimizes the chances of getting one hot and freshly-grilled. I'd rather roll the dice with something else and rely on the chance it's fresher. The plate set before me held a generous salmon filet, a vegetable medley, and wild rice. Everyone ate and the sounds of intermingled conversation flooded the room.

After lunch, more speakers took the podium. A local FBI agent talked about the hard and often unfortunate science of missing children and teens. Despite the long odds, he encouraged parents not to give up, saying hope and a resourceful child could improve the odds. I bought the resourceful child part but not the hope part. Wishing for something didn't alter the probability of it happening. A few parents who had lost children followed Agent Hess to the podium. Each shared the stories of their missing children. Two shared happy endings. There were many tears and much applause.

The Martin's staff served coffee for dessert. While everyone accessorized their coffee, a presentation played, talking about the foundation, its work with parents and law enforcement, and stories of several children located, ostensibly with the organization's help. After the presentation, Vincent Davenport got back up, thanked everyone for coming, offered a few pithy closing remarks, and bid all of us adieu.

The crowd filed out. The staff cleared the tables. Gloria and I lingered. Vincent Davenport joined us. He looked to be in his early fifties. Most of his black hair retreated before the advance of silver. Round glasses covered eyes never holding the warmth of his smiles. He wore a suit I would have been proud to own and shoes I could see my reflection in. Gloria introduced us. "Mr. Davenport," she said, "this is C.T., my boyfriend."

It marked the first time I'd been introduced as her boyfriend. As much as I cared for Gloria, and even loved her, it sounded strange. I hoped I hid it well as I shook Davenport's hand. "Nice to meet you," he said. "Your ladyfriend is an excellent fundraiser." Gloria blushed.

"She's great at whatever she puts her mind to," I said. The color remained in Gloria's cheeks.

"What do you do?" Davenport said, hitting me with the polite prick-waving question every man asks another shortly after meeting him.

Before I could answer, Gloria piped up. "C.T. is a private investigator," she said.

"Very interesting," said Davenport. I couldn't get a read on his tone, but it sounded sincere enough.

"It usually is," I said.

"Ever shoot anyone?" Davenport said with a sly smile.

"Yes."

My response made his smile run and hide. "Oh. Well, I'm sure it's a professional hazard."

"C.T. is working a case now," Gloria chimed in, "but when he's finished, maybe he could help with some of the foundation's cases."

I thought it was a dreadful idea but didn't say it and hoped my face didn't betray my thoughts. Neither Gloria nor Davenport reacted, so I must have hid it well. "It sounds promising," Davenport said. "Always good to have another professional pair of eyes look over things. It sometimes takes one break to solve a case and bring a child home."

Or find the child's body, I thought. Instead of throwing a wet blanket onto the conversation, I said, "It's true."

Gloria and Davenport chatted for another moment before he excused himself to go to his office. I shook his hand again, then Gloria and I left. When we got into the car, I said, "What the hell?"

"What do you mean?" she said.

"Volunteering me to look into the foundation's cases."

"You don't think you could make a difference?"

"Sure. Odds are I make the parents more miserable. Not the kind of difference I want to make."

"You don't know that."

"You heard Agent Hess. Missing persons cases rarely end well. I'd hate for someone to get their hopes up because I'm looking at their child's file."

"I think it could be worth it."

"Either way, I'd appreciate a heads-up if you're going to volunteer my time."

Gloria looked at me and nodded. "You're right. I shouldn't have sprung it on you like that. I'm sorry."

"It's all right."

She put her hand on my knee and slid it up my thigh. "Get us home quick, and I promise I'll make it up to you."

I put my foot to the floor. The Audi's engine complied.

CHAPTER 3

AFTER GLORIA AMPLY MADE UP FOR VOLUNTEERING MY services, I pondered how to attack the case. Ruby might not be out and about in mid-afternoon—she probably did most of her work at night. I didn't know where she lived or how to get hold of her. I had an idea who her pimp was, and I suspected talking to him wouldn't help me or her. The less he knew right now, the better for all involved. I called Detective Paul King to see if he knew anything.

"What favor do you need now?" said King.

"I don't always call when I need a favor," I protested.

"The hell you don't. What's up?"

"You used to work in vice, right?" King worked the drug detail now. I envied him less than the average member of the BPD.

"For a few years, yeah. Still know some guys there. What do you need?"

"I'm looking into a hooker who goes by Ruby. You know her?"

"Nope. Hookers are a dime a dozen, though. What's so special about this one?"

"She's being stalked."

"Maybe she should stop being a hooker," King said in a tone suggesting his obvious suggestion was the one true solution.

"I'll be sure to refer her to a career counselor when the case is over," I said.

"You want me to ask around in vice?"

"If you could."

"Your wish is my command," King said and hung up.

Ruby worked the Route 40 corridor. If she wandered a couple miles up the road, or veered off down North Point Boulevard, she would end up in Baltimore County. There were a lot of places along North Point Boulevard for a working girl to ply her trade. On the occasions I've worked cases in Baltimore County, I worked with Sergeant Gonzalez. I called him to see if he could tell me anything.

"You find another body in my jurisdiction?" he said.

"I haven't looked yet," I said, "but if you give me some time, I'm sure I could uncover one."

"Jesus Christ, I've got enough work. What do you need?"

"I'm looking into a hooker who goes by Ruby. Know anything about her?"

"No. What's her problem?"

"She says she's being stalked."

"She's a hooker. Being stalked is part of her job description."

"I think she might see it differently," I said. "This goes beyond the usual leering she has to deal with."

"If she's being stalked. You don't sound convinced."

"I only talked to her last night."

"Hookers think they get stalked a lot. Sometimes, a john gets pissed she didn't do something right. Maybe it's a pimp trying to move in on her. Who knows? It's probably nothing."

"Just the same, can you ask around and see if anyone knows her?"

Gonzalez snorted. "It's a waste of time, but it's your time. I'll let you know if I find anything."

"Thanks," I said. He grunted and hung up.

I wasn't optimistic.

* * *

LACKING any better options for now, I took a drive through the city and looked for Ruby. I didn't see her. This time, I went up and down Route 40, onto cross streets she might have strolled down, and even waited in the lot of the Deluxe Plaza Motel again. A couple other hookers went in and out, johns in tow, while I waited in the Caprice. One of them plied her trade in the same room Ruby used the night before. I didn't want to think about the motel's sheet-washing policy, if it had one. No hooker tried to solicit me, which I attributed to the Caprice—it looked like a cop's car.

When I drove back, King called. "Tell me something good," I said.

"I asked around in Vice," he said. "Ruby's been brought in a couple times but never actually busted and processed. One cop used her as a CI once."

"Who is he?"

"Rudy Giardello. He's a good guy."

"OK. I'll reach out to him if I need to."

"Let me know if you do," King said. "He's . . . not always easy to find."

I interpreted this to mean he spent a significant portion of his time undercover. King probably didn't want an amateur like me ruining things. I tried not to be offended and said, "All right."

Gonzalez did not call while I drove home. At least I went one-for-two.

* * *

Gloria and I changed back into our good clothes. I wore the gray suit again; I thought Gloria would have a seizure when I suggested the gown she wore earlier would be OK after only being worn a couple hours. Maybe women's clothes were different. Instead, she selected a charcoal dress with short sleeves and a hem showing only a hint of knees. I showered and put on clean shorts and a T-shirt under my suit. Gloria and I got into the Audi and drove to my parents' house.

I wished we went for an occasion as happy—or at least as non-sad—as the luncheon.

We drove up my parents' interminable driveway, and I parked the Audi in front of their garage. Gloria held my hand as I knocked on the door. My father answered. He sported a black suit with a pressed white shirt and a black and gray striped tie. My mother popped out from the kitchen long enough to see us and disappear again. She wore a black dress covering her from shoulder to ankle.

They were both dressed for a funeral.

Gloria and I walked inside. We went down the hall and to the right into the kitchen. As I suspected, my mother had done very little slaving over a hot stove. Instead, she hired Esmerelda, a cook and caterer she often used for soirees at the house. Most holidays and at random times throughout the year, Esmerelda turned my parents' kitchen into one which would shame many restaurants.

I poured Gloria some wine and fixed myself a rum and soda. As we sipped our drinks, my father finally broke the silence. "Thanks for coming," he said.

"Of course," I said.

"I was talking to Gloria."

"Oh," Gloria said, putting her wine glass down and smiling, "of course, sir. I couldn't say no when C.T. invited me."

"It means a lot to us knowing he wanted you to be here. Did he tell you why we're having this dinner?"

"I don't know that he told me everything."

My father flashed a small smile. "He probably didn't. Thirteen years ago today, we lost our daughter Samantha, C.T.'s older sister."

"I'm sorry."

"Every year, we get together for dinner. It just . . . seems right." My father paused as if something troubled him, then continued. "We didn't do it when C.T. was overseas, of course, but—"

"I Skyped in every year," I said in my own defense.

"It still would have been nicer to have you here, son."

"We're here now," I pointed out.

My father looked pensive. He started to open his mouth, frowned about something, then walked into the kitchen. "Odd," I said to Gloria.

"It looked like he wanted to tell you something," she said.

"I can't imagine what."

My mother came out, smiled at us, then she and Gloria hugged. "Thank you for coming, Gloria, dear," she said.

"Of course," said Gloria.

My mother and I embraced. I noticed she squeezed Gloria harder. "Coningsby, it's always nice to see you."

"You, too, Mom."

"I can't believe it's been thirteen years."

"Me, either."

"Why don't you two sit at the table? Coningsby, you check

to make sure everything is set out properly. This is supposed to be a nice dinner."

"I'm sure Esmerelda did a good job." I knew my parents hadn't set the table, not when they had someone in the house they could pay to do it.

"Check anyway, please, dear. I want everything to look right."

"I will," I said as I rolled my eyes. We walked into the dining room. The table looked like the White House staff set it. Each space sported a fancy napkin, two forks, a spoon, and two knives, all set out as Miss Manners would recommend. A dozen guests with plenty of elbow room could fit at the table. We would use but a third of it. Esmerelda would pop in and out, eventually joining us when the night was mostly over. It went the same way every year. Esmerelda, for her part, didn't mind.

My parents took their seats across from us a minute later. Esmerelda dropped off a large bowl of salad, then left and returned with a plate of steaming mushrooms stuffed with crab imperial. She put some salad onto each of our small plates. Gloria used some of the dressing—it smelled like a peppercorn ranch—and passed it around. I looked at the wall behind my parents. Samantha's high school graduation picture hung there, right next to a shot of the four of us as she entered Penn for her freshman year. It was the last photo we took together. My parents only displayed it around the holidays and when we gathered for this dinner.

After we ate our salads and started on the crab mushrooms, my mother began her usual speech. "Samantha left us far too soon," she said. "She was a bright girl who wanted to help people and the world. I wish she had gotten the chance to use her gifts and show everyone what she could do. She would be making a difference somewhere today. I know she would."

My father and I nodded. Gloria squeezed my knee under

the table. I told her this may not be an easy evening for me. Just when I thought I was over Samantha's death, something ripped the Band-Aid from the wound. I've come to the conclusion you never really get over something like losing your big sister when you're sixteen. All you can do is hope the intervening years make it a little easier to bear.

"We set up a scholarship in her name after she . . . passed," my mother said. I noticed her eyes glistened. "Every year since, we've helped a girl go to college when she might not have had the opportunity. I know Samantha would want to be a part of something like that."

"She would," my father said. He fidgeted in his chair. He looked at me again like he wanted to say something but said nothing. I never saw him act this way at one of these dinners before.

"Samantha loved the idea of peace and brotherhood," my father said. "She thought violence was ugly and war was dreadful. In high school and college, she involved herself with student groups who rallied around things like nonviolence and equality. I know she would have gotten a job helping people if she hadn't been . . . if she hadn't died so young." My mother and father exchanged a glance. I frowned anew.

Esmerelda walked back in and cleared the salad plates away. She returned a moment later, setting a juicy slab of filet mignon before each of us. When she joined us again, Esmerelda put a bowl of steamed asparagus and four baked potatoes onto the table, then disappeared into the kitchen.

We passed the asparagus around and worked on our steaks. Esmerelda used a dry rub and marinade on the meat. I have been to many a steakhouse in my day, and I've never tasted a steak to top Esmerelda's. I stopped trying. She spoiled me for premium cuts.

When I felt full about two-thirds of the way through my

steak, I set my knife and fork down and took a drink of water. The rum and soda would have helped, but I downed all of it except the last bit, which I needed to save. Now it was my turn to talk. Even though I would say the same things I said every year, nerves clawed at me. Maybe having Gloria here amped me up. The familiarity of the whole thing should have helped.

"I had a few friends growing up," I said. "None of them were better than Samantha, though." My vision swam as my eyes welled. I took a deep breath. "I called her Sam a lot because I knew she hated it." I smiled at the memory. "We saw a lot of things differently, but she was always there for me like a big sister is supposed to be. I hoped I could be there for her when she needed me." Past my blurry vision, I saw my father fidget again. What was going on with him tonight?

I paused to use my handkerchief. Once I could see again, I raised my glass. "To Samantha Elizabeth Ferguson," I said. "Daughter, sister, friend, and the finest person we've known."

"Hear, hear," everyone said and took drinks from their glasses. I let out a long, slow breath. Gloria squeezed my hand again. I smiled at her.

"Thanks," I said.

"You were great," she said. "I don't know if I could have done that."

"It never gets easier."

"Good job, son," my father said.

"Thanks, Dad."

My father looked at me. He shook his head so slightly I almost didn't see it. He'd been out of sorts all night. I wanted to ask him about it but not while my mother was still in the room.

"I think it's time for dessert," my mother said as if on cue. "Esmerelda and I are going to put the finishing touches on something amazing." My mother walked into the kitchen. Esmerelda came in to take our plates. I gathered mine and

Gloria's and carried them in over her objections. She'd done more than enough tonight.

Back in the dining room, my father stood behind his chair. He managed to fidget even while standing. I looked at Gloria; she shrugged. My father inclined his head and walked toward the hallway. I followed him.

"What's going on, Dad?" I said. "You look like you can't sit still, and I get the feeling you want to tell me something."

"I do," he said, "and I don't."

"Should we flip a coin?" From the kitchen, I heard a whirring sound. Esmerelda must have been using the blender while my mother supervised. Each did what she was best at.

My father looked back at the pictures of Samantha. Her smiles could provide all the light the room needed. "We never told you," he said after a minute.

"Told me what?"

He looked at me, frowned, and shook his head. "Forget it," he said. "Just forget it." He started to walk away but I grabbed his arm.

"I can't, Dad. You've had something on your mind all night. What's going on? Are you all right?"

"Hell, I'm fine. Your mother's fine, too." He paused, sighed, and bit his lip. I don't ever recall seeing my father bite his lip before.

"Now you have me concerned," I said. "What's going on?"

He looked around at nothing. Kitchen appliances still whirred and buzzed across the corridor. "I wish we would've told you."

"Told me what?"

"I shouldn't be telling you this now." He shook his head. "I shouldn't be."

"After all this buildup, Dad, I think you have to. What's wrong?"

My father looked down to the floor, then looked up at me and took a deep breath. He was gathering his courage for something important. "When Samantha died," he said, "we told you it was natural causes."

A rush of blood pounded in my ears. I didn't like where this was headed. "A heart defect, you said."

He nodded. "She didn't die of a heart defect, son. Someone killed her."

If I held a glass, I would have dropped it. "What?"

"Don't raise your voice."

My mouth fell open. I wanted to say something, but I couldn't form any words. From behind me, I heard Gloria's shoes on the hardwood. "You lied to me," I finally said. "All these years, both of you lied to me!"

"We wanted to tell you, son."

"But you didn't." I punched the wall hard enough to dent it.

"You took her death so hard already," he said. "It . . . it seemed like piling on."

"You should have told me thirteen years ago, goddammit."

My mother popped out of the kitchen, saw what was happening, and frowned. "What's going on?" she said.

"Dad told me how you two have been lying about Samatha's death all these years," I said.

"Robert!"

"The boy should know. He should have known long ago."

"There's the problem, Dad: I'm not a boy. I'm not fragile. You should have told me." I snatched my keys out of my pocket.

"Coningsby, where are you going?" said my mother.

"Away from the two of you. You can both go to hell." I stormed toward the door. Gloria followed me.

"Son, come back," my father implored.

"Coningsby!"

I opened the front door, let Gloria pass me, and turned around. "Anything else you want to tell me? Maybe I'm adopted! Why not?"

"Son, don't be like this." My father's eyes were down. He couldn't meet my stare.

"Like what? The most important person in my life dies, and you can't even tell me the truth about it."

"We did it to protect you."

"A fine job you did of it."

My mother's head appeared in the doorway. "Coningsby, come back inside."

"Go to hell. I hate you both." I slammed the door in their faces, marched to the Audi with Gloria, got in, tore out of the driveway, and never looked back.

CHAPTER 4

I THREW THE DOOR OPEN AND MARCHED DOWN THE HALL to my office. Gloria closed and locked up behind me. Her footsteps followed me. I'd already logged into my PC. "Are you all right?" she said.

"No," I said. I thought of a much harsher answer; it was a stupid question, but I knew Gloria meant well.

"Can I do anything?"

"No."

"Do you need any help?"

"No."

Gloria stood at the edge of my desk for a minute. I saw her in the periphery of my vision as I hunted for information on Samantha's death. My parents' deception gnawed at me. Gorge rose in my throat.

"Can I bring you anything?" Gloria said.

"A soda would be good."

She went to the kitchen and came back with a can of Coke Zero. I took it from her, muttered something meant as gratitude, cracked it open, and took a drink. Gloria kept standing at the end of the desk. I understood she wanted to be with me, to help, to try and do something, but I didn't want her there. I needed a way to tell her gently.

"Would you . . . rather be alone?" she said, giving me the opening.

I looked at her. "I would."

Gloria offered a tentative smile. "I understand," she said.

No, she didn't, but I appreciated the effort.

* * *

I COULDN'T BELIEVE I'd been so naïve at sixteen. My parents shouldn't have lied to me, but I should have sniffed something out back then. No one in the family showed a history of heart problems, yet I believed my sister simply dropped dead of an undiscovered hole in her heart one day. The shock and grief must have made me stupid. I could think of no other explanation.

Self-reproach didn't help. I took a deep breath and focused on what I wanted to do. Samantha was murdered thirteen years ago. When pretty college girls get murdered, there tends to be a story about it. I went combing through *The Sun*'s archives to see what I could unearth. As I looked for a story, I wondered if I really wanted to find anything. Unearthing a story would mean my parents lied to me, Samantha was indeed murdered, and I'd lived oblivious to this cruel ruse for almost half my life. Not finding a story wouldn't have made any of it untrue, but it would have softened the blow.

My parents called. I ignored it. A story popped up. Greg Elliot wrote the article about the murder of a pretty blonde college freshman at Penn. The victim's name was not released out of respect for her family. I read the article as my eyes welled again.

The unnamed victim—I knew her name, dammit—engaged

in extracurricular activities at Penn. She popped home for a long weekend and ended up in Patterson Park for unlisted reasons. Stabbed a dozen times, and any of them could have been fatal. The police announced no motive and no suspects.

Patterson Park. I could get there in ten minutes. I grabbed the keys to the Audi and started out. Gloria sat in the living room. "Where are you going?" she said as I opened the door.

"I found a story saying Sam's body was found in Patterson Park," I said.

"C.T., that was thirteen years ago. What do you expect to find tonight after all these years?"

"I don't know!" I shook my head. Yelling wouldn't solve anything, and I didn't want to drive Gloria away. "I don't know," I said in a softer tone. "Something. Anything."

"What do you want to do?"

"I want to find the bastard who killed my sister."

"And then what?"

I patted the gun holstered at my side. "Then I'm going to shoot him in the head." I stormed out of the house.

* * *

PATTERSON PARK IS A HUGE PLACE, bordered by Eastern Avenue, Patterson Park Avenue, South Linwood Avenue, and East Baltimore Street. The bulk of it is square in shape and at least 1500 feet per side. Across Linwood Avenue lay a couple more baseball diamonds and some jogging trails. Even without this additional acreage, Patterson Park comprised over two million square feet. The article offered a general description of where someone found Samantha's body. It helped.

I left the Audi and walked through the commons to the area mentioned, the quadrant near the Baltimore-Linwood intersection. I didn't know what the area looked like thirteen years ago; now it was mostly tennis courts, softball fields, trees, and jogging trails. It probably hadn't changed much over the years but regardless, I faced long odds of learning anything useful. The police would have found obvious physical evidence. Non-obvious proof would have been washed away in the rain, frozen in the snow, boiled in the summer heat, or any of a number of fates.

I needed to try. I needed to feel like I accomplished something. Darkness had long settled in, and even though street-lights illuminated the surroundings, not many people availed themselves of Patterson Park tonight. I took out my flashlight, found a useful stick on a tree, and used it to help search the ground, the trees, the dirt on the baseball diamonds, anything I could find looking searchable. I found a couple bottles, cans, papers, wrappers of various types, and two used condoms, but nothing I could point to as relating to Samantha's death—to her murder. I needed to think of it the right way. Thirteen years of deceit led to a hard mental habit to break.

My fruitless search cost me over an hour and a half and earned me my share of funny looks. True to form, no one said anything as if a dashing, well-dressed man with a flashlight and stick could be seen most nights in the park. I got back into the Audi and drove toward home, wondering what my next move would be.

* * *

ON THE WAY to my house, I detoured into downtown and stopped at the medical examiner's office. I walked in and headed back to the morgue. I sucked in a deep breath and pushed the door open. The rooms were well ventilated, but I always wanted to be ready if the system failed. I walked to the rearmost part of the examining room to see who was working tonight. In a stroke of good fortune, Dr. Gary Hunt looked up from a fresh cadaver. He frowned at me like he always does, and said, "Come to exploit your devil's bargain some more?" he said.

"You entered the bargain, doctor," I said. "I don't mind wearing the horns." A year ago, I discovered Dr. Hunt took a bribe to release a woman's body to her killer. I sorted the whole mess out, managed to keep Dr. Hunt away from it, and came to him for information when I needed it. He never seemed happy with the arrangement even though he got to keep his job.

"What is it this time?"

I sat on a stool at a desk near the table where Dr. Hunt worked. "Thirteen years ago tonight, my sister died. I just found out she was murdered."

"Wow." He looked up. "I'm sorry."

I nodded. "It's an old case, and I don't know what I can find at this point. I'm . . . I don't know what I'm doing. I have to figure out who killed her."

"Thirteen years is a long time for a trail to go cold. I'm not sure what I can do for you."

"I found an article. It said she was stabbed a dozen times in the chest." Hunt winced. I couldn't blame him. "Do . . . do you think she suffered?"

He put his tools down and sighed. "I don't know," he said. "For her sake . . . and for yours . . . I hope not, but I can't say without examining the body. If forced to guess, I would say she didn't suffer much. A deep stab wound in the chest is going to be fatal. More only speeds the process along." He paused. "Sorry, I'm sure my explanation sounded indelicate."

"It's OK," I said.

"If you uncover any evidence and want an opinion on it, come by and talk to me."

"I'm not sure what I can find after all this time but thanks."

"Don't mention it. Please." Hunt gave me an uncertain and tiny smile.

"I won't."

I left the ME's office and got back into my car. At least I could rely on Dr. Hunt if I found any evidence.

Now all I needed to do was find some.

* * *

I WENT BACK HOME and scoured any records I could. Thirteen years ago, the Internet had not been built into the technological behemoth it has become. Still, newspapers went online, people maintained blogs, the death spiral of newsgroups hadn't finished yet, and those combinations gave me more options for my search. I also jotted down a note to find and contact Greg Elliot. Maybe he remembered some detail of the story omitted from the final edition.

Before, I combed through *The Sun*'s archives. Now I expanded my search to other papers. The Baltimore *City Paper* and other assorted small local rags made a good place to start. I also looked for blogs and newsgroup posts related to Samantha's death. While my searches crunched, Gloria came down the stairs and poked her head in. "You feeling about the same?" she said.

I nodded. "Yes. Probably will be for a while."

"Your parents called me."

"Did you tell them to drop dead?"

"I would never say something like that to them. You shouldn't even think it."

"You're right," I admitted. "Suffice it to say I won't be talking to them anytime soon."

"I told them you were mad."

I looked up at her. Something in my expression made Gloria frown. "'Mad' doesn't even begin to cut it."

She leaned on the doorframe. "Do you want to talk about it?"

"Not now. I still have too much to do."

"Are you coming upstairs at all?"

"I don't know. Sleep isn't high on my priority list right now."

"I understand," she said for the second time—and for the second time, she was wrong. I let it go, though.

"Thanks," I said. I looked at my screen in time to see a newsgroup result. The gruesome alt.local.baltimore.homicides featured something about Samantha. The author was some twit with a handle I didn't want to figure out. He reiterated the information from the *Sun* article without adding anything new save some useless commentary on the frequency of crimes happening near Patterson Park. I checked responses and posts for the next few days on the newsgroup and found nothing related to Samantha.

The *City Paper* featured only a brief story of four paragraphs in length. It laid out the bare facts and little else, telling me nothing I didn't already know (though doing so with an impressive paucity of words). I jotted this reporter's name, Brad Allen, down as well, in case he knew something he didn't incorporate into his story.

It hit me how I'd exhausted all the options for finding news about a story happening years ago. No one knew much about what happened to Samantha. If I found any evidence, I could take it to Dr. Hunt, but I needed a lot more information before I could even figure out where to search. I couldn't give up. This was my sister's murder. I needed to solve it. I felt driven to succeed where everyone else failed. She deserved it.

Two hours into the case, and it had already bottomed out. It gave me an idea: I dealt with someone who saw bottomed-out people and heard horrible stories all the time. Maybe he would strike a spark of an idea and give me a new avenue to pursue. I looked at my watch. I knew he'd be asleep, but I didn't care.

I got in the car again.

*　*　*

I BANGED on Joey Trovato's door three times before I heard footsteps. Joey pulled open the door as far as the chain lock would allow. He looked at me through bleary, half-closed eyes. "C.T.? What the hell are you doing here?" Joey looked at his wrist, but it held no watch. "It's . . ."

"Halfway to oh-dark-thirty, I know," I said. "Can I come in?"

Joey undid the chain lock and pulled the door open. His right hand, hidden the whole time, held a 9MM handgun. Normally, I would make a crack about the pizza guy getting aggressive for a tip, but I didn't have it in me tonight. "What's going on?" Joey walked into his living room and plopped onto his recliner. The air hissed out of the cushion in protest.

I sat on the couch and turned a lamp on. Joey squinted in the brightness. "You remember my sister," I said. Joey and I remained friends since grade school.

"Sure," he said. "It's been a long time, though."

"Thirteen years tonight . . . last night, by this time."

"Wow. I didn't realize. My bad."

I waved it off. "Joey, my parents lied to me for thirteen years. Last night, my father told me Samantha was murdered.

"Holy shit." Joey's eyes went wide. "Why did they keep it from you all this time?"

"Some bullshit about protecting me. Even if they thought I

needed it at the time, they've wasted plenty of opportunities to tell me over the years."

"Wow, this is fucked up."

I looked at Joey. He was a black Sicilian of good humor—with allowances for being awakened at odd hours—and better appetite. After Joey's parents died in a car accident—less than a year after Samantha's death, in fact—my parents always hosted him for holidays and special occasions. They all liked each other. He might feel like he owed them something—something other than an enormous food bill. "You didn't know, did you?"

"What?" he said, looking genuinely surprised at my accusation. "No way! I would never keep something so important from you." Joey looked back at me. "Never."

"All right," I said. I believed him.

"What can I do?"

"I'm not sure there's anything you *can* do at this point. It's a thirteen-year-old case. I'm going to look into it as best I can, but it's possible I won't be able to uncover anything new."

"Let's say you do. Let's say you find the son of a bitch who killed her. What are you going to do?"

"Shoot him. Right in the face. I want to see his expression when it happens." I pictured the scenario in my mind. "I want to see the knowledge etched in his eyes he's getting what he deserves."

"You're not a killer, C.T.," Joey said.

"We both know I've pulled the trigger."

"Different situations."

"Whatever," I said. "I can be a killer this time."

"Maybe."

"You trying to talk me out of it?"

Joey shrugged. "You do what you think is right. If you do it, let me know when it goes down. I'll need a little time to prepare an alibi."

My smile was real for the first time since hearing the news."Thanks, Joey."

"What are friends for, right? Look, if I'm going to be awake, I'm going to put some coffee on. You want any?"

"Sure. I think I'll be awake for a while, too."

* * *

JOEY always demonstrated good taste in food, which showed in his waistline. His discernment extended to coffee. He brewed an Italian roast ("never trust the fucking French to make anything," he said), to which I added some sugar and milk. It'd been a long day and longer night, and I needed the caffeine to take the edge off of everything. The warmth cascaded down my throat. If it did nothing for my alertness, at least it tasted good.

We sat at Joey's breakfast nook. He owned a proper dining room table, but the smaller one worked for our impromptu *tête-à-tête*. Joey, never one to let any situation pass without food, crammed half of a bear claw pastry into his mouth. I long ago lost my surprise at Joey's capacity to eat. How he maintained the physique he did was a mystery. Joey wouldn't win any fitness contests, but his girth belied some actual conditioning, like a lineman in football. I wouldn't wager on Joey to win many races, but I knew a few people in better shape I'd pit him against, especially if a table of hot dogs awaited at the finish line.

"What are you going to do now?" Joey said when he finished chewing and swallowing his daily allotment of carbs and empty sugars.

"I'm not sure," I said.

"You working anything else?"

"I started looking into something for a hooker."

"A hooker? A bit outside your usual clientele."

"Rollins referred her to me. She says she's being stalked. He didn't see it but asked me to look into it."

"Did you?"

"I talked to the girl," I said. "She seems sincere enough, but who knows? Besides, I have a more pressing case now."

"You have a picture of her?" Joey said.

"Why, you need a party date?"

"No, I'm wondering if she's a past client. It's not like I've never helped a hooker before." Joey worked in the field of identity management in a very specific way: he knew how to create new identities for people and set them on the road to a different life. He worked with people who'd bottomed out and owned little but a bad beat story and the wherewithal to cover the fees.

"I do, actually. Rollins texted me a picture." I queued it up on my phone and showed it to Joey.

"Pretty." His eyes scanned the picture. "The hair's a distinctive shade of red. Hard to tell in the shot, but I'll bet she has nice tits."

"She does."

"Probably helps in her line of work." He paused. "What are you going to do if this girl really does have a stalker?"

I shrugged. "I don't know. I hadn't thought about it."

"Understandable. I know you want to find out who killed Samantha, but even you said the trail is cold. It's not like it's going to be consuming your every waking minute."

"Only my every thought."

"Not true. Gloria will bend over to pick something up, and I'll bet your thoughts shift."

"They would."

"So you can still find the time to help this hooker."

"Why do you care if I do?"

"Kinda like you, I help people when they don't have much other recourse. I guess I'm a softie."

"Certainly around the middle."

"You're hilarious."

"OK, I'll make some time for Ruby. I can't make her the priority, though. Sam has to come first."

"You look at the police report yet?"

I closed my eyes and shook my head. Of course. Even though my parents said otherwise for thirteen years, Samantha in fact was murdered. Someone found her body. The police would have investigated. Even if they found no compelling evidence to point to a suspect, they would still have notes and findings I could review. I knew what I would do when I got home. "No, but thanks for reminding me," I said. "I didn't think about it."

"You've got a lot on your mind." Joey tore into another bear claw.

"I have. Thanks, Joey."

"What are friends for?" Joey said around a mouthful of pastry.

CHAPTER 5

I GOT HOME AGAIN, CLOSED THE DOOR, AND HEADED TO THE office. During the first case I worked, my cousin Rich, then a uniformed sergeant with the BPD, left me at his unattended computer long enough for me to snag its IP information. Since then, the BPD's network has been my digital playground. Rich knows I access the network, but he never reports it or tries to stop me; huffing about it seems to temper whatever moral obligation he feels.

I accessed the BPD's network and prowled for anything I could find on Samantha. Nothing. I couldn't be surprised. What detective would have a thirteen year-old case file on the corner of his desk, waiting for a day with nothing else to do so he could dig up what no one unearthed before? I double-checked myself but didn't find anything on the second sweep either.

Despite the coffee I drank at Joey's, weariness settled on me. My eyelids felt heavy, and my eyes grew dry if I stared at anything too long. I heard Gloria pad down the hallway. "Still at it?" she said, coming into the office. She wore one of my T-shirts, which fit her like a short nightgown.

"I have to be," I said.

"You need to sleep."

"I need to find out who killed my sister!"

"C.T., it was thirteen years ago. How do you know that whoever killed her isn't already dead? Or in jail for doing something else?"

Her point was valid. "I don't," I admitted.

"It's almost four. You've been at this for hours. You'll be able to do a better job once you've had some rest."

"I feel like I'm letting her down if I give up and go to sleep."

"You're not giving up. You can try again tomorrow."

I looked at my monitor. A whole lot of nothing stared back at me. I'd spent hours tilting at a windmill after I left my parents' house, and all I discovered were the names of two reporters. Like Samantha's killer, they could have died in the intervening years. If they still lived, I doubted they'd be receptive to being awakened in the middle of the night by someone asking about articles they probably forgot writing.

"All right," I said. "Tomorrow." I got up and walked to where Gloria stood. She grabbed my hand, squeezed it, and smiled. I let her lead me upstairs, where I fell asleep almost as soon as I lay down.

* * *

THE NEXT MORNING, I rolled over to find Gloria gone. The alarm clock showed me it was 10:30. I'd slept about six and a half hours. It would have to do. I used some mouthwash and went downstairs. Gloria sat at the kitchen table drinking orange juice. "Good morning, sleepyhead," she said with a smile. I felt a dark cloud stir and blow away as she smiled at me.

"How long have you been up?"

"Long enough to get breakfast." Gloria pointed to the

counter near the coffee maker. "I picked up some things from Panera."

"I knew I loved you for a reason," I said as I investigated the bag. I grabbed a wheat bagel and popped it in the toaster. While it browned, I poured a cup of coffee and noshed on a fruit danish. I put butter and jelly on half the bagel and peanut butter on the other.

"What are you going to do today?" Gloria said as I joined her at the kitchen table.

I sipped some coffee. "Try to approach this rationally," I said. "Last night, I went after things half-cocked. If I'm going to find out who killed my sister, I have to be smarter."

"That's good to hear. I didn't want you to burn out or do something reckless and get hurt."

"I'm probably lucky I didn't."

"What are you going to do about the hooker you were working with?"

"I don't know. Hope she doesn't need me much for a while, I guess."

"What if she does?" said Gloria.

"This is more important."

"I know it is to you, but she might need you."

I nodded. "I know. I guess I'll talk to Rollins. Maybe he can keep an eye on her for a while."

"He needed your help with this, remember."

"I figured you'd be happy I wasn't spending so much time with a hooker."

Gloria chuckled. "I'm not worried about that. I only know she's someone who needs your help."

"I get it," I said. "I'll make time for her. But Samantha's case is the priority."

"I understand." Gloria said the phrase a lot recently. Maybe this time, she actually did understand.

After I finished breakfast, I went upstairs, showered, and got dressed. Shortly after I got back downstairs, someone knocked at the door. I looked through the peephole. Rich stood on my front step. I didn't want to see him, but I knew he'd persist until I answered. Might as well get it over with. I opened the door. "What do you want?"

"Can't I simply be making a social call?" he said.

"After last night? No." I moved aside and let Rich in.

"All right, your parents asked me to come by. They're upset and—"

"*They're* upset?"

"I see you are, too," Rich said.

I pressed him. "Wouldn't you be?"

"Sure, but I would still listen to reason."

"Maybe if I heard something reasonable, I would."

"Your parents are trying to show good judgment."

The urge to roll my eyes was too strong to overcome. "They should have told me thirteen years ago or any time since. They've had plenty of chances to do the right thing."

"They feel really bad about last night, C.T."

"So you're their olive branch," I said.

"Something along those lines."

"Can I break you and send you back?"

Rich now rolled his eyes. "I get you're pissed, but because someone killed Samantha doesn't change the fact she's dead or her family should gather to remember her."

"She was your cousin, too," I said. Even though Rich came in, we still stood in the doorway. Maybe he expected me to give him the heave-ho at any moment. "She always said she thought of you as the big brother she never had."

"You know I thought of her as my little sister," he said,

"I'm surprised you're not more upset by this sudden revelation." I glared at Rich. He looked away quickly and then met my gaze. "You knew, didn't you?"

"What?" he said, trying to sound innocent.

"You knew!" I insisted. "All this time."

"I'm just trying to look at the big picture here."

"Bullshit! You knew, and you didn't tell me, either."

"We wanted to protect you," Rich said, parroting a line I never wanted to hear again. "You took her death so hard."

"You should have told me," I said. "Even if they didn't, *you* should have."

"Maybe you're right," Rich said with a speculative nod.

"Get out." I pointed toward the door for emphasis. "Get out of my house."

"I came by to help you."

"And a fine fucking job you've done of it so far."

"There's a cold case file," Rich said. "It's not on the network. If you want it, you have to go to Records."

"Then I will."

"Our best detectives worked Samantha's case."

"Rich, you should know by now I'm better than your best people."

"You're going to need to be," he said.

"I will be. Now get out. Go back to the ivory tower and conspire with my parents some more."

"Good luck." Rich moved onto the front step.

"Thanks." He was about to say something else, but I closed the door in his face.

* * *

I'VE LOOKED at cold case files before. They're archived in a box (or multiple boxes) in the basement of the BPD, where the sun never shines, and the sergeants never smile. BPD members can check out the files and work on them. PIs like me can look at them there and make notes but can't leave with the file. I needed to take Samantha's data with me. Simply strolling out with it didn't strike me as a feasible plan. I walked into BPD headquarters, went downstairs, and tried to devise a strategy.

Sergeant Kelly looked at me from behind the cage as if seeing me for the first time. It had been a while, but I hoped I'd be more memorable. It would have made snookering him for the file easier. Alas, I played the hand I was dealt. "Good morning, Sergeant Kelly," I said, giving him a winning smile.

"Morning," Kelly answered in his best monotone. I've gotten warmer receptions renewing my driver's license. So much for the smile. I might have to practice it in front of a mirror when this case ended.

"I'm here to look at a cold case file." I put my ID on the desk.

"Name?"

"Ferguson. Samantha Elizabeth."

He wrote the request down, then looked at my ID. "Any relation?"

"My sister."

Kelly nodded and walked back into the archive room. I'd only glimpsed it through the door. Endless metal shelves held file boxes whose names and numbers didn't correspond to any system I knew. I drummed my fingers on the desk as Kelly searched for the file and emerged a couple minutes later with a box in his hands. He set it on the desk. The thud didn't make it sound too heavy.

"Sign here," Kelly said, pointing to a box on the records form.

I affixed my signature. "Considering this is my sister's file, do you think I could leave with it? I'll bring it back."

Kelly flashed me a thin smile. "It doesn't matter if it's your *mother's* file." He paused like he was stringing me along for something. "Normally."

"Normally?"

"I've been told you can take the file with you."

I blinked. "Really?"

"Hey, I just work here," he said. "I get the call . . . I do what the man says."

"Who's the man?"

"Does it matter? Take the box and do your best. We still want it back when you're finished."

"I'll bring it back," I said.

"You'd better."

I left with the box. Did Rich set this up? He knew about the cold case file. Did he have enough pull to swing this? Despite him being a fast riser in the department, I doubted he'd amassed quite so much clout. No, I harbored a sneaking suspicion who arranged this, and I would need to thank him. I called Captain Leon Sharpe's office, and after speaking to his secretary, got connected to the man himself.

"C.T., how are you?" he said.

"I'm OK, all things considered," I said. "I'm calling to say thank you, Leon."

"Thank me for what?"

"Someone arranged for me to be able to temporarily keep a cold case file in my possession."

"Sounds very nice of someone."

"It was," I said, "which is why I'm calling to say thanks."

"You assume I'm the someone."

"Rich was my first suspect, but I don't think he could do something like this. Letting a shady PI like me leave with BPD property takes a phone call from upstairs."

"I know you got the short end of the stick with the cop killer case," Sharpe said. "Rich told me late last night what happened. He said you'd be coming. I figured there was no harm in letting you borrow it."

"I'll make a copy of everything and bring it back."

"Keep it as long as you need to," he said. "Return it when you arrest the son of a bitch who killed your sister."

I cleared my throat. "Sounds good. Thanks, Leon."

"C.T., don't go off and kill this guy. I know you want to find him and make him pay. I don't want to hear about you being a murderer."

"You might need to close your ears, then," I said.

Sharpe sighed into the phone. "I'm a good judge of character. You're not a killer, C.T. Don't make a liar out of me." He hung up.

Leon Sharpe would have to be wrong.

CHAPTER 6

I took the file box to my office at the house. This reminded me that I'd been neglecting my regular office. A couple of incidents near the house compelled me to rent an office in the CareFirst building in the Highlandtown section of Baltimore. It allowed me to keep my personal and professional lives separate, something I should have been smart enough to do from the jump. This case, however, erased lines I'd spent time and money drawing.

The carton held three folders: a slender one containing the ME's report, a thicker one holding all the photos taken for the case, and one threatening to burst with all the archived notes. It would take time to pore over. The ME's report would be a quick read, and I could run anything I didn't understand past Dr. Hunt. The pictures folder called to me. I knew I wouldn't want to see what was inside, yet I had to look.

I took a deep breath and opened it. The photo on top showed Samantha lying face-down in the grass, presumably in Patterson Park, with blood pooled all around her. It drove the air from my lungs. I sat in the chair with my mouth open, unable to breathe as I stared. Finally, I gasped and breathed again. I closed my eyes, turned the initial picture upside down on the other side of the folder, and readied myself to look at the next one.

I wasn't ready.

This one showed Samantha lying face-up. Blood still pooled around her, and it covered her clothes. I could see a few areas where the knife tore holes in her body. Her blonde hair, caked with gore, lay scattered around her face. Her eyes, still open, bored into mine, looking right through me. I needed to turn away.

After a moment and a few deep breaths, I looked back at the picture, avoiding my sister's face. Her upper body was covered in blood. It had run down to her shorts and onto her legs. Her clothes looked intact. The Movado watch she always wore on her left wrist was gone. Did this make robbery a motive? Samantha would have surrendered the watch if someone threatened her for it. Why then kill her?

I flipped this picture over and looked at the next one. It was a close-up of Samantha's torso. I couldn't discern an area of her once-white polo shirt—I remembered it because of her high school logo on it—which dark crimson stains didn't ruin. The zoom allowed me to see the stab wounds. Darker areas where the blood tried to clot after being rent by a blade dotted her body. I shook my head as I looked at the picture.

Robbery didn't look like a motive. A random crime would prove tough to solve. I needed to operate from the presumption Samantha knew her attacker. How well she knew him—I presumed the attacker to be a man—I would probably never know. I hoped the first wound had been enough to kill her. Enduring eleven more would be agony I would only wish upon the man who murdered my sister.

I wiped my eyes and turned to the next photo, a wide-angle shot of Samantha's body as it lay at the crime scene. I looked for landmarks when I heard Gloria behind me. "I know you need to do this," she said, "but it's obviously torture for you."

"Like you say, I need to do it." I wiped my eyes again. My voice sounded unsteady to my ears; I knew Gloria would pick up on it.

"You don't have to do it now." Gloria put her hands on my shoulders. "Why don't you look at something else?"

I felt a tear slide down my cheek. "All this time, I thought she died of some heart defect. I thought she died in peace." I shook my head. "Now I look at these pictures." My voice cracked more. Tears started to flow. "She died in pain. Worse, she died alone, probably begging for her life and hoping her family would make it before . . . before she couldn't hold on anymore." I stopped talking. I don't think I could have said another word.

Gloria crouched beside me. I put my head on her shoulder and cried. I cried like I did when I first heard my sister was dead, and I sobbed harder because I now knew the terrible depths of the lie.

* * *

AFTER I'D COMPOSED myself and imbibed a good stiff drink—for all her kitchen ineptitude, Gloria made a rum and Coke capable of holding the straw up on its own—I went back to the file. Pictures would wait. I couldn't look at them right now. The fact my sister's murder file sat on my desk hammered home the lie my parents fed me all these years. Seeing gross photos made it even more acute.

I looked at the medical examiner's report. They conducted an autopsy as if the cause of death were a mystery. Not surprisingly, the ME concluded Samantha died of multiple stab wounds. Two pierced her heart, five shredded her lungs, and the remaining five ripped other internal organs. Many of the wounds by themselves would have been fatal. The doctor did not speculate on how much Samantha might have suffered or how long it took her to die. I could only hope the two piercing her heart came first. I rued the fact I needed to root for such a grisly thing to be a blessing.

I finished looking over the report. The ME, a Dr. Willett, included diagrams, showing the various wounds on Samantha's body. The unreality of inked marks on a generic drawing of a female body made those hurt a lot less than the pictures. I closed my eyes and took in a few calming breaths. If only I'd gotten the hang of meditation during my years in Hong Kong. Maybe then I could drive the thoughts of killing Samantha's murderer out of my head. Rich's and Leon Sharpe's wishes be damned: I would find the bastard and kill him. I could afford a good lawyer who could paint a very sympathetic portrait of me to a jury he would help select. My PI career would be over, but I could sleep well at night knowing the man who murdered Samantha finally paid for it.

Next, I opened the police file. The folder was packed with notes, findings, interview transcripts, a list of suspects, and anything the detectives thought relevant. Rich said their best men couldn't discern who killed Samantha, and they worked the case for four months. A quick glance at the pages showed eight men and women contributed something to the file. I needed to be better than they were. The trail would be older and colder, but I harbored a reason for wanting to solve the case other than the simple pursuit of justice.

I jotted down the lead detectives' names: Frank Beatty and Ted Pembroke. They didn't sound familiar. I conducted a quick search through the BPD's personnel roster and found neither man currently employed. Pembroke retired five years ago, and Beatty transferred to parts unknown a few months after.

Someone called 9-1-1 to report a girl's body in Patterson Park. Pembroke and Beatty took the call. Their notes said they sent some uniforms to canvass the area, but no one reported seeing anything unusual, hearing someone screaming, or anything else indicating my sister got murdered nearby. A forensics team worked on the scene and found no traces of the killer. In thirteen years, forensic science took great leaps forward. I wondered if any of the evidence collected still existed somewhere

There wasn't much to the scientific report. They found no weapon at the scene, no blood other than Samantha's, no finger-prints, no skin under her fingernails, and the only loose hairs belonged to a collie. The team concluded Samantha's killer had faced her and stabbed her in the torso. Then, he either let her fall and stabbed her eleven more times or held her up for another eleven blows and let her slump. Either way, her blood got on him. I went back to the detectives' findings; no one noticed seeing a man in bloody clothes in the area. Even if the same people still lived there, they wouldn't suddenly remember anything simply because I went to their doors with a PI badge and a sob story.

I spent another two hours scouring the file. My stomach rumbled for most of it, but I didn't stop. Other detectives hunted potential witnesses and chased down the scant leads they could uncover. Their most promising clues turned out to be Samantha's chat room conversations. She'd joined several progressive groups in college and took part in email and chat room discussions. A few weeks before she died, she often talked to someone with the handle "Rondel." He painted himself as a major pacifist and said he'd organized a group in Baltimore. Samantha went to see the group on a long weekend from school. Then Rondel (or someone else) murdered her.

Considering how little was known of computers at the

time, the BPD did a creditable job investigating everything. They learned Rondel's email address, rondel@erols.com. I remembered Blockbuster Video but not Erol's. I knew Erol's went online, where they reinvented themselves as an Internet service provider. Once high-speed internet caught on, companies like Erol's got bought out or swept aside.

At least I knew a place to start.

CHAPTER 7

GREG ELLIOT LEFT THE NEWSPAPER BUSINESS TO CREATE A technology consulting firm in Silver Spring. He agreed to meet me at 3:00, which allowed me time for lunch before heading south and enduring a trek around the Capital Beltway. To my surprise, I encountered normal traffic instead of the gridlock I expected. I maintained sixty-five as I got off at Georgia Avenue and headed toward downtown Silver Spring.

Elliot Technology Associates maintained an office in a bustling downtown environment. It would never be downtown Baltimore—it lacked the character—but Silver Spring's central area was easy to navigate, featured plenty of shops, an abundance of eateries, and a giant movie theater to bring hordes of teenagers in on the weekends. Maybe the last one wasn't such a big selling point.

Elliot's business office wasn't much bigger than mine. His receptionist spent more time looking at her nails and her Facebook page than anything work-related. A small conference area took up the back part of the suite. Elliot's section sat off to the right. All I could see to the left of the conference area was a closed door. Maybe they kept the technology the company name advertised in there.

Greg Elliot was short, no more than five-seven, with a round face and an easy smile. His salt-and-pepper hair thinned on top. He tried to compensate with a goatee, but gray dominated any black. He possessed the physique of a man who grew used to sitting behind a desk instead of working the streets. Still, his quick smile and easy demeanor would have served him well as a reporter and may have wooed a few clients to his side in this life as well.

I showed Elliot my ID as I sat in an uncomfortable guest chair. "You said this was about a story I wrote?" he said.

"Yes. Thirteen years ago, a girl was murdered in Patterson Park. You wrote the story for *The Sun.*" The office's small size was its best feature. Whoever chose the furniture and carpeting should retire. If I were Eliot, I would telework as often as possible.

"Thirteen years ago . . ." His voice trailed off. "She was a blond, right? Pretty young, maybe nineteen?" I nodded. "I remember. Why do you want to know?"

"She was my sister."

"Oh." Elliot's eyes went wide. "I'm sorry. Did you . . . only recently find out what happened?"

"Let's say I won't be sending my parents a Christmas card for about three hundred years."

"Man, that's gotta be tough."

"Do you remember anything about the case?" I said, refocusing the conversation away from my plight. "Any details not making it into the story?"

Elliot's cheeks puffed out as he sighed and contemplated my question. "They found her face-down. The police weren't sure if she died that way or if the killer turned her over . . . or even moved her from somewhere else. I didn't put that in the story because the cops asked me not to."

"It was in their report."

"You've read the police report?" he said. "They share those with civilians?"

"I think they know the futility of trying to hide it from me under the circumstances."

"I don't see how I can tell you anything you wouldn't be able to find in there."

"How long were you a reporter?"

"Fifteen years." Elliot showed the easy smile again. He liked talking. This company didn't suit him. "I spent the last six of them at *The Sun*, doing a few different beats around the city. I miss Baltimore."

"I'm sure they'd take you back. The paper could use the help."

"This is my life now," he said, smile vanishing.

"If you say so," I said. "My point is you spent a long time as a reporter. You probably have a good nose for the truth and a good bullshit detector when you're talking to someone."

"It helps out in this business."

"Did you talk to anyone who set off your alarms? A potential witness, someone in the neighborhood . . . anybody?"

Elliot frowned in thought. "No. No one seemed out of sorts to me. It was weird."

"Weird how?"

"How did no one see or hear a young, pretty girl get killed in Patterson Park?"

"It happened late at night," I offered.

"There are always people around. Someone's walking a dog, or a homeless guy is working the streets for handouts. No one saw anything."

"It was a weeknight and late."

"And unseasonably cool," Eliot said. "I remember that." Despite the years gone by, I recalled it too. "But nothing sticks out in my mind," he continued. "Everyone I talked to seemed unaware anything happened. Not surprised, of course . . . just unaware."

"It was a bad area back then," I said.

"It's gotten better over the years, from what I've heard. Different neighborhood demographics, the BPD does more in the area and all. Back then, though, you're right—Patterson Park wasn't the nicest place to be at night."

"Especially," I said, "if you're a young and pretty college freshman."

"I wish I knew more. When I paid attention to the case, the cops never came close to an arrest. I followed up a few times, then they sent it off to the archives. The BPD ran a cold case squad for a while. I guess they never looked at it."

"Maybe there were chillier ones out there."

"Maybe. Good luck, though. I hope you find the person who did this."

"Thanks."

"I wish I could tell you more."

"I'm not expecting to get a wealth of information this late . . . but thanks."

We shook hands. I left. The Capital Beltway exacted its revenge on me on the drive back.

I DISCOVERED Ted Pembroke lived in Cecil County near the Mason-Dixon line. He told me over the phone he didn't think he'd be able to add much to my case but agreed to meet me, anyway. When I told him I would be coming from Federal Hill, he made my drive easier by traveling to Aberdeen. It would cost me dinner at a place called the Olive Tree, but I hoped it would be worth it.

When I arrived, I saw no olive trees nor any living trees of any variety. I guess it made sense: Olive Garden didn't actually have its namesake planted outside the front door. It might have made their food better if they did. A sixtyish man in a loose windbreaker sat on a cushioned bench, watching everyone walking past. He eyed me up as I approached. "Mr. Pembroke?"

"You're Ferguson?" he said, standing with the cautious pace of a man who doesn't want to get a blood rush to his head.

"I am." We exchanged a quick handshake and got a table. Despite the crowd, our waitress appeared quickly, took our drink orders, and walked off to tend to her other tables.

"This is about the dead girl thirteen years ago," Pembroke said, not intoning his voice to make it a question. He kept his voice low like I expected.

"It is." I matched his quiet tone.

"You say she was your sister?"

"Yes."

"Why haven't you looked into this before now?"

"A disinformation campaign," I said. "I was lied to until a couple nights ago. Now I know a little of the truth."

"And you want to know everything," he said.

"I do."

"Shit, so do I. Never could learn it all, no matter what I did. Why do you think I retired?"

The waitress returned with our drinks and brought a large bowl of salad and a container of breadsticks. The salad popped with greens and reds. Maybe all "Olive" restaurants are required to dispense these appetizers. Pembroke ordered the soup *du jour* and something called chicken Amelia. I hadn't looked at the menu and opted for chicken parmigiana. A restaurant which can't do the dish justice should forever shutter its doors.

"You a detective?" Pembroke said. He hadn't asked me yet.

Maybe he just wanted the chance to talk shop with someone again.

"Private," I said.

He shrugged. "You just don't have to do all the paperwork."

"I try not to do any of it."

"How old were you when your sister got killed?" he asked.

"Sixteen. I was almost finished my junior year of high school."

"I'm sorry your parents lied to you."

I took a deep breath. "Me, too. By now, the trail has probably grown cold."

"It was never warm to begin with."

"I've read the case file," I said. A few more tables filled up. Ambient noise in the restaurant increased.

"I'm surprised they let a private detective take a case file," said Pembroke.

"Someone downtown likes me, I guess."

"I guess. Everything I found is in the folder you have. I know it ain't much. A bunch of other cops pitched in when they could. The brass wanted to clear this one. A pretty college girl murdered in a sketchy neighborhood? It was a red ball from the start. I'm surprised you never found out, though. No papers, no press?"

"My parents managed to keep my sister's name out of the paper."

"They must have some influence."

"They do all right," I acknowledged.

Pembroke sized me up as the waitress dropped off his minestrone. "How does a rich kid end up a PI?"

"How does a good cop end up retiring early?"

"Your story's bound to be better than mine," he said.

"Maybe, but it's irrelevant. Can you walk me through what

happened when you arrived on the scene? Maybe you'll remember something."

"You think I never tried?"

"The memory works in mysterious ways. You never know what might trigger something, and anything is useful for me."

"Hell, maybe it'll help." Pembroke put a spoonful of soup in his mouth. He closed his eyes. I transferred some salad to my plate and ate it while he remembered. "We got the nine-one-one call about a dead girl in Patterson Park. Never knew who put it in. When we got there, the girl was face down with a lot of blood on the ground around her. My partner, Beatty, and I started taking pictures and looking for evidence. We taped off the scene. Forensics got there and did their thing. They took a bunch more pictures, blood samples, bits of grass . . . you name it, they put it in a baggie. Once they were done, we rolled the girl over to see what happened to her." He shook his head. "Sorry. This is probably tough for you to hear."

"I've seen the pictures," I said. "The audio is easier."

"Once we were finished, the ME's men came and took the body away. We sent some uniforms out to canvass the area, see if anyone saw the girl before she got killed, maybe someone with blood on them, anything like it. We talked to residents, business owners who might have been open, dog walkers, everybody we could. No one saw anything."

"Had you seen a killing like this before?"

Pembroke paused for a drink of his soda. "I seen a lot of killings." His eyes took on a faraway look. "Plenty of people got stabbed. I don't know if I saw one like this, I gotta tell you. Just the . . . viciousness of it all. All those wounds, and they were deep. This wasn't some limp-wristed guy with a pen knife. This was a strong man with a good-sized blade who enjoyed what he did."

I winced. The pictures might have told me the same thing

if I could've looked past the fact my sister was dead in all of them. I recalled the picture of Samantha's torso. Depth of wounds was hard to determine in a photo, but a deep red surrounded each of the areas where the son of a bitch stabbed her. "You say he enjoyed what he did," I said.

"Speculation," said Pembroke.

"Do you think it's possible the same man killed anyone else?"

"If you're looking for patterns, we already did. Age of the victim, gender, height, hair color, where they were found, face up versus face down, number of wounds, size of the blade, anything we could think of. If this guy killed anyone else, he didn't do it in Baltimore."

There went another theory. The waitress brought our food. I ate a breadstick while I let my steaming entrée cool. After a moment, I cut a piece of chicken parm and tried it. The Olive Tree could keep their doors open. Pembroke's chicken Amelia consisted of a large chicken breast, pasta, broccoli, and a cream sauce. I hated cream sauces.

"I wish I could tell you more," said Pembroke. "There's just not much to tell. We worked the case for a while. The brass busted our balls about it. 'A pretty blonde rich girl,' they would tell us. The mayor was going to get involved or some shit. We did all we could." Pembroke almost sounded like he sought some kind of approval—or at least absolution. Cleansing someone of responsibility was well outside my pay grade.

"I don't blame you," I said, the closest I could offer to an absolution. "Sometimes, trails go cold, and killers aren't caught."

"You're not giving up, are you?"

"Of course not. Let me ask you one thing. I remember reading the BPD used my sister's online activity to point to someone who went by Rondel. Do you remember?"

"Yeah," he said, "some. I wasn't up on all the technology stuff. Still ain't, really. I send email and all, but the rest of it is just too much for someone like me."

I said, "So you weren't involved in the forensic side of the investigation?"

"I talked to the tech guys. Anything they found, they told me, and I put it in the report. We tried to figure out who the guy was, but it never went anywhere. You couldn't try to find him today?"

I shook my head. "His Internet provider went to the great bit graveyard years ago. There are way too many out there to search for one guy who might not even be using the same handle at this point."

"Your explanation actually made some sense," Pembroke said with a chuckle. "Scary."

We ate our respective chicken dinners for a while. The waitress refilled our drinks. I took some more salad but eschewed the now-tepid breadsticks. "Did you learn anything?" Pembroke said when he had put his fork and napkin down in surrender.

"I don't know," I said. "Any information can help me. Simply talking to someone else who knows the case could be a windfall."

"You get an idea you want to run past me, you call me and we can hash it out."

"Thanks."

"I won't even make you buy me dinner again."

"If you lead me to Samantha's killer, I'll buy you your own restaurant," I said.

* * *

I GOT HOME and looked at the file out of a dearth of better options. Dinner with the lead detective on the case didn't inch me any closer to unraveling what happened to my sister. It didn't disappoint me; I'd expected to come away with nothing. The hope of a better outcome got extinguished. Gloria walked into the office and sat in one of my guest chairs.

"How did it go?" she said.

"Pretty much like I expected."

"You still don't have enough to go on?"

"I don't have enough to be in the same ballpark as having enough to go on."

"You'll get there. You're smart and dedicated."

I knew what Gloria tried to do and smiled at her. "Thanks, but neither of those qualities will make evidence materialize."

"Why don't you call Rich?" I groaned. "I mean it; he might be able to help you."

"He doesn't know what happened either," I said.

"No," she said, "but he's more used to doing this than you are. Plus, he's not as close to the case."

Her point was valid. Before I could take out my phone to dial him, however, Rich called me. "Speak of the devil," I said.

"I'm almost surprised you answered," Rich said.

"Would it be like me to ignore someone's phone call?"

"I can ask your parents."

"Let's not."

"I was wondering how you're making out with the case so far. Any luck?"

"Not really," I said and blew out a breath. "I talked to Detective Pembroke. He didn't remember anything not already in the file, and he didn't know enough about the tech side of things."

"What are you going to do now?"

"I have no idea," I said. "I get stuck on cases from time to time, but this is different. I *have* to figure this one out."

"Have you considered the FBI?"

"The FBI? Why would I talk to them?"

"Samantha met the man who killed her online," Rich said. "Odds are good he came from out of state. Maybe he did something like this before."

"Pembroke said he didn't know of a similar case."

"Not in Baltimore. Maybe not even in Maryland. But there might be one somewhere. Hell, there might be a bunch."

"You think a serial killer murdered Samantha?" I said.

"I think you probably won't find out unless you talk to the FBI," Rich said. I heard forced patience creep into his tone. I'd gotten used to it over the years. "They have resources we don't. Just promise me you won't try to hack them."

"I probably could."

"C.T.!"

"All right, I won't. Is there someone in particular I should talk to?"

"I served with a guy named Jason Hess. He works in the Baltimore Field Office. If you're willing to go there at eight tomorrow morning, he's willing to meet you."

I remembered Hess from the luncheon Gloria organized. We didn't talk, but at least I knew the face. "I'll be there. How much does he know?"

"Not much," Rich said. "You know more about the file and the case than I do."

"All right. Thanks, Rich. I'll let you know how it goes."

"Good luck." Rich hung up.

"That sounded promising," Gloria said. I told her about the conversation. "I'm sure they'll be able to help you."

"I wish I could share your optimism," I said. "I'm hopeful. We'll see how it goes."

"You should get a good night's rest."

"I'll be up in a while. I want to look some things over again before morning."

Gloria went upstairs. I re-read parts of the case file and even looked at some of the more tolerable pictures. Talking with Pembroke desensitized me a little, but it still ripped at my core to see my sister ravaged by violence. At some point, it became harder to focus on the page. I woke up with my head on my desk a little past four o'clock. I trudged upstairs and was awake again before seven so I could take my chances with the FBI.

Gloria stayed in bed while I got up and showered. I went downstairs at seven-twenty to make breakfast. My refrigerator mocked me with its emptiness. I would have to remember to get groceries. With a lack of better options, I made coffee and ate a bowl of cereal, its flakes grown half stale. I could add it to my grocery list.

After my mediocre breakfast, I finished getting dressed upstairs. Most days, I wore jeans—Tommy or Ralph, but jeans nonetheless. Today, I broke out a suit. I opted for the blue pinstriped Armani. Maybe Hess would regard a fellow sharp-dressed man and be inspired to help me. Maybe he would think I was a label snob. I would confess to the charge—I certainly couldn't deny it—if it would spur him to action.

I took a cup of coffee for the road and drove to the FBI field office in Woodlawn. Getting up I-83 and around the Baltimore Beltway proved more challenging than I expected. Even with my usual aggressive driving, I stood no chance of being on time. When I got there at ten past eight, I considered it a small victory. I found Agent Hess in the directory and rode the elevator to his floor. A secretary directed me to his office.

Special Agent Jason Hess occupied an office on the

outskirts of a cube farm mostly empty on a Saturday morning. I didn't know if this made him some kind of supervisor or not, but it beat toiling in a cubicle. Hess' office looked like all the other ones carved out along the walls. In this dreadfully modern floor plan, even the offices presented a stifling sameness. I could never work in an environment like this. I knocked on the door.

Hess stared up at me. He had a full head of blond hair with some gray peeking in at the temples. I guessed him to be a couple years older than Rich, right around forty. He possessed a football player's physique and a piercing gaze. The Army and Quantico had taught him well. His stare reminded me of a few I received from the guards in the Hong Kong prison. Those were not happy memories. "Rich told me you'd probably be late," he said.

"Traffic."

"There's always traffic. Come on in."

I walked in and sat in a guest chair which didn't make me want to leap out of it right away. Hess typed a few keystrokes and then gave me his attention. I felt strange sitting on the other side of a desk. I had gotten used to being on the business side and now preferred it. "What can I do for you?" said Hess.

"Thanks for meeting me on a Saturday morning," I said.

He showed a brief smile. "Rich is a good guy. I don't mind. What's up?"

"I have a BPD cold case file. It's my sister's. She was murdered thirteen years ago in Baltimore."

"I'm sorry to hear it."

"Thanks," I said. "Unfortunately, I only recently learned she didn't die of natural causes." Hess gave me a funny look. "Long story. Anyway, I might have been able to do something with this if I'd gotten it sooner. Now, it's thirteen years after the fact. The police didn't have much luck the first time. I'm hoping to do better. I *need* to do better."

"How can I help?" Hess said. He held my gaze. He radiated sincerity. Maybe this would work out.

"The BPD did some online investigation. I think they were pretty new at it, so I'm wondering if your people could help there. Also, the lead detective on the case thinks my sister was killed by someone who enjoyed it. He said it could be a serial killer."

This time, Hess' smile rose from politeness. "Mr. Ferguson, serial killers are very popular on TV and in movies, but they're quite rare. Very few victims are actually murdered by serial killers."

I knew this already, but I didn't contest the point. I needed Hess on my side. "It can't hurt to look. Improbable doesn't mean impossible."

"Very true," Hess said. You have some information for me, then?"

I told Hess everything I could about Samantha, where and how she was found, the number of stab wounds, the length of the blade used, and anything else I thought could help. Hess entered it all on the computer. "We have a database to track patterns in crimes," he said. "It doesn't guarantee there is or isn't a serial killer involved, but it lets us play the odds better." He finished with a few keystrokes. "It takes a few minutes to run. What else do you have?"

I went over the BPD's foray into my sister's online activity and what they found. Hess asked for the spelling of Rondel, which I gave him. "I don't have anyone by such a handle in a database," he said.

"The ISP he used is long defunct," I said. "I was hoping you had some information on people who fit this kind of pattern."

"Mr. Ferguson, people are killed following online meetings a lot more often than we'd like. If I were to get all their files, I'd need a wheelbarrow and a lot of time."

"I figured. You don't have anything on this Rondel, though?"

"I'll look again." Hess did some more typing, then shook his head. "Nothing."

"What about your cybercrime folks?"

"The search I ran includes their databases."

I frowned. "Oh. I guess I'll cross my fingers for the other one, then."

A minute later, an answer showed. Crossed fingers didn't help. "This software plots a lot of factors," Hess said, "and assigns each a different weight. Based on the data you gave me, it's extremely unlikely your sister encountered a serial killer."

"How unlikely?"

"Odds are almost 96% against it."

"Still a four percent chance," I pointed out. A regular math ace, me.

"Do you play poker, Mr. Ferguson?"

"Occasionally."

"Would you push all your chips in with a four percent chance to win?" Hess asked.

"If it were the right time to make a stand, yes."

Hess nodded. "Fair point. I don't think this is that time. I'm sorry."

"Are there any serial killers who are possibilities?" I said.

"If I come up with any, I'll let Rich know."

"All right. Thanks."

"I wish I could find better results for you."

"I've heard it a lot the last few days."

"I'm sure you have." Hess stood and extended his hand. I shook it. "Good luck, and if you can, have a good weekend."

"I think my search will consume my time," I said.

"I'm having a geekend, myself. Some friends and I are going to watch the *Lord of the Rings* trilogy again."

"Sounds like you'll have more fun than I will. Thanks for your time."

I left the FBI field office no closer to finding Samantha's killer than when I walked through the front door. Everywhere I went, I spun my wheels. I was desperate to find a break in the case, but I had no idea from where.

I RETURNED HOME to discover Gloria left. Maybe she decided to take a tennis lesson. Maybe she realized she'd neglected her own house, which could hold three of mine. Regardless, I had the place to myself and little motivation to do anything except focus on Samantha's cold case file. I know the BPD's best detectives from thirteen years ago hammered at the case and couldn't get anywhere with it. Detectives routinely split their time. I could be single-minded.

Simply reading through the file didn't help. I needed to be more interactive. For the first time in my professional life, I wanted a whiteboard. A trip to Staples later, I had a 36" by 48" model hanging on the wall behind my desk. I wrote out a rough timeline for when things happened, including the electronic events leading up to Samantha's murder. Laying it all out helped me keep the events straight and think of them in a logical progression. Now, I needed it to help me solve the case.

I stared at the expanse of white for at least five minutes, but no breakthrough came. I went back to the case file, looking up at the timeline as I came across significant events. After about a half-hour, I grew tired. I rose early to meet Hess and have him waste my time, and I hadn't slept well since my parents finally revealed their deception. I didn't expect a rush of insight, so I went upstairs and lay in bed. Within a couple minutes, I fell asleep.

My ringing cell phone jolted me awake an indeterminate time later. I picked it up and glanced at the time; I'd napped almost two hours. I didn't recognize the number calling but answered anyway. "

"C.T.?" said a woman's voice my tired brain couldn't marry to a face.

"Yes, who's this?"

"Ruby. Remember me?"

How could I forget? I hoped her stalker situation would sort itself out. A distraction from Samantha's case was something I didn't want right now. "Of course," I said. "What's going on?"

"What's going on is the son of a bitch is back."

"Your stalker?"

"I just saw him."

"In the daylight?" I said, surprised.

"I never said he was a genius. Can you come down here?"

"Ruby, it's daylight. He can't stalk you in secret if you can see him. Are you sure it's him?"

"It's his car," she said.

"Can't you see inside?"

"He has the windows tinted really dark."

"License plate?" I said.

"Didn't catch one. I don't think he has a front tag."

"Look, I'm in the middle of something else. You have a million places to go to lose someone in the daytime. If he's still bothering you tonight, let me know."

"You're blowing me off." She sounded miffed but also not surprised. Ruby didn't strike me as very old, but she'd obviously grown used to disappointment.

"I'm telling you I can be more help to you tonight," I said in an effort to placate her while I hoped she wouldn't call back. So yes, I was blowing her off.

"Whatever," she said and hung up.

With any luck, I'd gotten the boot from the Ruby stalking case. It was a boring one from the start, and now I was immersed in something much more important. Rollins could deal with a stalker. He didn't have to know who the guy was to beat him up when he came around. I sat up in bed. Samantha's file wouldn't make any more sense to me now than it did when I came upstairs. I changed into lighter clothes and went out for a run. A few laps around Federal Hill Park would help clear my head. If nothing else, I might run into a pretty jogger.

I WALKED BACK inside my house about forty minutes later, having sweated my way through four miles and zero attractive runners. I needed a shower to wash away the exertion and the disappointment. After putting on clean clothes, I went back downstairs, frowned at the state of my refrigerator, and made a long overdue trip to the grocery store. An hour later, I walked back inside with a dozen Harris Teeter bags and a ravenous hunger.

I put rice on to boil while I oiled a skillet for a fantastic piece of salmon I bought at the market. I sprinkled the skillet with Old Bay and a pinch of dill as the oil heated. When it crackled, I put the salmon filet on. While it cooked, I finished with the rice and steamed some broccoli. About ten minutes later, I had a plate packed with a salmon filet, brown rice, and steamed broccoli so green it would make the Hulk jealous.

While I scarfed down my lunch, my thoughts drifted to Samantha's murder. My thoughts drifted few other places these days. Today, rational people kept their guard up online. Thousands of faux Nigerian princes duped people out of money, funny cat pictures bore malicious payloads, and too many children met way too many pedophiles. Thirteen years ago, the Internet had not facilitated so much mistrust. Samantha was a smart girl, and she knew enough to be careful online, but if she found someone else with a passion for the same causes, she could have revealed too much.

After lunch, I focused on the electronic component of the investigation. I would find Rondel even though I possessed no idea how to go about it at the moment. He'd talked to Samantha on many occasions, both in email and in chat rooms. The BPD collected a good amount of the email traffic. They seized Samantha's computer and printed any chat logs she archived. Many unsaved conversations could have been missing, however. How many important details did I now not have because my sister didn't save all the logs?

I earned a college education. Along the way to a master's in computer science, I took a few psychology and sociology classes —the former because it interested me and the latter because girls who majored in sociology tended to be easy. I wasn't a criminal profiler, but I might be able to pore over these emails and chat logs and glean a few things about the man who killed Samantha. I gathered all the printouts, got a legal pad, poured my third cup of coffee for the day, and got to work.

Sometime later, I heard the front door open. "Hello?" Gloria called from the foyer as she closed and locked the door.

"In the office," I said.

She walked in. I hoped she would still be in her tennis outfit with its tight top and tiny skirt. No such luck, however: Gloria wore a polo shirt and khaki capris. "I went back to my house for a while," she said, sitting in a guest chair. "Then I had a tennis lesson. Now I'm here." She smiled.

"Here you are."

Gloria looked at the whiteboard and my many scribblings. "I see you've been busy today."

I nodded. "Having a visual timeline will help me. I can stop rummaging through the file for the basics."

"What are you doing now?"

"Reading emails and chat logs to see if I can learn anything about the killer."

"Any luck?"

"I've made a couple notes," I said. We'll see if they turn into anything."

"How did it go with the FBI this morning?" I gave her my impressions of Hess and the meeting. "Sounds like a waste of time," she said.

"Looks like one now. Who knows? Maybe I'll uncover something and be able to go back to them with more evidence in hand."

"You think they can help you find this guy?"

"I think I have better odds with them than I do trying to brute-force an answer by myself."

Gloria sat in silence for a few minutes as I scanned another file. "You taking a break soon?" she said.

"I might," I said. "Why?"

She fixed me with a lascivious stare and licked her lips. "I'm a little wound up after the tennis lesson."

"I think we'll have to get you nice and relaxed."

"I think we will." She stood. "Come upstairs when you're ready for a break."

I finished the chat log I'd been reading, put it back in the box, and headed to the second floor. Gloria had already changed into a small nightgown unfit for network television. She grinned at me as I walked through the door and sat beside her on the bed.

"You've been working too hard," she said.

"I think we'll have to get both of us nice and relaxed," I said.

"I think we will," Gloria concurred.

* * *

LATER IN THE DAY, I cooked dinner. Gloria managed to distract me from Samantha's file for the better part of the afternoon. As I settled in to preparing our food, I realized I needed some distance from the file. It had consumed me ever since I carried it out of BPD headquarters. All I could show for it was a new whiteboard, a bunch of aborted theories, and some eye strain. I would keep at it, but I didn't need to hammer away at it nonstop in the stubborn hope of a breakthrough.

We'd barely finished eating chicken marsala when my phone rang again. I recognized the number this time: Ruby. I had blown her off earlier; the least I could do was talk to her now. "Hello?"

"You gonna blow me off again?" said Ruby.

"What's going on?"

"He's here again."

"Does he know you're on the phone?" I said.

"I don't think so."

"Where are you now?"

"Near the Gold Club," she said. "He's in the parking lot watching me."

"I'll be there shortly. Stay put unless you're in trouble. Call me if something changes."

"I will. Thanks, C.T."

"Sure." I hung up and grabbed my keys.

"Dining and dashing?" Gloria said.

"I always look dashing," I said. "But duty calls."

* * *

I CALLED Ruby when I got close to the Gold Club. "Is he still there?" I said.

"Hasn't moved."

"Describe the car."

"Silver, four doors. Looks like a Benz, I guess. He's on the side of the parking lot near the empty site. You know where I'm talking about?"

"Yes," I said. "It used to be a shipping company of some sort, I think."

"Yeah. I'm in what was their parking lot, talking to a couple of other girls and some guys in a blue SUV."

"OK. I'm going to drive to where you are. Let's see what happens."

I wheeled past the Gold Club. The lot was too crowded for me to pick out a specific car. The abandoned shipping company stood farther down Route 40. Ruby and a few other working girls gathered in the parking lot of Christian's Tires across Mapleton Avenue from the Gold Club. All of them wore skirts sized more like belts, heels tall enough to make my calves ache in sympathy, and tight tops leaving nothing to the imagination. Good thing we were having a warm late autumn. I pulled up next to Ruby.

"Where did you get this car?" she said.

"My first car came with a bumper sticker saying 'my other car is an Audi,'" I said. "I figured I should make it true."

She leaned into my open passenger's window. Her top loosened up around her breasts, and she showed me a lot more of them than I'd expected. At least it was a nice view unobstructed by a bra. "You see him?"

In the Gold Club parking lot, I saw a row of cars. Among

them was a silver Mercedes with no front plate. "I see the car you mentioned, but I don't know if anyone's inside it."

"We haven't seen him get out of it. He's up there, watching."

"I wonder how he would react if you got into my car," I said.

"I'd rather just go kick his ass."

"If he thinks you're onto him, he's going to drive away."

Ruby nodded. "We'd better get going, then. Transactions don't take this long to negotiate." I unlocked the doors, and she got in. As I pulled onto Mapleton, the front lights of the Mercedes lit up.

We had a pursuer.

THE SILVER BENZ PULLED OUT BEHIND US AND STAYED there, not even trying for subtlety. "Now what?" Ruby said.

"If he's smart, he's not going to follow us forever," I said. "We need to find a plausible place to go soon."

"Why not the motel?"

"Why not indeed?"

A few blocks later, I turned into the parking lot of the Deluxe Plaza Motel. They were still guilty of false advertising on two counts. "We getting a room?" Ruby said.

"You think he'd wait in the lot for you?"

"I don't know."

"We need to be careful not to spook him yet," I said. "Stick to the routine."

"Let's get a room, stud." Ruby gave me a playful pat on the thigh.

I paid for two hours of a room. The guy behind the desk, someone I hadn't seen here before, gave Ruby a key. She smiled and winked at him as she took it and led me down the walkway. The silver Benz sat at the back of the lot. Ruby unlocked the door to number eight, and we went inside. The room featured drab carpeting someone should have replaced years ago and paint deserving a similar fate. A queen bed took up one wall with a nightstand on either side of it. The furniture, which included a small desk, was all the same boring shade of brown. To my surprise, the room smelled fresh, though I shuddered to think about what nasty surprises lurked in the bedding.

Ruby sat on the edge of the mattress. I stood near it with no intention of sitting on the bed. The blue curtains were drawn, and I didn't want to look nosy by peeking out. "How long are we gonna wait?" Ruby said.

"How much time are you normally in a room?" I said.

"Depends what the john pays for." She looked at me askance. If she went for sexy with the look, it worked. "How long can you last?"

"I don't get any complaints."

Ruby smiled. "We have some time. Wanna fuck?"

"No thanks."

"You sure?" She pulled her top off, revealing first a toned stomach and then a nice pair of breasts no longer held in check by her shirt. I took a deep breath and steeled myself.

"It's tempting," I said. "But no."

"I'm clean. I get tested all the time."

I gave her a smile I hoped looked gentle. "I'm helping you because you seem like someone who needs it, not because I want you to trade sex for it."

She looked about to say something, but I got the feeling she didn't know how to respond.

"When's the last time someone wanted something from you other than sex?" I said.

"I don't know," Ruby said, shaking her head. "I guess I figure that's what everyone wants from me."

"I want to help you, and while I quite enjoy looking at you with your shirt off, you don't have to stay undressed on my account."

Ruby flashed a sheepish grin and slid her shirt back over her head. I hid my disappointment as her breasts once more vanished behind the white fabric wall. "Thanks, C.T. Not many people want to do things for me." Her voice cracked.

"Don't get all sentimental on me," I said. "How do you want to handle this asshole in the parking lot?"

"I figured that's your department."

"All right. He parked a distance from my car. If we went running after him, he'd just drive away." I remembered the parking lot. "There are two entrances, though. If I pull out of the back one, I might be able to do a quick loop and get behind him. Then we're the ones following him."

"I like it," Ruby said, nodding quickly. "Let's go."

I looked at my watch. "Not yet."

"Why not?"

"Because I don't want your stalker to think I'm a three-pump chump."

She laughed. "Fine. We'll go when your pride is sated."

"We could be here a while, then," I said.

* * *

We waited about ten more minutes and left arm-in-arm. I told Ruby to ignore the Benz, which remained in the same spot. We didn't need to let him know we knew he was there. I opened the door for Ruby—and wondered how many johns even drove her anywhere afterward, never mind opened the door for her—then let myself in. We went out the exit on the left, closer to where the Benz was parked. Traffic was light on this stretch of Pulaski Highway. The Benz pulled out behind us as we approached the second entrance to the Deluxe Plaza parking lot.

I stepped on the gas, turned hard, sped to the next exit, and pulled out behind the silver car. To my dismay, he only showed a temporary rear license plate. Years ago, Maryland shifted to paper temporary tags. If they get wet, they become illegible. This one was illegible. The Benz picked up speed as the driver realized he'd become the followee. I matched him. Ruby smiled in my peripheral vision.

The speedometer lurched above seventy as we blew past Moravia Road, then Moravia Park Drive. The Audi let out a supercharged hum as I downshifted for some more muscle on the hill. The Benz put down a good pace. I stayed about five car lengths behind in case of any shenanigans. The stalker swerved around a slower car whose driver laid on the horn in response. I followed suit. The horn persisted. We approached Chesaco Avenue going almost ninety. The light turned yellow. The Benz blew through it. So did a tractor trailer, making a left across Pulaski Highway, between the Benz and my Audi. I stomped on the brakes. The tires shrieked, and I felt the anti-lock brakes pulsating under my foot. We skidded to a stop barely in time.

I let out a deep breath. Ruby did the same. My heart thumped in my chest. Neither of us needed to say anything. The light turned green. I took off at a more reasonable pace, but we never saw the Benz again. At Rossville Boulevard, past the remnants of what used to be Golden Ring Mall, I turned around so I could take Ruby back.

"He got away," she said, breaking the silence.

"Do you think he'll come back?" I said.

"If he doesn't, then he scares easily. That would mean you did your job."

"I'm guessing he'll be the type who doesn't get spooked. He'll probably leave you alone for a couple days, though. Counts for something."

"You can't be around in your fancy car. He knows it now."

"Unfortunate," I said. "I prefer my fancy car to the other one."

"I'm sure you do," said Ruby.

"I'll keep an eye on you periodically. Rollins probably will too, but call me if you see this bastard again. He knows you know about him now. I hope he doesn't ramp up from being a simple creep."

Ruby nodded. "I will."

I dropped her off in the same place I picked her up. She gave me a kiss on the cheek. I smiled and waved as I drove off. In spite of myself, I actually liked the girl. Looking past the fact she took money to have sex with strangers in a shitty motel, she was very nice. On the drive home, I thought about the aborted chase of the Benz. We didn't need to tip our hands so soon. We could have merely driven back, and I could have watched Ruby and her stalker. Instead, we spooked him, he ran, and he might come back angry now.

The Ruby situation could demand more than my spare cycles. I already had Samantha's case occupying my thoughts full-time.

This proved an interesting night.

✳ ✳ ✳

WHEN I GOT HOME, I called Rollins. No matter when I phoned, he never sounded tired. Either he never slept, or he happened to wake up the moment he heard a phone ring. Having known him a while, I thought both theories rated some merit. "Hello?" he said in his usual alert voice.

"This hooker case is getting interesting," I said.

"What did you find out?"

"Her stalker drives a silver Benz. E class."

"Nice car."

"It's no Audi," I said, "but it's all right."

"He has money, at least. You catch him?"

"He used a tractor trailer to screen me at a light."

"You got his tag number, then." It was an expectation, not a question.

"No," I admitted. "Temporary tag ruined by rain. Couldn't read it."

"Real pisser," said Rollins, spreading wisdom.

"It sure is."

"What are you gonna do now?"

"I don't know. I think he'll leave her alone for a couple days and make sure she doesn't have a protector around all the time. Afterwards, he might become more aggressive now she's thwarted him."

"And used a man to do it," he said.

"Right." I told him about the motel setup.

"Sounds like you did it well," he said. "He got lucky and lost you with the truck."

"Can you look in on her for a couple days?"

"Yeah. You got something else going on?"

"I do," I said, "but a second shift on Ruby detail can't hurt."

Rollins paused. I knew he wanted to ask me what my other job was. I wouldn't tell him if he did. "You're probably right," he said.

We talked about dividing up the work of watching Ruby, starting tomorrow night. If the stalker defied our expectations and came back sooner, Ruby would call one of us. We hung up. I thought about her. She could fend for herself. If the stalker got aggressive, though, she would be in trouble. What if she didn't have a chance to call anyone? I wanted to work on my sister's cold case, but I couldn't consign Ruby to the mercy of a stalker.

I went back out to keep an eye on her.

CHAPTER 10

I took the Caprice this time. In case the stalker came back, I didn't want him to see the Audi and do something to Ruby. Or to the Audi. My job already cost me one car I liked. I found Ruby working the crowd in the Gold Club parking lot. She could make a mint there. Men staggered out in various states of intoxication, horny from getting lap dances from strippers they couldn't touch. It could also make them aggressive. I hoped Ruby knew the downside risk of what she did.

It took her a few cars, but Ruby found someone willing to go with her. She got into a Ford pickup driven by a balding man who looked both excited and embarrassed at the thought of having a hooker sit in the passenger's seat. They left, and I followed them to the Deluxe Plaza Motel. They went to the office and emerged a couple minutes later. Ruby opened the door to a room. The john looked around, as if wondering when his wife would find him, then entered after her.

I moved the Caprice closer so I could listen for screams or some sign the man became violent with Ruby. I didn't hear anything untoward. Soon enough, I heard the telltale signs their business transaction would reach a satisfactory conclusion. I moved back to my original spot. About ten minutes later, the john came out, got back into his truck, and drove off at a regular pace. Ruby emerged another ten minutes later with damp hair. I'd started to worry, but I should've guessed she'd opt for a shower afterward. She looked for the truck and shook her head upon not finding it.

She spied the Caprice and walked over. I put my window down. She leaned in, and I again noticed the lack of bra and the quality of her breasts. "What's a nice guy like you doing in a parking lot like this?" she said.

"I got worried about you," I said.

"You talk to Rollins?"

I nodded. "We both think it's likely the stalker backs off for a day or two. In case he didn't, I came back out to keep an eye on you."

"I can take care of myself."

"No doubt." I forced myself to look at Ruby's eyes. She smirked when I did. She had no intention of straightening up. "I knew you'd call me if you were in trouble, but what if he didn't give you a chance to?"

She nodded. "Thanks for coming back."

"You need to return to work?"

"I could go for some food."

"Get in," I said.

AGAINST MY WISHES and better judgment, we went back to the Happy Day Diner. It looked no happier, nor did any of its workers. We got a table in the rear corner near the bathrooms. People came and went, but few other patrons sat close. Maybe they didn't want to sit by a scantily-dressed woman and her apparent john. A waiter came, told us about the specials, and asked us about drinks. Ruby ordered a soda; I opted for a coffee.

"Did you learn anything about your stalker tonight?" I said.

"He's a better driver than you," Ruby said with a grin.

"Small sample size."

"Uh-huh." Her grin persisted. I liked this girl and again wondered how she fell into the life.

"You didn't recognize the car or the way he drove?" I said.

She shook her head. "Nothing."

The waiter dropped off our drinks. Ruby chose a burger and fries. I shrugged and got the same. It could be a few hours before I went back home. This case would play hell on my sleep schedule unless I figured things out quickly.

"Tell me about yourself," I said.

Ruby frowned. Her shoulders tensed. She was on her guard now. "What do you mean?"

"Whoever's stalking you might know something about you. If I know more, it could help me find him."

She turned the rationale over for a moment. Ruby was a smart girl; she could see the veracity in what I said. "I guess I can tell you a few things."

"OK. Can we start with your name?"

"No," she said quickly, shaking her head. "I'm just Ruby."

"I don't buy it. You're a smart girl. You've had a good education at some point. Private school, unless I missed my guess." Her pursed lips told me I didn't. "How did you go from there to here?"

"It's a long story."

"We have some time."

"OK, I went to private school. Then I went through a big falling-out with my family before college. Now I'm here."

"Why?" I said. "You could do a lot of other things."

"You don't need to save me. I like what I do." Ruby looked down at the tabletop.

I let the lie pass. Maybe I would learn the real reason at

some point. It was probably complicated. Pretty private-school girls don't end up turning tricks over a simple family argument. Other damage lurked beneath the surface. "How old are you?"

"Don't you know you're not supposed to ask a lady how old she is?" A faint smile played on her lips.

"I know. I'm asking anyway."

She unwrapped her straw and took a drink of soda before answering. "Twenty-three."

"So you've been in the business for five years?"

"More or less."

"There's a lot more to you than you're telling me," I said.

"Of course there is." She sighed. "Look, C.T., I appreciate what you're trying to do. Your heart's in the right place, but I'm nobody special. I'm just another girl with a sad story."

If she liked what she did, why was the story sad? I didn't press her. "Do you think this stalker is someone from your sad story?"

"I don't know. Nobody I know drives a silver Benz."

"Ignore the car for now," I told her. "He could have borrowed it from someone. Would anyone you knew, maybe someone you lost touch with over the years, stalk you if he happened to learn where you are?"

"I don't think anybody misses me that much," Ruby said. She sounded a little wistful, but I wasn't sure I believed her.

By the time the waiter brought our food a minute later, Ruby's story nearly depressed the appetite out of me. Something happened to turn her from private school girl to street prostitute. Baltimore featured a lot of good academies. They turned out few hookers. It was a long way to fall in a city poor at catching people. We ate in silence. I wanted to know more about her, but I didn't think Ruby wanted to stroll farther down the shadowy, twisty road of her past.

"Are you from around here?" I said when our paces both tapered off. She'd eaten more than me.

"Yeah," she said with a nod. "Baltimore County."

"Why work down here, then? There have to be safer places in the suburbs."

"Less money. Call it hazard pay, I guess, but I can get more in Baltimore for the same work."

I pondered other questions. What would she answer? How far could I push the envelope? Not very, I guessed, at least not tonight. Some other time, Ruby might be open to telling me more. Maybe I needed to get her a few drinks first. I wondered if she talked much to her johns afterward. Even if she got chatty with the pillow talk, I wasn't sleeping with her to find out about her past. I realized it was a moral line I never drew before.

It's hell getting older.

Ruby got up to use the restroom when the waiter collected our plates. I looked at the lighting. Two directly overhead cast plenty of illumination on our table. I took out my phone and brought up the camera with the flash off. When Ruby came back from the ladies' room and sat again, I snapped a picture of her on the sly. This one was a straight-on shot, better than the one I already had. "You ready to go?" she said.

"Just checking an email," I said, putting my phone away. The waiter came back with the check. I filled it out, signed it, and walked outside with Ruby. In my office, I could use the BPD's facial recognition software to see if the system knew who Ruby really was. She'd be unhappy with me for finding out, but if it helped me keep her safe from the stalker, I could live with it.

* * *

I KEPT an eye on Ruby for a while longer, then drove home. She went to the Deluxe Plaza Motel with three more johns. I followed her each time. Nothing eventful happened. Ruby showered again after the second one, and I drove her back up Pulaski Highway; the other two times, the johns were courteous enough to give her a lift back up the road.

When I got home, my house was dark. I called for Gloria a couple times and got no answer. She must have gone home. I went to the office, turned the light on, and sat behind my desk. An envelope waited atop my keyboard with my initials scrawled on it in Gloria's flowery handwriting. I opened the envelope and read the letter.

* * *

C.T.,

* * *

I HOPE *you're not out too late. My parents are going on vacation tomorrow morning, and I'm meeting them for an early breakfast at their house. You're welcome to come by if you're awake. I told them you might not make it. Try not to stay up too late with your head buried in a file. I know these cases are important to you, but I'm worried that you're burning the candle at both ends.*

* * *

I'LL SEE *you tomorrow even if you don't make it to breakfast. Sleep well.*

* * *

Love,
    Gloria

* * *

I smiled and ran the folded paper under my nose. No perfume. I pushed past my brief disappointment, put the letter down, and dug back into Samantha's case file. I knew I was missing something in the online investigation. Nothing useful jumped out at me. The defunct ISP put up a hurdle I couldn't leap. Samantha and her killer met in a few chat rooms. I checked into them; those service providers folded as well. Samantha's emails came from her Penn account. I felt confident I could hack an ivy league school, but who saved emails from thirteen years ago?

I kept looking through the file and at my whiteboard. Whatever effects lingered from the diner's coffee were coming to an end. My eyelids grew heavy. I pressed on but couldn't last much longer. Late nights with Ruby were wreaking havoc with my sleeping patterns. I compensated for it by zonking out at my desk.

* * *

I woke up when I almost tumbled out of my chair. This was no way to spend my nights. As much as I wanted to catch the bastard who killed my sister, I couldn't do it if I ran myself ragged. I trudged upstairs, rinsed my mouth with mouthwash, and brushed my teeth. The clock read 6:18. I'd slept about four hours. Gloria and her parents were doing an early breakfast. I wondered how much past sunrise it would be.

Gloria provided me a built-in excuse for missing breakfast, so I lay in bed. I still felt tired, but thoughts danced through my head. Ruby told me she received a good private education through her high school years. Then she said a falling out with her family led to her working the streets. There must have been a few steps in the middle she left out. Those would flesh out her story for me, but they might also give me some insights into her stalker. What if he knew her back then?

It made me think of my parents. They took the hint and stopped calling me. I couldn't talk to them yet. The wound still felt too fresh. Despite all their claims of protecting me, they let years go by before telling me. Even if I needed their protection in high school—I would argue I did not—the need for it died away since. If I thought about it, I could almost understand their motivation at the time. I couldn't forgive their silence over the years, however, and I didn't know that I ever could. Did this whole mess irreparably change my relationship with my parents?

I looked at the clock again: 6:35. Would Gloria be awake? As if in answer to my question, I heard a text come in. Gloria wondered if I was awake. I replied in the affirmative. She said breakfast at her parents' would commence at 7:30. I told her I'd be there. First, I needed a shower and some coffee, and maybe in the opposite order.

* * *

Clean and caffeinated, I drove to Gloria's parents' house. They lived near her in Brooklandville, a ritzy community in Baltimore County. Driveways as wide as some streets snaked up to the houses, cats wore diamond-studded collars, and even the dogs slipped into mink coats in the winter. I pulled into the driveway at 7:35. Even the java boost couldn't make me prompt. Gloria's Mercedes rocket and my Audi sat in the driveway—I think her parents would have fainted if I'd brought the Caprice—while the garage held a Jaguar and an Range Rover. No one drove a Honda in Brooklandville.

I rang the doorbell, expecting it to cue a small orchestra to play Brahms in the foyer and feeling a twinge of disappointment when it answered with a mere ring. Gloria appeared at the door a moment later. She smiled at me and after I walked in, wrapped me in a huge hug and planted a kiss on me. She wore what was for her an average dress, meaning it probably only cost a few hundred dollars. I'd pulled on a nice pair of jeans, a button-down silk shirt, and a tweed sportcoat. I always felt the Readings' house to be a jacket-required venue.

Gloria led me into the kitchen. Her mother, Susan, finished setting out an impressive breakfast spread. She walked to me, and we did the European cheek-kissing thing she liked because it made her seem worldly. Gloria's father, Hugh, shook my hand and almost smiled at me. Susan and Gloria dressed similarly; Hugh one-upped me by wearing dress pants. I sat at the table in my comfortable denims. A large pile of scrambled eggs steamed in the center. Plates of fresh fruit, sausage patties, bacon, toast, and English muffins surrounded it.

When Gloria's parents sat, we all passed the plates around. I ended with generous portions of bacon, sausage, and scrambled eggs. Figuring I needed some carbs to offset my plate of protein, I took an English muffin and buttered it. We all took a few minutes to eat. The bacon and sausage tasted so fresh I wondered if Susan butchered a pig in the kitchen before I arrived. Of course she hadn't—she'd hire it out.

"Gloria tells us you're working hard, C.T.," Susan said.

"Almost never by choice," I said.

"That's the spirit!" Hugh added.

"You're working two cases?"

"Officially, one. The other is more of a . . . personal interest."

"Gloria told us," said Susan. "How terrible to find out after all this time."

I couldn't be surprised Gloria told her parents. "It is," I said to keep up my end of the conversation.

We sat in silence for a few seconds until Hugh picked up on the fact I didn't want to talk about my sister's case or the way it affected my relationship with my parents. "What's your other case?" he said.

This would go over well. "I'm helping a girl who's being stalked," I said, omitting Ruby's profession.

"You've seen the stalker?" Susan said.

"I've seen his car. He drives it well."

"What does the girl do?"

I needed to tiptoe here. Hugh and Susan Reading, like many rich people, looked down on the working stiffs of the world, and I figured it counted double when the job itself was illegal. Then again, Ruby's profession formed the crux of the case. If she'd tumbled from her lofty perch and ended up as a waitress, everything would be different. "She's a prostitute."

Susan dropped her fork. I wondered if she would need to fan herself (or have someone fan her) because of the shock. Hugh took it all in stride. "You're sure she's being stalked?"

"I am."

"How did she come to find you?"

"She hired someone I know," I said. "When he realized there might be some investigating required, he called me."

"Is the girl on drugs?" Susan said, having recovered from the indignity of someone dropping the P-word in her house.

"No. She's quite smart. I could tell she's well educated from the way she talked. I asked her, and she said she went to private schools all the way through twelfth grade."

"What happened then?" said Hugh.

"A falling-out with her family. It led to her landing on the street as a working girl." I followed Hugh's lead.

"Sounds like an indirect path," he said.

"I thought so, too," I concurred. "She must be leaving a step or two out."

"I guess she hasn't told you her name?"

I shook my head. "I only know the name she uses on the streets."

"What is it?"

"Ruby." I paused and looked for a reaction. Maybe the Readings knew a wealthy family who had a daughter nick-named Ruby a few years ago. "Does it sound familiar?"

Hugh and Susan looked at each other. Both shook their heads. "I'm afraid not," he said.

"No one you know with a missing daughter? She says she's twenty-three and looks it."

"Can't think of anyone." Hugh looked at Susan, who shrugged.

"It's OK," I said. "I haven't been able to find out much about this girl so far. Some of it is because she just doesn't want to tell me a lot."

"What are you going to do?"

"Keep working. Hope she tells me more. Try to fill in the gaps if she doesn't. Ultimately, I want to find her stalker and persuade him to stay away from her."

"Do you think you'll be able to?" Susan said.

"I don't know." I said, glancing down at my plate. Most of the food would be cold by now. "I think I can, but some of it is going to depend on Ruby."

"Good luck," said Hugh. "Gloria tells us some of the cases you work, and your parents do, too. They're quite proud of you."

"They have a funny way of showing it sometimes."

"I hope it all works out with them," Susan said. "You're upset with them now, but they're good people, and they're your parents. It couldn't have been easy for them to bury a child."

I nodded to hide the fact Susan's comment compelled me to think. So far, I'd only focused on my anger at my parents' thirteen years of deception. However, to start the whole mess off, they buried their first child and only daughter. Parents aren't supposed to inter their children. Such upheaval in the circle of life can make people do things they wouldn't otherwise do.

I resumed eating my breakfast. The four of us chatted some more but not about my caseload. Gloria's parents were vacationing in France and Italy for a couple weeks. They rented a chateau and a villa for their stays. When breakfast was over and the dishes were put away, I wished them safe travels, kissed Gloria goodbye, and went back to my house. A lot occupied my mind.

CHAPTER 11

I got home, changed into workout clothes, and went to the dojo. I'd studied martial arts since high school, refined my knowledge in Hong Kong, and joined a dojo when I got back to keep in practice. I took a class once a week and sparred two other days, time permitting. When I arrived, I learned I would be practicing with Max, a black belt student and occasional instructor. He was a few years younger than I and wore his hair in a ridiculous Mohawk. Perhaps he first took up martial arts to offset the deserved beatings his hairstyle brought him.

Max and I stretched, geared up, and hit the mat. We wore cups, faceguards, and light gloves. He and I were veterans of sparring, but this was only the second time we'd opposed each other. We paced around the mat for a minute, going through a few simple punches and blocks to warm each other up. Once we both nodded to acknowledge we were ready, we got down to business.

I favored defense and counterstrikes while Max tended to prefer attacking first. True to form, he came in with a high kick I turned aside. He followed it with a series of punches, all of which I blocked before countering with an elbow from which

Max spun away. He banged his gloves together and came at me again. Low punch, block. High punch, block. Follow-up elbow, blocked. Knee to the midsection, countered with a knee of my own. I snapped off a quick kick after the block and hit Max in the chest. It didn't knock him over, but he scooted back a couple of steps.

Thoughts of my cases seeped into my consciousness. Samantha's continued to confound me. I needed some kind of a breakthrough and didn't know where to uncover one, even after a visit to the crime scene and several of the principals. Max led with a high side kick I blocked. He came right back with one at my midsection I also blunted. Though he couldn't get much behind it, he followed it with a lunging short left I didn't expect and didn't block. The faceguard soaked up the impact, but it rattled me out of my musings.

I went on the offensive. Max turned aside all of my punches and kicks. I felt myself ooze sweat. Who else could I talk to about Samantha's murder? The lead detective and *Sun* reporter added nothing to the little I knew. I could track down the *City Paper* reporter, but this held low expected value. Other detectives who worked the case could give me their perspectives. Two different cops, good as they both may be, can see the same scene and evidence different ways. I grabbed Max's arm after one exchange, but he wriggled out of my grip.

We continued trading turns on the offense with only the occasional minor hit getting through. My thoughts drifted to Samantha again. I must've missed something. Maybe I could ask Dr. Hunt to look over the ME's report. On the other hand, it lacked ambiguity even to a layman like me. As much as I hated looking at the photos, going through them could illuminate something new. Just as I decided to do it when I got home, Max's foot drove into my midsection and blasted the breath from my lungs. I doubled over and staggered back three steps before falling to the mat. Max broke his fighting stance and walked after me, frowning in concern. "You OK?"

I nodded as my wind returned. "You gave me a pretty good shot."

"I mean in general. You seem distracted. Everything all right?"

"Not really," I said, "but I'll manage."

Max asked me a couple more questions, but I didn't intend on going into further detail with him. We ended our session, and I hit the showers. After washing my hair, I stood under the spray pondering my next move in the case. Ruby crept into my thoughts. I couldn't forget about her as much as I wanted to focus on Samantha. For the first time, I considered a link between the two cases but dismissed it. These two cases being related required enormous feats of coincidence I couldn't buy into. Besides, if the same man who killed my sister now stalked Ruby, she should've been attacked by now.

The hot shower grew tepid. I turned the water off, dried myself, got dressed, and went home to see if I could figure anything out. I wasn't optimistic.

THE FIRST THING I figured out was lunch. My recent trip to Harris Teeter left me with a refrigerator burgeoning with options. I put some turkey bacon on a skillet while I assembled the rest of a sandwich: a hearty bread, thin slices of roast beef, mustard, and lettuce. While the bacon finished, I spooned some hummus into a small bowl and put it and bag of pita chips onto the table. The bacon sizzled to perfection. I took it from the skillet, added it to my sandwich, sliced the whole thing in half, and sat at the kitchen table.

Gloria unlocked the door and came in while I ate. She hung

her purse on my coat rack, usurping a space larger than any coat I would have hung there—to say nothing for the weight of the purse. Hefting it could have been the thirteenth labor of Heracles. Gloria joined me at the table. "My parents are off to Europe," she said.

"I'm surprised you didn't go with them," I said after swallowing a large bite of my sandwich.

She shrugged. "Trips with the parents aren't what they used to be. They expect me to pay my own way now."

I grinned. "How beastly of them."

"I know, I know . . . I can afford to. When I was younger, I liked traveling with them. Now, I think I'd rather go by myself." She smiled at me. "Or with you."

"Don't book us any trips until I finish these cases. At this rate, you might want to call a moratorium on travel for the rest of the year."

"You'll work it out." Gloria patted my hand. "You always do."

I appreciated her confidence in me but at the moment, I couldn't share it.

AFTER LUNCH, I went back to the office and took up my vigil with Samantha's file. I read the ME's report again. Nothing changed, and no new insights sprang to mind. Next, I looked over the police report. The result was the same. I pulled out the pictures, steeled myself, and flipped through them.

Seeing Samantha lying on the Patterson Park ground, more blood out of her than in, walloped me right in the gut. I used Google Maps and Google Earth to compare the present park they showed with the pictures. The lay of the land hadn't changed in thirteen years even if specific details had. I went back to the police report and read the interviews with nearby residents and anyone who may have been a potential witness. Nothing. At least, nothing on the surface.

Baltimore is an insular town. We don't like outsiders, and many residents don't have the BPD on their Christmas card lists. I knew no reason to suspect any of the nearby residents lied to the cops, but even taking them all at their word, I looked to see if a pattern would emerge. Six residents on Eastern Avenue saw nothing. Ditto Baltimore Street with four and Patterson Park Avenue with five. On South Linwood Avenue, only one resident claimed he saw nothing. All were small sample sizes. I wondered if the police interviewed anyone else, and those notes didn't make it into the box when it all went into cold storage.

It wasn't much, but a single cord can unravel a sweater. I learned this in a song. Linwood Avenue featured few businesses breaking up stretches of classic Baltimore rowhouses, and it crossed other streets with the same configuration. The best place for someone to hide—other than in a random house—was the Hatton Senior Center a few blocks down Linwood at the corner of Fait Ave.

Did Samantha's killer dash away from the scene, escape the notice of the one person the police found to ask, and hide in the old folks' hangout? What if the killer had a relative there? What if he worked there? I wondered if I could find employment records from Hatton going back thirteen years?

Database administrators use a language called SQL to interact with their quarry. While it's fine for what it does, someone like me can exploit vulnerabilities in SQL and gain access we weren't meant to have. A simple injection attack opened their network, and I prowled around for HR records. Current employee files resided in a folder. Past organizational charts had been shunted off to a different location. I found the closest one I could to the time of Samantha's murder, dated March of the same year. A quick comparison to the current employee roster showed only two people still worked there. I noted their names, then went hunting for files on the old employees. Along the way, I found a policy stating erstwhile employees would have their folders deleted one year after they left the company. Swing and a miss. I settled for taking a screen capture of the old organizational chart and printing it. Once I had what I needed, I covered my tracks and disconnected from the center's network.

I hopped onto the BPD's system and looked for any information I could find on Hatton employees. I entered all the names and sent a query to their database. A few seconds later, three files popped up. The lack of deviancy among the staff didn't help my case. The first file belonged to a man whose only transgression had been a DWI. An unlikely murderer. The second was of a woman who vandalized two cars belonging to her ex-husband. I ruled her out. The third held promise.

Tim Green worked at the Hatton Center thirteen years ago. Five years prior, he got arrested for assault relating to a bar fight. Two years after, Green displayed a thick skull, getting arrested for assault again. Four years later—two years following Samantha's murder—he got popped for armed robbery The case ended up getting thrown out. Still, he showed a history of violence, and it gave me more to go on than anything else I'd seen.

I dug into Tim Green. The first thing I noticed was he died six years ago. Maybe he killed Samantha. I hoped not. I wanted her killer brought to justice at the business end of my .45, and Green, a good candidate, inconsiderately expired. I went back and looked at his BPD file. Two bar fights and an armed robbery charge. He'd been a man unafraid of violence, but it didn't make him a killer. I took my printout of the senior center org chart and spiked it into the shredder.

Any leads I could cobble together were evaporating. Now I knew how the BPD detectives felt thirteen years ago when this happened. However, other cases landed in their inboxes all the time, and I kept mine clean. I could afford to devote more time to Samantha's, for all the good it had done me so far. Without anything else coming to mind, I went back to the pictures.

Samantha looked a lot like our mother—by contrast, I favored our father. She had soft green eyes, a shade of blonde hair no woman could get from a bottle, and delicate, pretty features. When some people die, especially when they're murdered, their faces contort in horror. Sometimes, they stare forward in eternal surprise. These expressions fade when a mortician works their faces into a more calm and neutral one. At her funeral, Samantha looked like she'd fallen asleep. I could still see her lying in the casket. The memory made my eyes well again. Samantha's face in the pictures didn't look the same. Her eyes were open, the last thing they saw being the man who stabbed her a dozen times.

I took a deep breath and kept flipping through the pictures. The BPD photographer snapped copious pictures of Samantha, both as they found her face-down and after they rolled her onto her back. The cameraman also took pictures of interesting detritus the uniforms and detectives marked. The police report said none of it came to anything.

I looked through all the pictures. Seeing my sister lying on the Patterson Park grass saddened me, but none of the images enlightened me. The possibility Tim Green killed Samantha served as my light bulb moment. Maybe he did. I figured it to be unlikely and would go forward as if her killer were still out there.

What else could I do?

* * *

I TOOK A NAP.

Between staying out late with Ruby and getting up early this morning to have breakfast with Gloria and her parents, I was running on four hours sleep, max. As I neared thirty, the combination of a late night and early morning wore on me more and more. Gone were the days where I could carouse until the wee hours in college, then ace an exam at seven-thirty the next morning. I lay down for two hours and woke up with more energy but no more insight into either of my cases.

An image of Ruby—without her shirt on, of course—fluttered to the forefront of my mind. I'd been treading water with Samantha's case. Could I do any better with Ruby's? I sat up in bed. Someone stalked her. I'd seen and chased his car, and he drove like someone who'd spent years handling horsepower and speed. The car didn't lead to anything. However, I didn't even want to ponder the number of silver E-class Mercedes in Maryland. Half the residents of Brooklandville or Roland Park probably garaged one, to say nothing of ritzy suburban areas like Fallston or Potomac. I required much more specific information about the stalker to do much about him.

The whole case cried out for more specificity. Hell, I didn't even know Ruby's real name. What if—despite her claims to the contrary—the identity of the stalker could be gleaned from her unhappy past? Without knowing much about her, my hands were tied.

I called up the picture of Ruby I snapped in the diner. Though unaware I took it, she looked right at me, a small smile crossing her lips. The happiness didn't make it to her eyes, though, giving her the look of a girl who wanted to smile and hadn't found a compelling reason in a long time. Just about every hooker could dredge up a bad beat story. Bumper stickers proclaimed well-adjusted women seldom made history; they also seldom wound up selling themselves on street corners. Where did Ruby's life come undone?

I went downstairs and transferred the picture to my PC. I accessed the BPD's network and brought up their facial recognition software. They added the feature within the last year, and it pulled from state police records. I put Ruby's photo into the software, set it to run, and went into the living room. Matching a picture against thousands and thousands of records took a while, despite what TV shows might tell you.

I flipped channels while I waited. Gloria must have gone back out. When the TV bored me, I got up, toasted a piece of hearty bread, and slathered it with peanut butter. After sparring earlier, I could afford the calories. I ended up watching a show about baseball. They talked about every team other than the Orioles. Typical, I thought in my provincial Baltimore way.

When it ended, I walked back to the office. The search finished. Ruby got detained for a scuffle when she was younger but never got herself arrested for anything. Her record made no mention of prostitution. I looked at the most important bit of information about her: her name. I didn't believe it when I saw it.

Melinda Davenport.

A quick Google search told me Melinda was the daughter Vincent Davenport said disappeared five years ago . . . the missing girl who compelled him to start a large charitable foundation.

What the hell had I wandered into?

CHAPTER 12

GLORIA COULDN'T HAVE KNOWN ABOUT DAVENPORT. A man like him would hide a bombshell like a daughter working the no-tell motel circuit, especially from the people who helped him raise money. It's hard to say you run a charity to support finding missing children when your own daughter turns out not to be missing. Did Davenport know Melinda ended up as Ruby? I could ask him. He wouldn't like it, but I didn't care. My gut told me he knew.

Armed with this new knowledge, I looked up everything I could about Vincent Davenport, Melinda, and the whole family. Ruby—or Melinda, or however I should think of her now—told the truth about going to private school. She graduated from Seton Keough, an all-girls Catholic School in Baltimore. At graduation, Williams College offered her a scholarship. Williams could produce no record of her ever attending a class. Something—or someone—caused Melinda to disappear the summer of her graduation. Did the same someone stalk her now?

Melinda was born to Vincent and Sheila Davenport twenty-three years and seven months ago at St. Joseph's Hospital. Sheila died of cancer when Melinda was ten. Six years later, Vincent married the former Helen McMurray, who had a son three months older than Melinda. They all lived in Davenport's house for about two years; then, everything went to hell. Melinda disappeared and resurfaced as Ruby, Helen left for places unknown, and her son Jackson cycled in and out of drug rehab centers throughout the state. He no longer lived with Davenport, and his last known address belonged to an expensive rehab facility in Harford County. I called; they said he no longer resided there.

After Melinda left, Vincent Davenport started the Nightlight Foundation. The charity's website made no mention of his daughter's name, nor did it specify how long she'd been missing. I wondered if Davenport even searched for her. Something bothered me about the whole situation. Helen Davenport leaves and doesn't turn up anywhere. Jackson McMurray is in and out of rehab and as far off the grid as his mother. Melinda has some kind of family falling-out and winds up a hooker along Pulaski Highway.

What drove the Davenports apart? Did it have something to do with Melinda being stalked now? I would need to dig into the family and find out. Vincent Davenport was a big player in Baltimore. He'd accumulated a lot of friends in high places. I would need to be careful. He would also have enemies, and maybe I could uncover them.

As I pondered the fall of the house of Davenport, Gloria walked in. She sauntered down the hall and came into the office. "How's it going?" she said, sitting in a guest chair and smiling at me.

"I'm still hitting my head into a wall with Samantha's case," I said. "Ruby's, however, has been . . . interesting."

"What do you mean?"

"I snapped a better picture of her last night. This morning,

I ran it through the BPD's facial recognition program. Want to guess who she is?"

"You know who she is?" I nodded. Gloria pursed her lips. "I wouldn't even know where to start."

"Her real name is Melinda Davenport."

Gloria started to say something, then paused and frowned. "Davenport?"

"Yes. As in your friend Vincent Davenport's missing daughter."

"Oh, my gosh! You found her!" Gloria got up from the chair. "I have to tell him."

"No," I said.

"But he—"

"Knows already."

Gloria recoiled as if something hit her in the face. "You think he knows?" she said, slumping into the chair.

"I think he must." I provided her the rundown of the Davenport family history since Melinda's birth.

"That doesn't mean he's aware his daughter is Ruby," she said.

"It's likely. The whole situation stinks. His wife and stepson vanished. His daughter is a hooker. Something bad happened in his family. Maybe it was his fault, and maybe it wasn't, but I'll bet you my Audi he knows his daughter isn't really missing."

"But . . . his foundation?"

"Good for him for starting one," I said. "I'm sure his rich friends expected no less. I'm glad he's raised all the money for a good cause, but the whole thing becomes pretty cynical when you factor in his family history."

"He cares, C.T. He cares about the parents whose children have disappeared. I've seen it."

"Maybe he does. Maybe it's guilt from his own situation.

Look, he's done good by a lot of people, no doubt. Even if his foundation hasn't helped find a single missing kid, he's brought publicity to the problem and given families some hope. It doesn't mean his hands are clean, though."

"You think he killed his wife?" Gloria said. She fidgeted in the chair, and Gloria was not prone to this behavior.

"I'm very curious what happened to her," I said.

Gloria shook her head. "What a mess."

"It is. It's a lot deeper than an ordinary hooker getting stalked."

"What do you think I should do?"

"About what?" I said.

"About his foundation. I'm involved with it. What have I really gotten into?"

"Stay involved. There's a chance he's innocent in all this. If not, I'd rather he not have an idea you know what might've happened."

She nodded. "All right. What are you going to do now?"

"Keep looking into the Davenports, I guess."

"Be careful, C.T.," Gloria warned. "Vincent is a powerful man."

"I know. I've thought about it. I'll do my best to be discreet."

"You're already in trouble, then," she said with a grin.

"Don't I know it."

THE ANSWER to Ruby's particular puzzle had to lie with her family. She'd gone through a lot even before her home life underwent an upheaval with the addition of a stepfamily. Plenty of people managed these situations without ending up in the sex trade, but everyone is different. Melinda could have experienced a worse time of it than most. I would need to figure this out. For now, I wanted to focus on the stalking angle.

Armed with Ruby's identity, I could presume her father may be involved in the stalking. Vincent Davenport was certainly wealthy enough to hire someone to keep tabs on the daughter he knew didn't go missing. The guy let himself be seen, which put a mark against his professionalism, but he drove the Benz like someone who'd evaded pursuit before.

If Davenport knew his daughter walked the streets as Ruby, it meant he also was aware of her pimp, Shade. Shade could be in trouble. Melinda hadn't talked to him about the situation yet, and I doubted she would. I didn't relish the idea of conversing with another pimp, but this job forced me to do a lot of things I didn't enjoy. With no idea where to find Shade, I turned to the BPD's resources for help.

Shade, real name Donnell Shadrick, enjoyed the amenities of Central Booking on two occasions. The city prosecuted him for being a pimp once but couldn't make the charges stick. The BPD speculated he "managed" a stable of seven prostitutes and ascribed to him a territory including Ruby's stomping grounds near the Gold Club. His favorite hangouts included The Wagon Wheel, an establishment like the Gold Club, minus the polish and plus several factors of seediness. I hoped to find him somewhere else as I drove there.

Unfortunately, Shade occupied a table at the Wagon Wheel. He shared it with a massive white fellow who looked at everyone, even the naked dancers, through narrow, distrusting eyes. Way to be inconspicuous. Some people showed no respect for tradecraft. The table featured three large cushioned chairs facing the stage. This left one open. I sat in the remaining chair when Shade's bodyguard looked in the other direction.

"What the hell?" said Shade from my left.

"Just enjoying the show," I said. On stage, a moderately attractive dancer peeled off her last scrap of clothing and gyrated to some dreadful rock song. She looked around the assembled patrons with empty eyes, scanning for dollar bills and easy marks.

"Well, enjoy it somewhere else." The bodyguard, two seats to my left, now fixed his narrowed eyes on me.

"I also came here to talk to you."

"You a cop?" asked Shade.

"Hell no."

"What do you want to talk about?"

"You might be in trouble," I said.

Shade snickered. "When I get in trouble, Jacko takes care of things. Why don't you show the man how you take care of things, Jacko?"

A small smile broke the line of the bodyguard's lips as he stood. He must've been six-five and close to 280 pounds. I'd seen smaller linemen on football teams. Like a lot of larger guys, he carried too much weight for his frame but also a good amount of muscle. I wouldn't want to stand—or sit—around and let him hit me. The muscleman stopped in front of my chair and stared down at me. His expression didn't change. It was more uninterested than menacing.

"Why don't you sit somewhere else, bub?" said Jacko.

"I have some news for your boss," I said.

"You can tell me."

"I think it might get lost in translation."

Jacko pondered my remark for a second, then pointed at me, putting his thick index finger a few inches from my nose. "You need to beat it, or I'm gonna beat you."

"Wow," I said, "pretty clever. You trademark it yet?"

He jabbed his digit into my cheek and pulled it back. "I ain't gonna tell you again, funny man."

I grabbed Jacko's finger and bent it the wrong way. When he tried to recoil, I used my other hand to bar his wrist. He squirmed and thrashed even as he grunted in pain. "Struggling just makes it worse," I said. "Give me a reason and all I have to do is twist a little harder." I put some more pressure on his lower arm to drive the point home. "You won't be pointing at anyone for a while, and you'll have a broken wrist to complete the lesson. Is this what you want?" Jacko shook his head. "There's the first smart thing you've said. Now sit down and be quiet while the grown-ups talk."

I let go of Jacko's hand and arm. He rubbed the sore parts and glared at me. I pointed to the seat he vacated. He walked back to it and sat down. "Like I was saying," I said to Shade, "I think you might be in trouble."

Shade looked at Jacko, shook his head, then regarded me. "What kind of trouble?"

"One of your girls might have someone after her."

"Who?"

"I'm not at liberty to say," I told him.

"You ain't telling me much."

"Let's say an interested party has the means to keep an eye on her. The logical conclusion there is he knows about you. It means he could be watching you, too. If this man decides to act, he'll use someone who won't think twice about putting Jacko down to get to you."

Shade tried to look tough, but the furrow in his brow and the big gulp he swallowed spoiled the illusion. "You ain't gonna tell me who it is?" he said.

I shook my head. "It might be nothing. I don't want to see anyone getting hurt—even you two clowns—because someone harbored a vendetta."

"What should I be on the lookout for?"

"People you don't know hanging around."

"You mean besides you?" he said.

"I mean not out in the open." The song stopped, and the dancer left the stage. Once the announcer finished talking, the din lowered, and it felt like a smidgen of order returned to the universe. "Someone you see in the shadows watching," I continued. "A car around more than it should be. Those sorts of things."

"OK." Shade nodded. "I'll make sure we keep our eyes open. What about the girls?"

"I don't think they would be in any danger."

"Not even the one with this nutbar looking for her?"

"I don't think the nutbar wants to hurt her," I said.

"But he might want to hurt me."

"I think he would see you and Jacko as part of the problem." A new dancer came to the stage in a slinky negligee. She wiped the pole down before she started her routine. She probably needed hours to disinfect it properly. Instead, the beginning of the next song overlapped with her disinfecting routine.

"All right." Shade still sported a frown. Jacko cast his distrusting eyes around, settling mostly on me. "I'm not sure what to do about this news, but thanks for telling me."

"Sure," I said, standing up. "Try not to get killed. And stop pointing at people," I said as I passed Jacko. "It's impolite."

I didn't wait to hear his response.

* * *

SHORTLY AFTER I GOT HOME, Ruby called my cell phone. Even though I still thought of her by her *nom de rue*, I knew her real name and resisted the temptation to use it. For now. "C.T., some bad shit went down," she said.

I wondered if my conversation with Shade started a chain reaction. "What happened?"

"I was with a girl, and she got beaten. Someone came up . . . I think he was after me. She got in front of me and ended up taking a pounding. I felt bad, but I had to run."

"Did you see the guy?" I said.

"No, he wore a mask. He found us in an alley. I don't think anybody saw what happened."

"What about the other girl?"

"I came back for her," Ruby said. "I called nine-one-one and said some crazy guy beat the shit out of her. They took her to the hospital."

I would probably need to talk to this girl. "I want you to come with me when I talk to her," I said.

"What am I going to do?" Her voice cracked.

"Not be a target while you're with me."

Ruby sighed into the phone. "All right. Pick me up outside the Deluxe Plaza in a half-hour."

"I'll be there," I said.

* * *

I COLLECTED Ruby thirty-five minutes later, and we drove downtown to Mercy Hospital. We parked in the garage and got visitor badges in the main lobby. The security guard leered at Ruby the entire time he processed us. She wore a small skirt barely covering her thighs and a thin shirt which could have shipped without its top four buttons. The lace bra she wore underneath poked out all the time.

Ruby knew the name the other hooker would use at a hospital. Maybe they sat around and discussed such things on slow nights. Jeanne d'Arc, a name which should have fooled no one over the age of eleven, shared a semi-private room on the fifth floor. The other patient lay sacked out in the next bed, two bags of medicine pumping into her.

"Joanie," said Ruby quietly as we stood by her bedside. Her voice took on a tender, soothing quality when she tried.

Joanie's eyes fluttered open. "Ruby?" she said.

"I'm here." Ruby squeezed Joanie's hand. She was a white girl with auburn hair and brown eyes who looked a few years older than Ruby. Her face may have been pretty, but whoever beat her made it impossible to tell. Bruises and swelling dotted her features. She sported a shiner around her right eye; the left one was swollen shut. Someone did a number on her. I clenched and unclenched my fists. If the stalker did this, he needed to answer for one more thing, and I would see he did.

"Who's with you?" she said.

"He's been looking into the stalker thing for me."

"You a cop?"

I stood beside Ruby. About a year and a half ago, when I first started this job, a hospital room with two hookers would have ranked among the last places I thought I'd end up. Ten years ago, it would have sounded like a fun way to pass an evening. Now, the nature of the situation gnawed at me. Ruby came from a wealthy family, and her activities couldn't have been a secret from her father. Someone, presumably Ruby's stalker, pummeled poor Joanie. This case went downhill fast, and I still didn't know if I could step hard enough on the brake. "No," I said, "just a private investigator who might be able to help."

"Lot of help you were earlier today." Joanie's voice, which a moment ago sounded weary and distant, took on new life with the injection of bitterness.

"What happened?"

"Some guy beat my ass is what happened."

"Did you see him?" I said.

"He wore a mask."

"I told him that already," Ruby said.

Joanie fixed me with her good eye. "Why'd the hell you ask me, then?"

"Because you might have noticed something, or recognized someone, in spite of the mask."

"I don't know who the hell he was, if that's what you mean."

"What about by body size?" I said. "Is he built like anyone you know?"

She thought about this for a moment and then said, "He's a little shorter than you and thicker."

"Was he white?"

"Yeah."

"Could you tell anything about his face, like eye color, moustache . . .?"

"For not a cop, you sure ask a lot of questions."

"I'm trying to figure out who did it."

"Good luck. Cops ain't gonna care. A whore gets beat up, she musta had it coming. That's how they see it."

"It's not how I see it," I said.

Joanie stared at me with her half-good eye. I did my best not to fixate on the swollen one. "I don't know who did it. He seemed interested in Ruby. Maybe it was a stalker, maybe it was some asshole john. I don't know."

I got the feeling Joanie didn't tell me everything, but I didn't think I'd get anymore out of her. "If you can think of anything else, Ruby knows how to get hold of me."

"You keep her safe," she said. "Ruby's a good girl. She could get out of this life if she wanted." Ruby sighed behind me. "You keep her safe from this asshole."

I nodded. "I will," I said.

I hoped I could.

* * *

Ruby and I hopped back into the Caprice and left the hospital. "You really going to keep me safe?" she said.

I looked at her as we sat at a red light. Her lips were pursed, and she wore a small, delicate frown. Her lip quivered occasionally despite her best attempts to hide it. "You're spooked, aren't you?" I said.

"I don't scare easily. You can't survive on the streets if you do. But yeah, this has me pretty spooked. Some asshole looks for me, finds me, then beats the shit out of poor Joanie. And what do I do?" She snorted. "I run while the running's good."

"You survived."

"What if Joanie hadn't? What if he had killed her?"

A tear slid down Ruby's cheek. I popped the console and handed her a tissue. "It didn't happen. You can't get lost in hypotheticals. You made the best decision you could at the time."

"What am I going to do now?" she said as the tears flowed. "I don't feel safe anymore. I know there's danger in my job. I think about it every time I get into a car or go into a motel room with a john. What if this one is crazy? What if I remind him of his mother?" She sobbed a few times. "I can live with that. This . . . this hit too close to home."

"So stop," I told her. "Get out of the life."

"And do what?"

"Put your private school education to use."

"You think it's that easy?" She turned and stared out the window. Her reflection wore a wistful expression. "How do I explain a five-year gap of no school and work?"

"International travel." I shrugged. "Caring for a sick relative. It doesn't matter. Make it sound convincing and sell it in an interview."

"I appreciate your confidence, but I'm not sure it's so easy to get out of this life."

"You don't think Shade would let you go?"

Ruby's head snapped around to me. "You know Shade?"

"I'm a detective," I said. "You don't think I can find out who your pimp is?"

She wiped a stray tear from her eye. "Shade treats me well. A lot of girls have it worse."

"And you could have it better if you got out."

"Maybe."

Did Ruby know her father set up a foundation after she disappeared? I wondered if they were ever in contact. Vincent Davenport must have known what his daughter did, but what did Melinda know? I thought about dropping my knowledge of her family on her but decided against it. Ruby had been through enough for one night. She didn't need thoughts of her family problems chasing dreams of a beaten Joanie through her head. "You could probably do whatever you set your mind to," I said. "You just need to aim higher."

We pulled into the Gold Club parking lot. Ruby looked over at me, smiled, and kissed my cheek. "It's sweet that you think so."

"I'll keep an eye on you when I can. Call me if something gets bad."

"I will." She gave me another smile, then got out of the car. Evening settled in, and cars crowded the parking lot. I pulled onto Pulaski Highway and made a U-turn about a block down the street. As I drove back up the road, I noticed a silver Benz make the U-turn behind me.

CHAPTER 13

As a snooty car consumer, I knew the general specs of a new Mercedes E-class sedan. I also knew the specs of my Caprice, which did not sport its stock engine or exhaust. The Benz might be a little quicker, but I felt confident my American-made V8—much newer than the car's blocky body—possessed more top-end power. He couldn't catch me on a long straightaway. Problem: downtown Baltimore features few of those unbroken by a string of stop lights. I knew the city well, but a lot of stops and quick turns favored the Benz.

I didn't let on I spotted a tail, and the other driver did his best to remain inconspicuous, even falling in behind a minivan. Instead of heading home via the most efficient route, I took my follower on a tour of the city. If we ended our game of follow-the-leader in the wrong neighborhoods with some seedy characters on the streets, they would ignore my older Caprice and focus on the newer, shiny silver Benz. It could be enough interference to allow me to escape.

I considered calling Rich. He could probably quote me chapter and verse from the BPD manual on what to do if you're being chased in a car. If nothing else, he could find us and come up behind the Benz. I decided against it—the reminders I would get of how I needed his help to bail me out would be too much. Instead, I called Rollins. "I'm being followed by Ruby's stalker," I said after he picked up. "I'm in the Caprice, and he's in a silver Benz."

"Where are you?"

Pulaski Highway split farther in Baltimore, becoming Orleans Street to the right and merging with Fayette Street to the left. I took it left. "I just got onto Fayette from Pulaski."

"I'm not far. I was headed to the Gold Club." Tires screeched through the connection. "Lead him to Fells Point. We can probably lose him in the traffic down there, but if not, there are plenty of places to box him in."

"OK. I'm going to head over and take Broadway into Fells."

"I'll find you," Rollins said and hung up.

Patterson Park Avenue was the next light. I made the left. The minivan did not follow me, but the silver Benz took the turn behind me. I didn't carry a gun tonight. If I got stuck at a light, I would have to rely on the Caprice's fortification against small arms fire and my own lead foot to affect a getaway. I resolved to leave the house armed for the duration of this case.

After a block, I hit Baltimore Street and drove past Patterson Park. I wondered if my subconscious chose this route. There were myriad ways to get to Fells Point from where I called Rollins. Hell, I could have continued down Fayette and hit Broadway without diverting onto any other streets. Ruby's case consumed a lot of my time recently. Was this my subconscious' way of telling me I needed to prioritize Samantha's murder? I regarded the park as I drove past. A few people walked on the trails, one being led around by a powerful Rottweiler on a leash. A Frisbee game wound down as dusk settled over the area. Behind my left shoulder lay my sister's murder scene. I took a deep breath as I drove past and glanced in my rearview. The Mercedes hung back several car lengths, trying to give the impression we were simply going the same way. Another peek in the mirror revealed the absence of a front plate.

I made the right onto Eastern Avenue. The Benz took the turn behind me. I looked in my mirror again. A black pickup now followed the silver car. Rollins had acquired us. Now I needed to drive in such a way as not to spook the stalker. The same went for Rollins, but I knew he could shadow drivers without letting them know he tailed them.

The light at Wolfe Street went yellow as I approached. Normally I would have driven through it. This time, I stopped. Rollins called me. "You want to take him now?" he said.

"Too public. This is a big intersection." I looked around. People trolled for parking spots and walked deeper into Fells Point. "Too many folks around if it gets bad."

"All right. You lead us where you want to go." Rollins hung up. The light turned green. I drove forward. Business picked up in Fells Point. Broadway was a main thoroughfare, packed with bars, restaurants, and curiosity shops. If this got ugly, especially with gunplay, innocent bystanders could be hurt. I avoided Broadway and made the next left onto Ann Street.

Ann Street wasn't free of watering holes—no road in this part of Fells Point could make such a claim—but it featured far fewer than Broadway. People still drove around trolling for parking spots, but this street saw much less foot traffic. After a few blocks, we hit old Fells Point, and the road shifted from asphalt to cobblestones. It made for a rocky ride as I crossed Thames Street and started down Fell, which ended at Henderson's Wharf and my old apartment building. The Benz waited for a couple of cars on Thames, then followed me, Rollins in tow.

I drove down Fell Street at a pace allowing the Benz to catch up. Once he did, I made a show of looking for parking.

Rollins' black pickup crept closer. We passed the Dead End Saloon. It didn't mark the end of Fell, but it did announce the end of any attractions. Parking grew scarcer as the road narrowed, and Henderson's Wharf loomed ahead.

We passed Wolfe Street on the left. I slowed a little more. The Mercedes made the hard turn, and I watched it speed up Wolfe as fast as the cobblestones would allow. Rollins tried to follow, but his truck didn't have nearly the turning radius of the agile German sedan. He stopped, backed up a few feet, and then finished cornering. His truck bounced on the cobblestones. I swung around and followed him.

"I think he just went down Aliceanna," Rollins said when he called me a moment later. As we approached, the light turned red. "Dammit!" Rollins yelled. We waited for the light. Cars lined up coming down Wolfe. The signal turned green. Rollins burned rubber and jumped the left ahead of the oncoming cars. I waited for the four vehicles to pass before I made the turn.

"Any sign of him?" I said.

"Don't see him yet," said Rollins. "He had time to lose us. There are so many turns he could have made."

We drove around the area for five minutes and didn't see any sign of the Benz. "This asshole is pretty clever," Rollins said.

"He's dangerous, too." I filled him in on the beating Joanie took for Ruby.

"You're gonna need to be careful."

"I know."

I wanted to work Samantha's murder. Something needed to shake loose somewhere. If I could devote my time to it, I would uncover something. Instead, I got immersed in this case, where hookers were stalked and beaten, and their stalkers followed other people. I missed the weight of a pistol at my side as I drove home.

* * *

I TOOK A NAP. Why not play further havoc with my sleep patterns? I woke up about fifty minutes later. Gloria watched a movie in the living room. I heard what sounded like fireworks and laughter. I walked into the kitchen and foraged in the refrigerator to see what I could make for dinner. Gloria must have heard me rummaging around. "Are you cooking?" she called from the living room.

"If I find something," I said. I had a full refrigerator and enough culinary talent to put it to use. I sought inspiration as I looked in drawers, hunted around on shelves, and checked the contents of the freezer. I pulled out a fresh turkey breast, some baby carrots, an onion, and several small red potatoes. I chopped the onion, quartered the potatoes, and arranged them around the bird in a pan. While the oven heated, I brushed the vegetables with a mix of olive oil and soy sauce and sprinkled rosemary over the potatoes. I put the pan in the oven and turned around to see Gloria in the doorway.

"What's for dinner?" she said, grinning at me. I knew the look.

"Turkey breast and vegetables," I said. "If I get industrious, I might whip up a salad, too."

"I paused the movie." She sashayed into the kitchen. Yoga pants—one of man's finer inventions—hugged her hips. Gloria wrapped her arms around me and kissed me. I took a couple steps backward into the counter and thought she might throw me down atop it.

Which I would not object to, of course.

"You've been working so hard recently," Gloria said, her breath hot on my neck. "Want to get industrious upstairs?"

Nearly an hour remained on the kitchen timer. I put my hands under Gloria's backside and hoisted her up; she wrapped her legs around my waist. "I would love to," I said.

* * *

GLORIA LAY SNUGGLED AGAINST ME, her head on my shoulder, her hair spilling over my chest. I blew a few stray strands out of my face. I told her about Ruby being spooked by Joanie catching a beating meant for her. "This guy is escalating things," she said. "Does she know you know who she is?"

"No," I said, "I figured she'd been through enough for one night. She seemed surprised I knew who her pimp was. I tried not to be offended."

"Did you succeed?"

"Barely," I said in my best faux hurt voice.

"Doesn't she want to do something else with her life?" Gloria said, ignoring my tone.

"I think she does, but she needs a serious push to overcome self-doubts."

"Her friend getting beaten in her place wasn't enough?" said Gloria.

"Apparently not."

"You said this girl is educated, right?"

"Seton Keough for high school," I said.

Gloria nodded her approval. Just like game recognizes game, so does ritzy private school education. "She should be able to find something."

"She doesn't believe it, though. There's a lot of self-doubt there."

"Should there be?"

"I don't think many strong and self-confident women end up as prostitutes," I said.

Gloria nodded against my shoulder. A wisp of her hair blew into my face. I pushed it away. "And you said she had some traumatic experience that caused her to leave home. Who knows what kind of damage it did?"

"I'm going to keep after her to get out of the life. One of these days, I'll hit the right combination to unlock something to allow her to believe in herself."

"Or you'll drive her away."

I shrugged. "I can't control how she reacts."

"But you don't want anything to happen to her," Gloria said.

"Of course not."

"Any stalker sightings since the attack on the other girl?"

"He followed me earlier tonight."

"Why didn't you say something?" Gloria propped herself up on an elbow and frowned at me in concern.

"It was no big deal," I said. "I saw him right away and called Rollins. He picked us up heading into Fells Point. The guy got away, though."

"This is the second time he's done that to you."

"Thanks for reminding me."

"You should take your mind off it."

"What do you think the previous forty-five minutes accomplished?" I said with a grin.

Gloria's cheeks colored. "Come on . . . let's have dinner. I'd just started the first *Lord of the Rings* movie before you got in. Curl up on the couch with me and take a night off. You deserve it."

I pondered her words for a second. "I believe you're right."

* * *

GLORIA SAT at the end of the couch. I lay on my side, facing the TV, my head on her lap. After dinner and a bowl of popcorn, she restarted the movie. She offered to go back to the beginning, but I assured her I'd seen *The Fellowship of the Ring* many times already. We watched the end of the fireworks celebrating Bilbo's birthday. My thoughts drifted.

Driving past Patterson Park reminded me I needed to devote more time to Samantha's case. I'd planned to eschew Ruby entirely once I learned my sister had been murdered, but I couldn't abandon her. My lack of progress in trying to learn anything about my sister's killer helped, too. I walked a cold trail and didn't know where I could build a fire to heat it.

Gloria crunched popcorn above my ear as I pondered. I couldn't think of anyone else to talk to. Even if I tracked down every cop who worked the case and every reporter who followed it, what would they remember after thirteen years? People got murdered in cities all the time; pretty girls in Baltimore didn't constitute a special class. No, whatever evidence I uncovered would be what I found on my own. I kept hoping for some small clue allowing me an epiphany. Then I would have my revenge.

My thoughts drifted back to Ruby. Joanie's beating spooked her, but I couldn't convince her to get out of the business. What if I could help her get a job? The BPD wouldn't hire her. I knew a few lawyers, both with the Public Defender's Office and in private practice; these were also dead-ends. Everyone else I could recommend her to didn't exactly work a legal trade. I doubted Joey Trovato needed (or wanted) an assistant, and working with someone who looked like Ruby would distract Joey too much.

"Are you paying attention?" Gloria said, pulling me back from my reverie.

"Of course," I said.

"OK, what did I just say?"

"You asked if I was paying attention," I pointed out.

"What about before that?"

"I wasn't paying attention then."

I turned my head up. Gloria shook her head and smiled down. "You're lucky I love you."

"No doubt. What did I miss?"

"I was asking you if you read these books before you saw the movies."

"I read them in high school and again in college."

"Are they good?" she said.

"It probably helps if you like the genre. I don't know if being a fan of the movies is enough. I like Tolkien, but he's not for everyone."

Gloria thought about it for a moment. "I might like to try them."

On my TV, Arwen brought a wounded Frodo to Rivendell. I remembered seeing this movie in theaters for the first time and thinking Hugo Weaving had come a long way since Agent Smith. Who wouldn't want to play Elrond? Playing the king of the elves must've constituted an upgrade over the last two dreadful Matrix movies.

Elrond. The name tugged at my brain. I couldn't figure out why. I watched the scene and looked for anything that would spur a memory or an insight.

Then it hit me. Elrond.

I got up from the couch and marched down the hall to my office. This might be my first chip at the stone.

* * *

I sat at my PC. I'd come in here with an idea and the determination to act on it but not a clear direction in which to proceed.

The revelation hit me and now, I didn't know what to do with it. Gloria's soft footfalls moved down the hardwood. "What is it?" she said. "You took off like you just had a breakthrough."

"I should have seen it sooner," I said. I started typing out a list of all the names I could remember from the three *Lord of the Rings* books, even characters like Thom Bombadil who got snubbed when the big screen came calling.

"What? Seen what?"

"The guy my sister talked to—the guy she met, the guy who killed her—used the handle Rondel. It's just a corruption of Elrond. I didn't see it before."

"It couldn't mean anything else?"

"I can't imagine what," I said.

"So now what?"

"Now I'm going to come up with a bunch of similar names. Then I'll have to find out if any are in use."

"You think this guy is still using the same kind of screen name?" Gloria said.

"People are creatures of habit."

"Can I do anything?"

I glanced from my screen to Gloria. She wore an expectant look, like I would give her some vital task at any moment. I smiled at her. "You've already done it," I said. "You pointed me down this road. When I couldn't figure out how to get started, you gave me a direction. Now I have to see where it goes."

Gloria blushed. "All I did was put on a movie."

"You never know where inspiration will strike," I said. "I'm going to be crunching this stuff for a while. If you want to watch the rest of your movie, go ahead."

"I want to be in here with you," she said.

"I appreciate it, but you'll be terribly bored. So will I, but it's necessary work."

"All right." Gloria showed a gentle smile. "I'm glad you're on the right path."

"Me, too," I said. "And thank you."

Gloria padded back to the living room. I kept pulling character names from my memory and Wikipedia.

* * *

TOLKIEN POSSESSED a fertile imagination manifesting itself in many ways, notably the breadth of characters he created and their colorful names. Some were rooted in dialects and languages Tolkien himself invented. None of this made my task any easier. After exhausting Wikipedia and my dog-eared copies of the book, I stared at a prodigious list. Now I needed to mangle and corrupt the names into something a killer might want to use as a handle online.

Like many menial tasks, this could be solved with scripting. I found the code for an anagram generator. Some tweaking removed its ability to list only English dictionary words for output. I doubted the real words I could glean from a name like Aragorn would lead me to Samantha's killer. Once I compiled the code, I fed my list into it. The newly-minted program ran them through the paces. I waited for the results, saw they would be a few minutes, and went back to rejoin Gloria in the living room.

I told her about my plan to come up with potential handles. She looked at me as if I sported a hideous facial tattoo but nodded as if she understood. We settled in to watch the rest of the movie. The Balrog shall not pass, Boromir met a volley of arrows, and the ending invited the second movie, which I doubted Gloria would watch tonight. I returned to the office to see the fruits of my labors. The result was in droves—I uncovered way more anagrams than I could use in a lifetime. Along with an embarrassment of riches in this department, I also had no guarantee the killer used any of them. Thousands and thousands of names and only a hunch told me one would be in use today.

Those weren't good odds.

I banged away at the keyboard for a while, starting and then stopping a half-dozen hare-brained ideas to cull the list into something more meaningful. Even the paring down I baked into my script left me with too much noise and not enough signal. The rise of broadband began the slow death of chat rooms like the one Samantha used. Still, I could hunt around on a service like Internet Relay Chat and see if anyone used any of the handles on my exhaustive list.

IRC has existed for ages, basically as a chat service and a place to share files. Like most ancient Internet technologies, security has always been something of an afterthought. Despite gains in this area, IRC's decline in popularity meant some servers were more open than others. I went after those. I dumped my list of anagrammed names into a text file and bypassed the nonexistent security. Once I was in, I checked if anyone used any of the handles on my list.

I knew it would take a while. I used my other computer and split the text file into much smaller chunks and ran Google searches on a batch of potential handles at a time. It wasn't the most scientific method, but I could see if any results showed merit. I expected this to take a long time, too. I went into the kitchen and turned on the coffee maker. While I added water, Gloria padded in. "I'm going to bed," she said. "I have a feeling you'll be up for a while."

"I'm sure I will," I said. "I'm testing a few things and don't want to stop."

"I understand." She said those words a lot during this case. I still didn't think Gloria understood, but I figured she came closer each time she said it. Before the end of this mess, we just might be on the same wavelength.

"I'll be up when I'm finished," I said.

"All right." Gloria walked to me, put her arms around my neck, and kissed me. "You'll puzzle it out." She added a reassuring smile. "You have the best motivation."

"Revenge?"

"Your love of your sister."

I would list those at 1 and 1A were I writing out my motivations, but I saw no need to quibble. Gloria was ready for bed, the coffee maker brewed the nectar of life, and I had work to do. I bid Gloria good night, poured myself a cup of java, and walked back to the office. Results were still pending. IRC was a big place, and their most popular servers still housed many thousands of users. I might need a second cup before everything finished.

* * *

While I sipped my coffee and waited, Ruby called. I hoped her stalker remained distant; I didn't want to leave before I got results. "Did I wake you, C.T.?"

"No, I'm working on another case."

"Oh." She paused. "I don't want to bother you, then."

"You're not," I said, even though she was. "I'm just

watching data fly by on my screen." I didn't hear anything. "Are you still there?"

"Yeah." Another pause. "I'm still spooked. I guess I wanted to hear a friendly voice."

"I'm glad you think of me." I offered it as an automatic response, but I meant it, something I didn't expect when I started working her case. She grew on me.

"You're easier to talk to than Rollins," she said. "He's pretty dry."

"He is . . . and he won't be appreciative when you take your top off." She chuckled. "How's Joanie?"

"Better, I guess. She doesn't have any permanent injuries." Not physical ones, at least. "The doctors want to observe her overnight, make sure the swelling around her eye goes down . . . things like that."

"What happened to her isn't your fault."

"The hell it's not."

"It isn't," I insisted. "Someone made the decision to follow you around. He then made the decision to assault you. Joanie chose to get in his way. None of it is your fault. You don't control other people's choices." I felt strange giving a hooker a pep talk, but I meant what I said. Ruby shouldn't view what happened to Joanie as her fault even though her doing so was inevitable. In her place, I might have felt the same way. When I thought about it, twinges of the same feeling plagued me over the years. What if I went with Samantha on the fateful night? What if I'd pressed her for details about what she was doing? Going down the what-if path led to heartache and destruction. I came to realize this in the months following Samantha's death, though the thoughts resurfaced on rare and unpleasant occasions. Ruby would learn to get past the Joanie incident as well.

"What you say makes sense," she said.

"It usually does."

"And you're modest, too." She offered a humorless laugh. "It'll take me a while to get there."

I realized Ruby didn't know her stalker followed me after I dropped her off last night. I wouldn't tell her. Joanie's pummeling caused her to feel lousy enough; I didn't need to pile on with my tale of a harrowing car chase through the streets of Baltimore. The fact the stalker eluded capture again would make for an unhappy ending. Ruby didn't need those problems right now. "How are things tonight?" I said instead. "Any signs of trouble?"

"No. Rollins says he's around so I think I'll be OK tonight."

"You're in good hands."

"I guess . . . I guess I just wanted to talk. Thanks, C.T."

"You're welcome."

"Good night."

"Good night, Ruby." I hung up. The conversation proved easier than I'd expected.

A few minutes after I reheated my coffee, my phone rang again. This time, it was Rollins. "I'm on Ruby detail," he said.

"I figured you couldn't stay away."

"She grows on you." He paused. "I was wondering if you could take over for me in a few hours."

I glanced at my screen. I didn't know how long it would take to get results, but I expected it sooner than a few hours. Once I got them, further research awaited. "Probably not," I said.

"Probably not?"

"I don't think I'll be able to."

"You sound preoccupied," he said. "You sounded the same earlier, and then you kind of got over it."

"I *am* preoccupied."

"Something important?"

"Yes," I said.

"More important than a scared girl who needs our help?" Rollins said. This marked the first time I'd heard genuine annoyance in his voice.

I rolled my eyes at the guilt trip. "If I didn't think it were more important, I'd probably be out watching her right now."

"Well, when you're not so *busy*, maybe you can take another turn looking after the girl you agreed to help." Rollins hung up before I could say anything else. He would've understood the nature of my preoccupation if he'd given me a chance to tell him. One day, I would, but I wanted more information first. In the meantime, he would have to live with me splitting time and prioritizing my murdered sister ahead of a hooker, no matter how much the hooker grew on me.

I finished my coffee and realized I never shared my discoveries about Ruby with Rollins. I would need to, but other priorities consumed my time, and he needed to come down off his huffy cloud. As long as tonight passed without stalker incidents, he would be more willing to listen tomorrow. I got up, went back to the kitchen, and made another cup of coffee. I stared into the refrigerator, pondering a snack. I ate dinner earlier, plus some popcorn on the couch with Gloria. I didn't feel hungry right now, but if my queries kept grinding, I would. I closed the refrigerator and went back to my office.

When I sat down, I saw results.

Thirty-seven names from my anagram list used IRC's major chat servers. If each one belonged to a different person, I had thirty-seven potential killers to wade through. It would make for a long night.

* * *

I RAN INTO A PROBLEM. I should have expected it, but not using IRC since college, I didn't recall its transient nature.

Anyone can use a screen name when logging in to an IRC server. Just because someone is Rondel one day, does not mean the person must be the next. Users can cycle through an array of screen names if they so choose, and there is little account-ability to pin a verifiable identity to a handle.

While I could do a thorough investigation of each name I found, this came with no guarantee I could act on the results. If I were going to beat my head into the wall, I needed tangible results to show for it. On top of it all, some IRC servers allowed different people to use the same handle, though not at the same time. Even if I found someone suspicious, I would have a hard time proving a certain person used the handle while the activity occurred.

Like a salesman selling something at a razor-thin margin, I would make it up in volume. Armed with the results, I now sought the handles used most often, and if I could glean rele-vant information about their use. While this crunched away, I went upstairs and got ready for bed. When I slipped in, Gloria stirred and rolled over to face me. "How's it going?" she said, sleepiness giving her voice a husky tone I found alluring.

"I don't know," I said. "I have some results, but I'm not sure I can do anything with them. Right now, I'm trying to sort them and see if I have anything to act on."

"Do you think you will?"

I shrugged. "No way to know. I hope so, but the Internet really does allow you to be hard to find sometimes."

"You'll find him," Gloria said and rolled back. I heard her snoring not ten seconds later. I envied her ability to wake up, have a conversation, and fall back asleep almost right away. If anything roused me from slumber, I spent at least a few minutes tossing and turning. I pulled the sheet over me and settled in.

* * *

SAMANTHA WAS HOME FROM COLLEGE. I woke up early—for me, at least—but she'd already left. I spent the day at lacrosse practice, went to the dojo to train, and then finally deigned to do some homework. Samantha came back before dinner. My mother fixed something she called hunter chicken featuring mushrooms in a tasty brown sauce. She always served it over rice, which I didn't care for but went along with because it was easier than arguing about it.

Whenever Samantha returned from college, my mother prepared hunter chicken and a bunch of other dishes she liked. I wondered if I would get the same treatment. When my team won the JV lacrosse championship last season, I didn't get a special meal. Still, I liked the dish, and I always enjoyed my sister's company, so I didn't rock the boat at the dinner table. Samantha and I could bag on Mom later, when she couldn't hear us.

After dinner, my sister and I lingered at the table. Our parents went off to do whatever boring things middle-aged people did when dinner ended. "How's college?" I said once our parents disappeared upstairs.

"Pretty good," she said. "I'm on the dean's list again."

"I had no doubts."

"Thanks. How about you? Didn't lacrosse season just end?"

I frowned and nodded. "Yeah."

"What happened?"

"We did all right, but not well enough to play for the title. It's weird—it's a lot of the guys from the JV team last year, and we won it all. We should have done better, but we came up short."

"That's too bad," my sister said with a sympathetic grimace. "What about you? How did you do individually?"

"I started the last six games. I did pretty well. Well enough I should start next year, too. I just wish we'd had a better season."

"Can't win 'em all, little brother," Samantha said with a grin.

"It won't stop me from trying," I said.

"I wouldn't expect it to."

"Mom said you have a boyfriend this year. What's up with that?"

Samantha shook her head. "It's over is what it is. He was a jerk."

"What happened?"

"He decided he liked having sex with the girls in the next dorm room," she said.

"Oh."

"At the same time."

I liked the fellow more now but could never tell Samantha my opinion. "You really need to introduce me to these assholes you date." I pounded my fist into my palm. "I'll keep them in line for you."

"Gee, thanks," Samantha said with a chuckle. "I think I'm supposed to take care of you, though. I'm the older sister."

"I'm taking care of myself pretty well."

"So I hear."

I smiled. "Guilty as charged."

"Be careful, C.T. You're a good-looking guy, and I know you can talk to pretty much anyone. You'll probably live it up for a while, but if you treat a girl badly, she'll get hurt. You don't want to get a reputation."

"I'll keep it in mind." I said the words to placate Samantha. I knew she realized it when she rolled her eyes at me. "Are any of your friends home for this long weekend?"

"Don't even think about it," she said, kicking me under the table.

Samantha got up and went into the kitchen. I followed her a moment later. She rummaged around in the freezer before closing the door. "Mom and Dad have lousy ice cream. Want to go out and get some?"

"Sure," I said. "Let me get my shoes."

I ran upstairs, found a pair of tennis shoes, put them on, and came back down the stairs. Samantha stood in the foyer, waiting with her back to me. "Ready to go, Sam?" I said, grabbing her shoulder. She toppled backward onto the foyer. Blood covered her torso, and stab wounds perforated her clothes and flesh.

I screamed.

CHAPTER 15

I must have screamed when the nightmare woke me because my throat was dry and raw. Gloria sat upright beside me, looking around with wide eyes. My heart raced in my chest. I gulped in deep draughts of air to calm myself. Gloria put her hand on my shoulder. "Bad dream?" she said. I nodded, unable to speak yet. "Want to talk about it?"

My pulse still pounded. I sucked in a few more deep lungfuls and shook my head. "No," I managed to say. The breathing exercises slowly calmed my thumping heart.

"Was it about your sister?"

I nodded. "Yes."

"Sure you don't want to talk about it?"

I shook my head again before relenting and telling Gloria what happened. The conversation between Samantha and me in the dream mirrored one taking place on the fateful weekend she came home. "We went out, got some ice cream at the store, came back, and watched a couple of cheesy movies," I said.

"That sounds nice," Gloria said, her reassuring hand rubbing my shoulders.

"It was." I smiled at the memory. "She was nineteen and I was sixteen. We could have been out with other people on a

Friday night and instead, all we did was eat ice cream and watch B movies on our parents' couch. We did stuff like that a lot. Have you ever seen *Mystery Science Theater 3000*?"

"Once," she said. "I had an ex who liked it a lot."

The surprise of Gloria knowing what *MST3K* was almost rendered me speechless again. "Samantha and I loved riffing on those cheesy movies ourselves. We started it when I was thirteen, I think."

"What movies did you watch that night?"

I recalled them right away. They were the last films Samantha and I would ever watch together. "The original *Night of the Living Dead* and *Highlander 3*."

"It sounds like you recall that night vividly."

"I'll never forget it," I said.

"Embrace your memories," Gloria said as she rubbed my arm. "The dream wasn't what happened. Don't give it any power over you."

I understood what Gloria said, even if it came out sounding like psychobabble. "I'll do my best," I said as I lay back down. True to form, Gloria snored about fifteen seconds after her head hit the pillow. I remained awake for a while, turning the nightmare over in my head. I thought people who rushed to assign meaning to their every dream were idiots, but this must signify something.

As I drifted off to sleep, I gained no insights as to its potential meaning.

* * *

THE NEXT MORNING, I poured a cup of coffee and considered the breakfast options in the fridge when I heard a knock at the door. Gloria made it halfway down the stairs in her small nightgown, then dashed back up when she heard the rapping. I watched her disappear around the corner before I went to the door and looked through the peephole. Rich stood on the step. I rolled my eyes and opened the door. "Back for another try, Ambassador?" I said.

"I'm here on my own this time." Rich sniffed the air. "You making coffee?" he said, and walked in past me.

"Sure . . . come on in." I used my most sarcastic tone.

"Thanks," Rich said amiably as he went to the kitchen. I closed the door and followed him. Gloria joined us a moment later, wearing a track suit I'd never seen before. "Hello, Gloria."

"Good morning, Rich."

I snagged my coffee mug before Rich could get his hands on it. He opened the cupboard, took out another, and fixed a cup for himself. Even if I filled the water reservoir with vinegar, my brew would still taste better than the swill in the BPD's pots.

"So, what's for breakfast?" Rich said, sipping his black coffee and sitting at the kitchen table.

"Maybe some bacon in your honor," I said.

"You're still angry about the other night. I get it. I probably would be, too. But I told you, I'm here on my own. I want to know how the case is going."

"What case?"

"Oh, please. Like you're not investigating Samantha's murder. The circles under your eyes tell me you haven't been sleeping well. All things considered, it's not a surprise."

"You're here to help me?" I said. Gloria busied herself with preparing coffee for herself while Rich and I bantered. The right balance of too much sugar and too much cream was delicate.

"If I can. Why don't we discuss it over breakfast?"

"I hope your advice is worth the meal," I said.

"Isn't it always?"

"I shopped at Harris Teeter."

"I'll bring my A game, then," said Rich.

* * *

As promised, I made bacon but of the turkey variety. Rich sniffed it while it cooked, and his look told me he knew it did not come from the flesh of swine. In addition to the faux hog, I toasted three whole wheat bagels, put butter and cream cheese out with them, and set out a plate of scrambled eggs. Everyone took a bagel and some meat; Gloria eschewed the eggs while Rich and I helped ourselves.

After we all ate enough to slay the worst of our morning hunger, Rich spoke up. "How's the case coming along?"

"Not so great," I said. I filled him in on what I'd discovered so far, whom I talked to, and the issues with what I found in my poached IRC records. I needed to go back and check my results.

"It's an old case," Rich said when I finished.

"I could have heard the same from anyone at the precinct house without having to cook a good breakfast," I said.

"It complicates things, but it doesn't make them impossible."

"Thanks for the pep talk. By the way, never go into coaching."

"You're looking for some great insight to unlock everything for you," Rich said. "I don't have one."

"What the hell are you doing here, then?" Gloria took in a sharp breath. I glanced at her. Rich paid her no mind and stayed above the verbal jabs I threw at him.

"Telling you what I would do."

"Which is?" I said.

"I'd go see the FBI."

"The FBI?"

"Yes," said Rich. "You have some information now, and you don't have to tell them how you got it. Take it, plus what you need from the case file, and see if they can help."

"Like your boy Hess helped the first time?" I said. "I could've gotten as much from the goddamn janitor."

"A zealous FBI agent—yes, like Hess—could look into things on his own. Also, it sounds like you need service provider records. You'll probably tell me you can hack the ISPs, and maybe you can. But you don't want Samantha's murderer getting off on a technicality because you couldn't be bothered to do things the right way. Use the proper channels."

I entertained no intention of seeing Samantha's killer in a courtroom, and I also didn't plan to tell Rich of my intentions. He probably suspected it, though he remained quiet. "I hadn't considered going back to the FBI," I said with the most diplomacy I could summon.

"I didn't think you would. It might turn out they can't do much for you, but you never know until you try."

"All right," I said. "I'll get some information ready and see what they can do for me. Thanks." Waiting on the FBI would also allow me to pay some attention to Ruby's case again, which would placate Rollins.

"Agent Hess will be expecting you again," Rich said.

"I'll make sure to see him today, then."

"He's expecting you after lunch. I told him it would take you some time to get everything together."

I nodded. "All right. Thanks, Rich."

Rich nodded. When he finished his breakfast, he said, "So was it worth the price of admission?"

"I think I want a refund on the bagel," I said.

* * *

AFTER RICH LEFT, I went back into the office. Everything long since finished running. I pored over the data. IRC still provided a veneer of anonymity, but I saw many legitimate email addresses behind the handles. I dumped the raw text output into Excel, sorted by email address, and highlighted the ones I judged valid.

"You're really going back to the FBI?" Gloria said from the doorway. I didn't hear her approach. She walked into the office and sat in one of my guest chairs.

"I hope it's a good idea," I said.

"It's an unexpected idea."

"How so?"

"They didn't seem like much help before," she said. "Why are you so willing to work with them again?"

She posed a valid question. "I have more information now. They have resources I don't have and couldn't easily get, even with my usual methods. I'd rather not hack the feds. Working with them allows me to avoid it. They're good at catching killers, even across state lines. We don't know Samantha's killer was a local. And I've never worked with them before." If I said all this to convince myself, it was effective.

"What do you think they'll do?"

"Get user info from ISPs and email providers I couldn't acquire without a lot of effort."

"You *could* get it, though."

"Yes," I acknowledged. "It would take a while and be very illegal. This way is easier."

"What if they shut you out of the case?" Gloria said.

I'd failed to consider it. Gloria chose her questions well. The FBI and local cops created tenuous relationships turning on issues of jurisdiction and access. Why would they play ball with a PI? Rich may have gotten on great with Agent Hess, but he could still shut me out if he thought it best for his case. "I don't know," I said. I felt Hess understood me and the case well enough not to do it, but at the end of the day, he was a fed, and I was a PI. "I hope it doesn't happen."

"It may be better than the alternative."

"What do you mean?"

"If they share their information with you, and their suspect ends up dead, they're going to come looking for you."

"No doubt," I said.

Gloria sucked in a breath and stared at me with warm eyes. "I love you, C.T., and I don't want to see you go to jail."

"I'm not going to jail."

"What makes you so sure?"

"Because I would get an alibi," I said.

"Someone would lie for you?"

"Basically. Don't worry; I wouldn't ask you to do it. I wouldn't want to put you in such a position."

Gloria regarded me with a mischievous smile. "I can think of some other positions I'd rather you put me in."

Her comment compelled me to smile. "After my meeting with Agent Hess," I promised.

"Hurry back," Gloria said. She stood and walked out of the room.

I watched her hips sway as she left. Once she cleared the door, I resumed work. I printed the Excel dump of my IRC data. The assembled pages rolled up could swat a baseball an impressive distance. I put them in a large manila envelope. I added the ME's and detective's report, along with a few photos and newspaper clippings. For the first time, I typed my own notes, based on my conversation with Ted Pembroke and Greg Elliot, and printed them out.

The envelope had a nice heft to it. I hoped it held enough to get the FBI to help me find Samantha's killer.

CHAPTER 16

I rewarded myself for my hard work in the morning with a homemade omelet. I would have rewarded Gloria, too, but she left for a tennis lesson. I downed my mug of coffee and took a shower before my meeting with Agent Hess. To enhance my chances of making a good impression, I shaved off the scraggly stubble I'd accrued over the last two or three days. I thought about wearing a suit but opted for a nice pair of khakis and a Polo.

When I arrived, Hess sat in a meeting. I busied myself watching the news in the waiting room. I trusted their coffee machine about as far as I could flick it with a finger. If the BPD brewed dreadful coffee, I figured the FBI's to be one step away from being declared toxic by the CDC. I used the hot water to make a cup of tea. Watching my water darken to a nice brown proved more exciting than the news, which consisted of two people yelling at each other despite the large overlap in their opinions. How did people watch this every day?

A moment after I finished my tea, Agent Hess fetched me from the waiting room. "Ready when you are," he said. I followed him into his office and sat in the same uncomfortable guest chair as last time. "Rich told me you've been banging away at this, so I figured it might be worth a second look. What do you have?"

I dropped the manila envelope on his desk. It landed with an impressive thud. "It's a lot from the BPD's case file, plus some notes I made of interviews I've done, all the online stuff the BPD found, and some IRC information on people with handles similar to Rondel."

"Similar how?"

"My girlfriend got me to watch *The Fellowship of the Ring* with her." Hess gave me a funny look. "I've seen it a bunch of times," I clarified. Keeping my geek cred mattered. "I wanted to work on my sister's case file, but I figured a break from it couldn't hurt. Anyway, we got to the scene when Arwen brings Frodo to Rivendell, and they meet Elrond."

"Rondel," said Hess with a nod.

"I didn't see it sooner. It might not have made a difference considering thirteen years have passed, but I still wish I'd recognized it. I anagrammed the character names from the series and then tried to find anyone using those handles. You have the results of several hours of work."

Hess lifted the folder and tested its weight. "Rich told me I'm better off not asking you too many questions about how you gather your intel."

"I think it would be better for both of us," I said.

"Here's the deal," Hess said, going into full agent mode. "We don't take shortcuts at the FBI. We work with US attorneys and federal judges, and they make sure we cross every T and dot every fucking I. I'll look at what you have here, and I'll do my best to spin it into something I can act on. If your information is good, and I can sell it well enough, we can get a warrant."

"I understand."

"You say you have a lot of information from IRC?"

I nodded. "I dumped it into Excel so it's easier to read."

"So I might need to go poking around ISPs?" Hess said.

"You might."

"I'll have to be a pretty good salesman, then. Let me take a look at this. Give me a day or two to read it all over and see how good your intel is. I'll let you know either way but I hope I can do something with it."

Were I the type to believe in regrets, I would've harbored some at coming here. Still, I couldn't just snatch the folder off Hess' desk and storm out in twin fits of disappointment and pique. I managed to say, "I hope so, too."

"I'll be in touch."

We shook hands. "Thanks," I said.

I walked back to my car. When my parents told me the truth about what happened, I couldn't have imagined giving Samantha's case to anyone else, even Rich. Now I handed what I knew to a virtual stranger based on my cousin's recommendation. Was this the right thing? I *could* hack the ISPs and email providers to get the information I needed, but the tactic ran the risk of detection. I couldn't do much for Samantha if I got busted for hacking Verizon. The FBI represented the safer route.

This numbered among the few times in my life I had opted for the safer route. I felt uneasy as I got back into my car and drove away.

*   *   *

AT HOME, I doffed the khakis and polo in favor of a T-shirt and running shorts. This combination of cases left me sedentary: either I spent time in the office working on Samantha's murder, or I sat in my car watching Ruby take strangers into motel rooms. Neither was good for my long-term cardiovascular health. I decided to climb back on the wagon with some laps around Federal Hill Park.

I arrived too late for the lunchtime runners but too early for the dinnertime crowd. A couple people walked dogs, and the only jogger I saw had at least twenty years on me and wore them well. I kept a good pace, using the downtime to think about my dual cases. I didn't care for working two at once, even if I took up the second one out of love for my sister.

It got me thinking about not talking to my parents since they dropped the Samantha bombshell on me. To their credit, they stopped calling. I wondered if Rich gave them updates. If he did, they knew I carried what I learned to the FBI. Still, I needed to call them at some point. I would remain mad at them for a while, but I couldn't punish them with silence forever. As difficult as it had been for me to bury my sister, how much greater was the ordeal for them to inter their first child, especially knowing she didn't die of natural causes?

I looked out from the park, down Federal Hill, and across the Baltimore Harbor. Afternoon sun glistened off the water and reflected off the windows of the National Aquarium and the Rusty Scupper. I loved the fact I could walk to either of those places if I wanted. Parking was bad enough where I lived without having to deal with lots and garages near the harbor.

My workout app told me I ran 4.3 miles. I counted it as a victory and headed home. Gloria remained away. I went upstairs, took a much-needed shower, and changed into a pair of jeans and the Polo I wore to visit the FBI. No sooner did I walk back downstairs than Rollins called. "You have time for me now?" he said, his tone sharp.

"Don't I always?"

"Unless you're preoccupied, which you have been recently."

"Yeah," I admitted, "I have been."

"We need to talk about the Ruby case."

"OK. I want to bring you up to speed on a few things."

"I'll come by."

"I need to make a phone call first," I said.

"An important one?"

"Yes, and I don't know how long it'll take. Want to meet me for dinner?"

"Pick a place," said Rollins, annoyance in his voice again.

I saw it on my run, so it lingered on my brain. "How about the Rusty Scupper?"

"I'll see you there in an hour," Rollins said and hung up.

An hour should be plenty of time to talk to my parents, presuming it didn't take me most of the time to overcome the sense of dread.

* * *

I STARED AT MY PHONE. I rarely experience trouble talking to anyone, but I could think of no way to open this conversation. On some level, I still felt pissed at my parents and thought they should apologize. On another level, I knew I didn't handle the situation in the best way possible, and I realized they'd been carrying a lot of pain for the last thirteen years.

After another minute of unproductive staring, I called their house line. I hoped my father would answer and breathed a small sigh of relief when he did. "Hi, Dad."

"Hi, son." His voice perked up. "How are you?"

"I'm all right, I guess. How are you and Mom?"

"We were worried about you . . . the way you stormed out

of here and then wouldn't answer your phone. Rich said you were angry."

"A mild word for it," I said. I heard the edge in my own voice.

"You understand we did it to protect you," my father said.

"I'd rather not talk about it, Dad. I think you made the wrong call, but I also know what you and Mom have had to live with every day since Samantha died. It couldn't have been easy."

"It hasn't been," he said in a small voice.

"I called to say I've been looking into her . . . into what happened to Samantha." Mentioning her murder out loud to my father still felt weird. "It's a cold case file, so I didn't have much to go on. I may have turned up a lead, though."

"Are you still looking into it?"

"I gave it to the FBI. Rich suggested it. We'll see what they're able to do."

"Sounds promising." He paused. So did I. We didn't fill in the conversational gap until my father continued a few seconds later. "You think they'll be able to do something with it?"

"I don't know," I said. "I gave them enough to identify potential suspects and work from there."

"What if they can't get anywhere?"

"Then I'll try on my own."

"Be careful, son. You know Samantha wouldn't want to see anything happen to you."

"I can take care of myself, Dad."

"I know you can." Another pause. "Do you want to talk to your mother?"

"No, I have to go look into something else I'm working on. Tell her . . . give her my best, I guess."

"You guess?" he said.

"Let's not add to the awkwardness, Dad."

"All right. Good luck."

"I'll let you know what the FBI says," I told him.

"OK, thanks. Goodbye, son."

"'Bye, Dad."

I hung up and let out a long, slow breath. Whatever Rollins would tell me, I could handle it after this conversation. Talking to my mother would have made it worse. She would have tried to make me feel guilty and then tsked and sniffed when I didn't play along. Once this mess was over, whatever the outcome, my parents and I would need to sit down and settle our recent dysfunction.

Now, however, other obligations took precedence.

* * *

I WALKED from Federal Hill Park to the Rusty Scupper. I enjoyed the scenic stroll out to the harbor. It also eliminated the need to park at the restaurant. When I arrived, Rollins was already there, of course, and the hostess led me to his table. We were treated to a nice view of the water looking out at the Pier Five hotel and restaurant complex.

"You're late," said Rollins.

"I walked," I said.

"So did I."

"You're an overachiever." I looked over the menu. A pretty waitress who wore the bland white shirt and black skirt like she owned it came to take our drink orders and review the restaurant's daily specials. They all featured seafood of various types, though I tuned out and focused more on the waitress than her routine pitch.

I asked for an unsweetened iced tea and a shrimp cocktail appetizer. Rollins opted only for a tea. "Gotta watch my figure," he said when the waitress left. "Sitting in the truck and watching shit happen isn't good for my diet."

"I feel you,'" I said.

"Hope you don't mind if I mooch a couple shrimp."

I shrugged. The waitress came back with our drinks and my appetizer. An array of peeled shrimp sat balanced on the edge of a large wine glass, with a petite bowl of cocktail sauce in the center. Rollins, true to his word, used his fork to spear two prawns from around the rim of the glass and put them on his bread plate.

Our waitress returned after dropping off another table's check. I ordered the glazed salmon; Rollins opted for crab cakes. "You're paying, right?" he said when the waitress left to key in the order.

I watched the waitress' hips as she walked away. "Sure." I tried not to sound too distracted.

"She's wearing a nice skirt," said Rollins.

"I doubt people are admiring her sartorial sense. When a waiter in tight pants walks by, I'll point him out to you."

"I'll see him before you will," Rollins said with a grin.

"I'm sure."

I went back to my appetizer. The sauce needed a touch more horseradish, but the shrimp were plump, flavorful, and deveined by an expert. When only a couple remained, I said, "What have you learned these past couple days?"

"Ruby's pretty popular," Rollins said. "I saw a couple of return customers."

"But no stalker?"

"If he was there, he didn't make a move."

"I wonder if we've scared him away," I said.

"I don't know. I doubt it. He's probably figuring out how to get past us to get to her."

"Reassuring."

"It's what those people do," said Rollins. "Stalkers don't think like everyday folks. They got something going on in their heads, and a car chase through Fells Point isn't going to fix it."

A few tables around us filled up. I lowered my voice. "You've dealt with stalkers before."

Rollins nodded. "When you do bodyguard work, stalkers are a part of the job."

The waitress returned with our dinners. The aroma of glazed salmon wafted up to my nostrils. It disintegrated into delicious fish slivers in my mouth. As good as it was, Rollins' crab cakes looked just as savory. I saw lumps of crabmeat bursting from the surface. When he cut into one, I spied precious little filler inside. The next time I came here, I would need to order them.

After Rollins had finished his first crab cake, he got down to business. "You said you knew some things about Ruby."

I nodded as I finished a bite of salmon. "I do."

"Feel like sharing?"

"She's very guarded. I'm sure you've noticed. Every time I thought she was going to discuss something private with me, it was like she realized it and shut down. So I went the indirect route."

"What do you know?"

"Her name for one. Melinda Davenport."

Rollins stared at me and then shook his head. "Supposed to mean something?"

I lowered my voice more. "Melinda Davenport is the girl who went missing and spurred her father to start the Nightlight Foundation. Her father is Vincent Davenport."

"Never heard of him," Rollins said.

"You're not very familiar with the Baltimore power brokers, are you?"

"I'm not from Baltimore."

"Vincent Davenport's family started a bakery a couple generations ago. Now it has operations in several states and a couple thousand employees."

Rollins frowned in thought. "D and S?"

"You got it," I said.

"And Ruby is this guy's daughter?"

"Yes."

"He started some foundation. Does he know she's a hooker?"

"I think he must. He's too well-connected, and Baltimore isn't too big. A girl like Melinda could disappear in New York. Not here."

"What are you going to do now?" Rollins said.

"I'm not sure. I doubt her father is stalking her."

"It'd be pretty creepy," Rollins said with a shudder. "If he knows about her."

I nodded. "I'm operating under the assumption he does."

"You gonna talk to him?"

"I might have to at some point."

"He sounds like a powerful man."

"He is," I said with a shrug. The reality was Vincent Davenport operated on a different plane than people like my parents and Tony Rizzo. I rubbed elbows with the B-team of Baltimore power players.

"How does this get you closer to the stalker?" Rollins asked.

"Who would want to stalk a nameless hooker? The list is endless. Who would want to stalk Melinda Davenport? There's risk there because of her father. It's a more manageable list."

"And maybe a more dangerous one." Rollins frowned in thought. His eyes scanned the restaurant. "She says this started recently. How long has Melinda been Ruby?"

"A few years," I said. "It's possible the stalker only recently learned who she really is."

"Sounds like a good blackmail opportunity against the old man."

I hadn't considered the possibility. If I needed to chat with Vincent Davenport, this would make an easier conversation starter than saying his daughter worked as a hooker. "It is."

Rollins polished off his second crab cake as I finished the last scraps of my tepid salmon. "You still want me to stick around Ruby?" he said.

"When you can."

"What about you?"

"If I land in the soup, I'll let you know."

"I'll be waiting for your call," Rollins said with a smile.

"Go to hell," I said.

* * *

I PAID THE CHECK, bid Rollins adieu, and walked back to Federal Hill. I took a lap around the park at a brisk walk, figuring it might burn off the calories of a few of the shrimp I enjoyed as my appetizer. Staying fit had been easier before I started meeting people in restaurants to converse about cases.

After my brief constitutional, I headed home. As I walked down Riverside Avenue, I noticed a silver Mercedes parked on the other side past my house. It could have been the stalker's car. It could have been anyone's car. Maybe vehicular anonymity went into being a successful stalker. Rolling in an Aston Martin like James Bond tends to get a body noticed.

My house grew closer. I heard an engine start. The headlights on the silver Mercedes glowed to life. The car pulled out. I reached inside my coat and took out my .45. I stopped behind another vehicle, holding the pistol up so the driver could see it. The Mercedes sported no front plate as it approached.

I stared down a darkened window which never lowered. A

door never opened. Maybe the gun discouraged the driver from taking a shot. Maybe he did all this to show me he knew who I was. The car eased past me. I turned my head and watched it. No rear plate. The driver sped up once he got past me and then turned toward Key Highway.

I let out a deep breath. Whoever this guy was, he knew who I was and where I lived, and he made a show of telling me tonight.

Point taken.

CHAPTER 17

I WENT INSIDE AND CLOSED THE DOOR. GLORIA WATCHED TV and lay on the couch. She looked up at me and smiled, then frowned when she glanced down. It made me realize I still held the .45 in my hand. "Would you believe I was doing some bicep curls?" I said.

"No," she said, shaking her head. A yawn broke her face, but the look of concern returned quickly.

"I think I saw Ruby's stalker."

"Here?"

I nodded. "Waiting down the block."

"So he knows where you live now."

"It would appear so." I put the hand cannon away and double-checked the lock on the door.

"What are you going to do?" Gloria sat up now. Any weariness vanished from her face.

"Keep working," I said. "I can't let something like this scare me off. If you want to stay here, I think you should use the parking pad and back door to enter and leave. Don't park on the street. Don't come and go via the front door if you can help it."

Gloria shook her head. "Is every case you take going to be like this?"

"I tend not to take the easy ones. They're too boring."

"I could use some boring right about now."

I gave her a grin I hoped she found reassuring. She didn't reciprocate. My smile game was mired in a slump. "This case has become bigger than I thought, but I can't abandon Ruby now."

"I know," she said. "You wouldn't be you if you could." She paused. "I wonder if the stalker knows where Ruby lives, too."

"*I* don't even know where she lives."

"But he might."

She posed a excellent point. Ruby made a habit of not opening up to me. I'd learned more about her through observation and research than the sum of everything she told me. She practiced the art of circumlocution when talking about where she lived. Maybe girls who did what she did in the areas she did it rarely enjoyed steady residences. The fact remained I never tried to find where she lived, but her stalker might have put in the effort.

She deserved to know.

* * *

"I'm working," Ruby said when I called her.

"I hope I didn't interrupt you while you're . . . with a client," I said.

She chuckled. "I never answer the phone . . . even if they're lousy. What's up?"

"Your stalker turned up outside my house tonight."

Silence served as my only reply for the few seconds it took Ruby to find her voice. "You're sure it was him?"

"If it wasn't, it was someone else in a silver Benz who desperately wanted me to notice him."

"Shit." Her sigh hissed in my ear. "No plates on the car?"

"We wouldn't be so lucky," I said.

"What are you going to do?"

"I can take care of myself. The question is what are *you* going to do?"

"Me?" she said. "Why?"

"This guy found me. Yeah, I'm in the phone book, but it's not like I handed him a business card. He figured it out." My tag number would have been all he had to go on. If he converted the information into my name and address, he was resourceful. I paused to ponder this before I continued. "If he can find where I live, who's to say he can't do the same to you?"

"You think he knows who I am? Who I really am?"

"Why not?" I said. "I do."

Silence again. It lasted so long this time I pulled the phone away from my ear to make sure Ruby didn't hang up. "I guess it was inevitable," she finally said, her voice resigned.

"You could have saved us both the time and told me. Regardless, if I discovered it, and your stalker deduced who I am, he could solve for Ruby and get Melinda."

"I guess," she said after another delay. Losing her anonymity must've weighed on Melinda. "Besides, I don't really live any one place."

"Doesn't matter," I said. "You need to find somewhere safe to stay."

"What about with you?"

"I don't think it would be a good idea."

"Your girlfriend wouldn't like it?" Melinda said. I heard mirth in her tone for the first time tonight.

"Of course she wouldn't. More importantly, why would staying at a place the stalker already knows make you any safer?"

"Shit. I hadn't thought of that."

"Can you get somewhere safe tonight?"

"I'm working."

"Take the night off," I insisted. "Tell Shade what's happening. Send him to see me if he gives you any shit. You can't make money for him if you're dead."

"He'd just find another girl."

"Would this be a bad time to suggest a career change?"

"I think it's a little late for that," said Melinda.

"You're twenty-three. I didn't find my career—if you want to call this a career—until I was older than you."

"Really?"

"You still have time. You have to want to do it first. Your job might have led this stalker to you or made it easier for him to fixate on you. It might have nothing to do with anything. Can you really take the chance?"

"OK, OK." She took a few contemplative breaths into the phone. "I can find a place to crash tonight. I'll tell Shade I'm going on leave. If he doesn't like it, I'll send him to you."

"Good. Call me tomorrow, and I'll see if I've found a spot you can stay."

"I will." Melinda paused. When she spoke next, her voice threatened to break. "Thanks, C.T. It's been a while since anyone really did anything for me."

"You're welcome, Melinda." Calling her Ruby seemed inadequate now.

"I'll call you tomorrow," she said and hung up. I did the same.

Melinda would be safe tonight. Until tomorrow, I could focus my attention back on Samantha's case.

* * *

AGENT HESS ASKED for a day or two. I would give him until tomorrow to judge his progress. Even though I'd hit several roadblocks along the way, it still chafed me to hand my sister's murder investigation over to a bureaucracy like the FBI. They possessed reach and resources I didn't, but they were also constrained by laws. In theory, I was too, but I'd always found those constraints to be loose. Hess and his fellow agents couldn't think in those terms.

Gloria already went to bed. After my encounter with the stalker and conversation with Melinda, I felt amped up. I thought about where I might be able to stash her until the case ended. My parents' house was out of the question, even if we were on good terms. Rich's girlfriend would have the same objections Gloria would to a hooker staying in the house. I didn't want to put her in a hotel, even a nice one, because I couldn't control the security there. Part of leaving Melinda with someone was knowing I didn't have to be around all the time.

I got a beer from the refrigerator, opened it, and sat on the couch. Maybe Melinda could stay with Rollins. He knew her, could protect her even better than I could—despite the protests of my ego—and would be immune to her charms and come-ons. Rollins freelanced a lot, however, and he couldn't take Melinda with him, nor could he leave her unguarded in his house. No, I needed someone who would be able to stay home and keep an eye on Melinda.

Midway through my second beer, I experienced an epiphany: I could ask Joey Trovato to take Melinda in for a while. He worked out of his house so leaving for long stretches wouldn't be a concern. He owned guns and knew how to use them. I didn't doubt his ability to protect her, and despite the crust he sometimes put up, his heart was good, and he would want to help me and Melinda. Unfortunately, he'd be very vulnerable to her charms and come-ons. I didn't know if a hooker houseguest was the best situation for Joey, but I would let him make that decision. Tomorrow.

I finished my second beer and went upstairs to bed.

* * *

I woke up, ran a few laps around Federal Hill Park, came back, showered, and set about making breakfast. After a careful inventory of the refrigerator and pantry, I made pita sandwiches with turkey bacon, eggs, and fresh spinach. Gloria came downstairs to join me for breakfast and coffee. There were days I wished Gloria would take the initiative to make breakfast. Then I remembered her disastrous forays into the kitchen and scuttled those wishes.

After breakfast, I needed something to do. I wanted to wait for Agent Hess and the process—his process—to play out. Not working Samantha's case chafed at me. Rich vouched for Hess. He seemed like a stand-up guy, and I thought he would do what he could. I'd be salty if all this waiting led to Hess telling me I didn't give him anything actionable.

I sat in front of my computer. Temptation gnawed at me. Given time, I could find Rondel or Romirbo or whatever he wanted to call himself now. ISPs, like any monolithic entities, harbored weaknesses. They hid them well, and the law was on their sides, but I could find their vulnerabilities and get in. I did it in China against entities more secure than American Internet providers. The keyboard mocked me. I should have been at work bringing some electronic walls down.

My phone rang. I snatched it from the desk and looked hopefully at the caller ID. Instead of Hess, however, it was Rich. I answered anyway. "Hello?"

"Any word from Hess?" said Rich.

"Not since I handed over everything I had on Samantha's killer."

"It's bothering you."

"Yeah. I could be working her case. I *should* be working her case."

"You'd be doing something illegal."

"We both know I'm all about law and order," I said.

"You get what I mean. Hess can put this guy away."

"I'm not interested in putting him away."

"Look," Rich said, "Hess is a good guy. It sounds like you did a lot of work. If there's something there, he'll go after it."

"He'd better. I trusted you on this."

"You did the right thing. I want to make sure you're giving the process time. Hess has to talk to attorneys, go after warrants, and all."

"I'm familiar with how the process works," I said, "even if I do my damnedest not to use it."

Rich chuckled. "Give it a chance, then. How long did he say?"

"He told me to give him a day or two." I took a deep breath. "What I don't want to do is wait around and then find out he can't do anything."

"I know. Just don't do anything stupid. Remember, if Hess can do something with your information, you might end up being a witness. Keep your credibility."

"I'm almost impressed how you think I have some to offer," I said.

"I'm feeling generous today."

"Your guy better come through, Rich."

"Give him a chance," Rich said again. "You won't regret it."

"I hope I don't," I said and hung up. Rich usually broke the connection on me without saying goodbye. I derived a tiny bit of satisfaction from turning the tables on him.

* * *

WHEN I WAS GROWING UP, my parents liked to tell me idle hands were the devil's playthings. They weren't very original. I tried to keep busy as a kid, mostly because I hated being bored and in part because I wanted them to stop abusing the poor cliché. When my non-idle hands discovered computers and how to compromise them, my parents stopped encouraging me to find something to do.

I stared at my keyboard. Hacking always came naturally to me. Computers were stupid and operating systems were easy. Most people, even those who worked in the field, didn't understand security enough to close off all avenues of attack. Even state-run websites in communist China showed vulnerabilities. I knew the ISPs would have weakness somewhere. I'd just promised Rich I would give Agent Hess a day, but I couldn't shake the feeling he would come back to me with a sad look and palms upturned. Going after the providers would be hedging my bets.

Gloria regarded me from the office doorway. "You look like a man who needs to be distracted," she said in a come-hither voice nearly compelling me to leap from the chair.

I took a breath to calm myself. "I'm trying to trust the process," I said.

"The process?"

"Agent Hess. I gave him all the ammo in my belt. I'm trying to believe he'll come through with the warrant."

"But you don't think he will."

I shrugged. "I don't know. It's a tossup. I don't want to sit around and do nothing in case he fails."

"What did Rich say?" asked Gloria.

She knew Rich called. I smiled and wondered if the two of

them talked about me. "He told me to trust the process. Where do you think I got the phrase?"

She smiled. "And that's what you're trying to do?"

"It's very tempting not to."

"Well," she said, turning on the come-hither voice again, "I think I know a way to distract you for a while."

Gloria's plans occupied me for a long while, it turned out. We went upstairs, came back down an hour and change later, and then resumed watching *The Fellowship of the Ring*, which my epiphany forced Gloria to watch alone. Thoughts of my sister's killer flashed into my head every time I heard the names Elrond or Boromir. Boromir's death at the end felt satisfying. I never liked him in the movie anyway, and now with the name connected to Samantha's murderer, I enjoyed every arrow puncturing his body.

"Are you planning to distract me again?" I said as the credits rolled.

"If that's what it takes," said Gloria.

"I would hate to impose."

"I think we can find something to do in the meantime." Her face brightened. "Come shopping with me."

"What?" I felt my good mood fleeing at the thought of being in a store with Gloria.

"I want to look at some clothes. You can give me your opinion on them."

"Do you at least know where you're going to go?"

"I'll figure it out."

I couldn't conceive how Gloria or any woman could use such a shopping method. Whether I needed clothes, books, or anything, I knew where I wanted to go and possessed at least some idea what I wanted to look at. I did research. I scoffed at salespeople trying to sell me crap for the sake of their commissions. Maybe it was a guy thing. Gloria employed an entirely different process.

"You coming?" she said with a grin.

It seemed like the boyfriend thing to do. I shrugged. "Why not?" I said.

* * *

I DISCOVERED a myriad of reasons why not almost as soon as we began. Gloria chose the Galleria under the Renaissance Hotel downtown. There were better places to go for shopping, and while they all required more driving, the payoff would have been worth it. Instead, Gloria frumped her way through some place called Loft. Because the prices were confined to only two digits before the decimal point, Gloria presumed something was wrong with the clothes. She looked at the sale rack as if she expected a snake to uncoil from it at any moment.

Her trip to Victoria's Secret lifted my spirits. There, awash in a sea of overpriced pink, Gloria found more happiness. She tried on a negligee making me want to slip into the dressing stall with her. If two employees weren't lingering in the uncrowded store, it might have happened. Gloria crooked her finger at me when she spied a sales girl shooting her the hairy eyeball. I wondered how often people had sex in the changing rooms. Probably not too often with the coitus police working the register.

She bought the negligee but passed on a couple other things. We walked across to Harborplace to have lunch at McCormick and Schmick's. They made a passable crab cake, featured superior fish, and cooked a good steak. We'd barely put in our orders when my phone rang. I ignored Gloria's frown and looked at it.

It was Hess.

"I have to take this," I said, and excused myself from the table. "Hello?" I said after a jaunt to the lobby.

"C.T., it's Agent Hess," he said. "How are you?"

"Depends on what you have to tell me."

"Look, it's taking a little longer than I wanted. There are a couple judges I like to go to, and I can't get in to see either of them until after courts are done for the day."

"So we're in a holding pattern."

"More or less."

"I'm chafing at not doing anything," I said.

"I'm sure you are." His tone sounded genuine. "It's just taking some time."

"Longfellow told us the mills of God grind slowly, Agent Hess. I expect the mills of the FBI to be a little faster."

I cut off his reply when I hung up.

CHAPTER 18

I GOT TO WORK WHEN WE GOT HOME. TO HER CREDIT, Gloria wanted to go somewhere else to keep me from the temptation. I couldn't be away from it any longer. I trusted Rich, Hess, the FBI, and their damnable process. So far, all I could show for it was an ache to do more and the vague semi-optimism of Agent Hess. None of it would ever be enough.

In Hong Kong, my cohorts and I hacked our ways into pretty much anything and never left any traces. Companies learned more about security in the intervening time, but so did I. Hackers always stayed a step ahead of the people trying to keep them out. Getting into the ISPs would not be fast; I would need to conduct serious reconnaissance work first, plus make sure my online footprints would be invisible. Gloria watched TV and puttered around while I did the legwork. She tried to come in and convince me to come up for air a couple times but quickly learned the futility of it.

I smelled something wafting from the kitchen a couple hours later. Did Gloria try to cook? If so, I expected the smoke alarm to go off any minute now. After a few moments, relief flooded me when I realized my house would not be a cinder by the end of the evening. Gloria materialized in the office door a short time later. "Want some pizza?"

"You made a pizza?" I said.

Gloria snickered. "Delivery from that place we like nearby. You want any?"

I'd been working without a break since we arrived home. Sitting in a chair, mapping some networks, and typing would never qualify as hard work, but I'd immersed myself in it. My stomach grumbled with the onset of hunger. "I'll get some in a little while."

"Hard at work?" She walked into the room and stood behind my chair.

"For a change." I stopped. Someone looking over my shoulder always served to distract me. I reminded myself my sister's murder outstripped my peculiarities and went back at it.

"It's amazing all of that makes sense to you," Gloria said, leaning closer to the monitor as if searching for insight.

"Hopefully, it'll lead me to an answer soon."

Gloria lingered and watched me work for a few more minutes. I guess the excitement of a network mapper and a terminal shell became too much for her, and she needed to leave the room to escape the thrills. The TV clicked on a moment later. I finished a couple of network scans and then went into the kitchen. Gloria ordered a plain cheese and a mushroom and onion pizza. I took two slices of the latter, poured myself some iced tea, and went back to the office. After an additional two slices of pizza and another glass of tea, I secured the network information I needed.

A few minutes of research told me all I should know about the intrusion detection systems I would encounter. From there, I made sure I took all the necessary precautions to remain invisible as I poked and prodded the ISPs. I wasn't stealing anything. I wasn't exfiltrating a bunch of data I shouldn't have. All I wanted to do was search their records for users with handles in the format of Rondel and Romirbo. Where was the harm? I didn't expect them to agree with my philosophy, but someone like me could have been doing a lot worse.

It took longer than necessary, but I wanted to make sure I set everything up correctly. My scripted searches fired, running against the large national ISPs, as well as the consequential local and regional ones. I got up and vowed to do something else. Melinda tugged at my memory. I was supposed to talk to Joey about her.

No time like the present.

To my great non-surprise, Joey already ate dinner. I told him I would pick up dessert and bring it by. Armed with three pieces of decadent cheesecake—two for Joey—I knocked on his door. He let me in, and we sat at his breakfast nook. He brewed some coffee. I took the cheesecake out of the bag and arranged the pieces on the table. Joey came back with two coffees and two forks.

I let him indulge in some velvety goodness before I got down to business. Given the choice of the three pieces, Joey chose black forest and red velvet, leaving me with strawberry. No objections from me. I sipped my coffee and took a small bite of the slice. By contrast, Joey devoured his one-fifth at a time. "What brings you by?" he said after wiping his face on a napkin.

"I need your help with something," I said.

"Samantha?" Joey said after an enormous bite,

"No, the other case. The hooker."

"What about her?"

"Her stalker turned up on my street."

"You sure it was him?"

I repeated what I told Melinda. "If it wasn't, someone else has the same car and a keen interest in being seen driving by my house."

Joey shook his head. "You told her?"

"Yeah," I said. "She's spooked. It took a while, but she's finally spooked." I ate another bite. The strawberry ripples breaking its surface tasted natural and fresh.

"What now?" said Joey.

"I need to put her up somewhere, and it can't be my place. I was hoping she could stay with you."

"With me?"

"Her stalker doesn't know about you," I said. "She won't get in the way of your work, and I know you can protect her if it came down to it."

Joey pursed his lips in thought. "There are probably some perks to having a hooker for a houseguest."

"I knew you'd see the positives." In reality, I hoped Joey wouldn't fixate on such an obvious benefit. Melinda might be too spooked and cautious to express her gratitude in the way Joey wanted. Going off the other end, I didn't want him to wind up smitten with a prostitute after a few romps in the sack.

"Give me a call when you want to bring her by," Joey said.

"It'll probably be tonight. If I can, I'll get Rollins to handle the transfer."

"You expect to be occupied with Samantha's case?"

"I do," I said.

* * *

I GOT HOME and walked down the hallway to my office. My illicit inquiries could be finished. I might have my answers and then get revenge for Samantha. I stood in the doorway. Giving my word meant something to me. I told Rich and Hess I would trust their process and hope for the best. I already did the legwork; all Hess was required to do was find a judge who liked him enough to sign a piece of paper. How hard could it be?

If it were so easy, how come I didn't have the good word from Hess yet? Did he experience a problem with the judge? Had he already been denied and now slow-rolled me because he didn't want to call and tell me? Courts would long be finished for the day—lawyers and judges avoided overtime as if they were afflicted by a terminal allergy to it. Hess said it was taking longer than he expected. I felt confident my expectations differed from his.

Gloria already left, probably to go back to her own house. We weren't living together full time, which was fine with me. I rarely stayed with her even though her place could have held two of mine and still allowed room for a swanky kitchen. Despite its size deficit, I liked my house and the stuff in it. I liked having an office on the first floor and being a short drive from a real office I didn't use often enough. Tonight, Gloria would probably have tried to distract me from working on the case. She did it out of my best interests, which I understood and appreciated. I would have let her distract me for a while. At some point, the anticipation of waiting for Hess' call would make me poor company. The witching hour dawned.

I pried myself away from the office door and sat on my couch. The emptiness of the rooms only made me restive. I could smell Gloria's fragrant and expensive shampoo in my couch cushions, and the scent reinforced her absence. I missed her. This didn't help. I grabbed the remote and turned the TV on. I tend to be a channel flipper and my mood only amplified it. Shows or movies I liked to watch got only a few seconds on the screen before I went to the next channel. The lack of focus on the TV allowed me to relax a little.

As I flipped up to the premium channels, my phone rang. It was Hess. I hoped for good news while bracing myself for something else. "Hello?" I said.

"C.T., it's Agent Hess." I heard disappointment tinge his voice. He failed. He'd failed my sister and failed my trust.

"I trust you have some news for me?" I fought to keep my voice neutral.

"I haven't been able to get a warrant. I know it's not the news you want, but it's reality. This is a . . . complicated case."

"It's a very simple case. My sister is dead. Someone killed her. I handed you a wheelbarrow of evidence to find him."

"Fruit of a poisoned tree."

"I knew I shouldn't have bothered. You and your system are useless."

"I'm still going to try—"

"No," I said, cutting him off. "Don't. Don't bother. I know how to proceed, and it doesn't involve groveling before some asshole in a black robe. Thanks for your time, Agent Hess." His reply died on the line when I hung up on him.

I got up from the couch, not even pausing to turn off the TV, and walked into my office. As soon as I sat, my phone rang again. This time, it was Rich. "Did Hess ask you to call?" I said.

"He told me what happened," said Rich. "I'm sure you're disappointed."

"I am, but I wonder why. I should have known this would fail."

"The system works."

I laughed. "Yeah, sure it does. And you wonder why I don't want to be a part of it. It works like a fucking charm . . . right up until it doesn't. When it happens, people can't get their heads out of their asses to figure out how to fix anything."

"Your spin is unfair. C.T., I don't want you to go and do something you'll regret."

"I don't believe in regrets," I told him. "But if I did, trusting you and Hess and your precious *system* would make the list." I hung up on Rich, too, before he could say anything.

I was on a goddamn roll.

CHAPTER 19

THE ROLL ENDED AS SOON AS I REALIZED SOME RESULTS were still pending. I'd put a lot of work into this information extraction, but it was dependent on other processes. My anonymizer needed to run, then the meticulous ISP detecting and bypassing scripts, and others set to wipe away my electronic footprints. I could have obtained results faster but at the risk of being visible. I settled for slower results and the extreme likelihood of being untraceable. It was a tradeoff I'd been glad to make at the beginning. Now, after my frustrating conversations with Hess and Rich, I wanted results, and I didn't have them yet.

My phone rang again. I considered spiking it into the wall until I looked at the caller ID. Melinda. "He found me again," she said between ragged breaths.

"Slow down. What happened?"

"The stalker. He's onto me again."

"Even where you were staying?" I said.

"He found me walking around. I didn't even go where I normally do. C.T., what am I going to do?"

"Where are you now?"

"I ducked into a restaurant," she said. "He's parked nearby.

I can see his car through the window." Her breaths still came quickly. "What am I going to do?"

"What's the name of the place?"

"The Golden West Café. You know it?"

"I'll be there in ten minutes," I told her.

* * *

MORE PEOPLE in Baltimore should know and visit Melinda's hiding place. Hampden could boast of many other attractions—as well as copious neighborhood charm—but none of its eateries stood up to the Golden West Café. I loved the eclectic menu and the fact they supported live music and performers, even though I'd never heard of a single artist who took the stage there. I called Melinda as I drew near. "Where is he?" I said.

"On Thirty-Sixth. He's just parked there, looking at me."

"OK. I have an idea. Sit tight for a few minutes. I'll call you again."

A while ago, to close out a pesky case, a spy shop owner required a bribe to show me his receipts. In return for my contribution, I got the receipt I needed plus some gadgets. I'd snagged one of those gadgets as I left the house. This would be a great time to use it. I drove up Falls Road, past 36th Street, made a right onto 37th, then a right onto Hickory. I found a parking spot near the intersection of Hickory and 36th. Finding a place to leave your car in Hampden neighborhoods felt like parking in Federal Hill: you competed with residents for spots which should have been theirs, and sometimes they let you know it.

I got out of the car and called Melinda again. "Do something distracting," I said.

"What do you mean?"

"Just cause some kind of scene for about a minute. I want

everyone's attention on you inside and not me outside." I hung up and crouched behind a car on 36th, making my way down to the silver Benz. I dropped to all fours and crawled to it. If the stalker looked in the mirror, he would see me. Other patrons could see me from the restaurant. If Melinda made a scene, I would probably have less than a minute of invisibility while everyone rubbernecked the crazy girl in the restaurant. I took a small, nondescript black box about half the size of my pinky out of a jacket pocket. I scooted behind the Benz, reached under it, and stuck the small box to the inside of the frame.

Then I crept backwards away from the car, crouched again, and skulked back down 36th. When I hit Hickory, I stood up, walked to the Audi, and called Melinda again. "How did the scene go?"

"Well enough that everyone thinks I'm a nut," she said. "I hope it accomplished something."

"It did. Get up and walk toward the bathrooms. Then leave via the back door. You'll come to an alley. Turn left, and I'll pick you up on Hickory."

"Got it," she said and hung up. I drove the Audi across 36th and waited outside the alley. Melinda emerged a minute later and climbed in.

"What was all that about?" she said.

"I wanted to do something to his car, and I needed everyone to look at you," I said.

"What did you do?"

"Put a GPS tracker on it."

Her eyes went wide, and she grabbed my arm, thankfully not when I needed it to change gears. "So we'll find out who this asshole is?"

"It's the plan," I said.

Melinda sat back in the passenger's seat and let out a deep

breath. Tension left her body as her posture relaxed. "Where to now?"

"You're going to stay with a friend of mine named Joey. He works out of his house, so he'll be home a lot, and he can protect you if things get ugly."

"What's he like?"

"He's a good guy. Big heart . . . equally big stomach."

"Can I fuck him?"

Now she sounded like the Ruby I'd first come to know. It only reinforced how far she needed to go to divorce herself from this life. "I guess it would be up to him," I said, "but you don't have to. He's doing this as a favor to me, not for what he might get out of it."

"You really are no fun sometimes," she said, a smile playing at the edges of her mouth.

"As long as I keep you alive and stalker-free, you're welcome to think what you want."

My words snapped her back to reality. "Thanks, C.T.," she said. "Will you let me know who it is when you figure it out?"

"Yes."

"Good," she said. "I want to know who this guy is and why he's stalking me."

"The why is something you may have to answer for yourself," I said.

"Isn't it always?"

I pondered Samantha's case and found veracity in Melinda's words.

* * *

The app to monitor the GPS tracker resided on my laptop, which I picked up from my house. I hid the device well. If he found it, then Melinda's case could drag on far longer than I expected it to. I wanted to help her, but I also wanted to focus on Samantha's murder. My thoughts flashed to my results. They could be displaying right now. I should check. I took a deep breath and made myself focus on the screen. The tracker moved, heading northeast away from Baltimore.

I got in the car and followed its trail for miles of highway It stopped in Fallston, a swanky area of Harford County. I got there about a half-hour after my target. The silver Benz sat in the driveway of a small house bordering on swankiness. It needed more square footage and nicer construction to earn the title. Other homes farther down the street lorded over it. Houses at the front of the street ran small, as if the homeowners association decided to put the paupers away from the business end of the cul-de-sac.

I jotted down the address: 12124 Rochelle Drive. The Benz now showed a rear plate, so I noted it, too. Then I left before the homeowners took offense to a mere Audi besmirching their fine neighborhood. I arrived home, ignored my curiosity at the ISP results, and focused on finding out who Melinda's stalker was. First, I used the BPD's network to run his license plate. It gave me a name I looked at a few seconds before I believed. I needed to be certain, so I used an MVA search to match the address. Same name.

Jackson McMurray. Melinda Davenport's former step-brother.

The family weirdness hit a new level.

* * *

I DROVE to Joey's house and called to let him know I was en route. When I got there, Joey and Melinda sat at the kitchen table. They both looked like someone roused them from a deep sleep. I briefly wondered if they woke in the same bed before a shudder drove those thoughts from my mind. Each of them sipped coffee from a mug. I poured myself one before I joined them at the table.

"What's going on?" Melinda said.

"I found out who your stalker is," I said.

Her sleepy eyes looked more alert right away. "That's great! Who is it?"

"Before I tell you, we might want to have this conversation in private." I looked at Joey. "No offense."

He shook his head. "None taken. I understand." He got up from the table, went into the living room, and turned on the TV.

"What was that all about?" Melinda said. "You trust Joey to look after me but not to know who he's protecting me from?"

"When was the last time you saw Jackson?" I said, not answering her question.

"Jackson?" She frowned. "It's been a few years." The furrowed brow remained on her face. "I guess I can't be surprised you found out about my family. Why do you ask?"

I sat and stared at her. She looked back. The frown pulling her eyebrows down did a sudden reversal. "Oh, my god!" she said. "You're saying Jackson has been stalking me?"

"I am."

"Are you sure?"

"I followed him to his house," I said. "The plate on the silver Benz is registered to him at the address I saw."

Melinda put her head into her hands. It took me a few seconds to realize she was crying. In lieu of tissues, I grabbed a few napkins from Joey's counter and handed them to her. She peeked out from behind her fingers, nodded, and took them. The bawling continued a few more minutes.

I waited as Melinda's crying grew softer, and the sobs came less frequently. She wiped her eyes a few times and cleared her throat to compose herself. "Why did it have to be Jackson?" she said, her voice a shade above a whisper.

"I'm afraid I need you to answer the question," I said.

"It's complicated."

"So I gathered."

Melinda took a drink of her coffee. "Fuck, I wish this were stronger right now." She paused. "I wish *I* were stronger right now."

"You're doing fine," I said to reassure her.

She needed another swig of coffee. "Jackson's mother married my father. You already know that." I nodded. "We were both sixteen. He was a couple months older." Something resembling a smile cracked her face, but it disappeared immediately. "He was really cute. He told me I was cute, too." She shrugged. "Things just . . . sort of happened from there."

"You had sex with him."

She nodded. "It took a couple months. I think we felt the attraction while our parents were dating. Once we were both under the same roof, it was hard to see him and not . . . you know. We were careful. Our parents liked to socialize a lot and be important, and we were old enough that they'd leave us at home. So they'd go out on the town, and Jackson and I would stay home and fuck."

I suppressed another shudder. Melinda and Jackson weren't related by blood, but their relationship still creeped me out. It felt too *Game of Thrones* for me, even if it stopped shy of being incestuous. I wondered at the damage a relationship like theirs could do. Did Melinda become Ruby because of her affair with Jackson and its inevitable aftermath? I needed a few more semesters of psychology to puzzle it out. "Did this go on for a while?" I said.

"Yeah. They went out a lot."

"But your parents eventually found out."

"I guess they had to at some point," she said.

A large part of me didn't want to ask the next logical question. This grossed me out. I needed to know, however, so I said, "What happened?"

"We were both eighteen. Seniors in high school. Consenting adults. Jackson dated a couple girlfriends, I went out with a couple boyfriends, but none of it lasted. Anyway, our parents went out again. Jackson cancelled a date so we could . . . anyway, they came back way earlier than we expected." Melinda closed her eyes. "They caught us in the shower."

I blew out a deep breath. The rift in the family traced its genesis here. This must have set Melinda on the path to becoming Ruby. For the first time, I realized how difficult it would be to reverse. "What happened afterwards?"

It took Melinda some time to answer. She used another swig of coffee to buck herself up. "They knew they couldn't leave us alone. My father blamed Helen, of course. She blamed me for corrupting her little boy. Jackson and I didn't blame anyone. We were just two teenagers."

"But you didn't love each other."

She shook her head after a moment. "On some level, maybe. Not in the conventional sense. Like I said, it was complicated."

"This is what drove your family apart," I said, not phrasing it as a question.

"Yeah. Daddy tried to bring in some expensive shrink. He paid a lot for discretion. When you're *Vincent Davenport*, you can't have it get around that your daughter has been fucking her step-brother. The shrink was an asshole, though. None of his shit worked. Daddy and Helen couldn't get along. He still blamed her, and she still blamed me. Neither of them even thought how unnecessary it was to blame anyone. We were two good-looking, horny teenagers thrust under the same roof." She shrugged. "What did they expect?"

"What happened to Helen?"

"Daddy made them leave. He paid her to go away and never contact us again. I don't know where she went."

"And Jackson?" I said.

"He blamed me for us getting caught. Like it was my fault they came home early. He would try to get with me on the sly, but we never really stood much of a chance. Daddy installed alarms on our bedrooms, so we couldn't even sneak down the hallway in the night. When it was obvious Jackson and Helen needed to leave, Jackson and I . . . had a fight."

"When you say a fight—"

"He hit me. Called me a whore . . . all of that." Melinda paused to collect herself with a few deep breaths. "Once he realized what he'd done, he tried to apologize. He said he'd come back for me." She shook her head. "I guess I pushed a lot of that out of my mind. Suppressed it or whatever."

"You couldn't presume it was him," I said. I sipped my coffee. It was lukewarm.

"But I should have realized it was possible. That night . . . I don't know, he sounded obsessed. 'I'll find you. I'll come back for you.' I think he thought he was rescuing me from a bad situation."

"He might really feel he is now."

"Jesus, I didn't think about that." She put her head in her hands again. "He found me, C.T.," she said in a muffled voice. "He found me. What am I going to do?"

"For now, you're going to stay here. He doesn't know where you are, and he doesn't know I know who he is."

"What are you going to do?"

"I need to talk to some people," I said. "The rest is going to depend on what Jackson does."

Melinda whisked her head out of her hands. "Don't kill him," she said, her eyes looking like a puppy's when begging for scraps. "Please."

I frowned in surprise. "You care about him?"

"In some weird way, yeah. I don't want to be with him again. I'm not even sure I want to see him again. But I don't want him to die. Promise me you won't kill him."

I shook my head. "I promise I'll do everything I can not to kill him. It's the best I can do. If he pulls a gun on me, all bets are off."

"I can't go back to work, can I?" Melinda said after a moment.

"You need a career change," I said. "We can figure it out once this mess is settled. For now, stay here with Joey and don't go back to any of your old stomping grounds. Don't even talk to anyone. Don't give Jackson an easy way to find you."

Melinda nodded, but her eyes looked at something far away. "It wasn't him in the alley," she said, "when Joanie got beaten up."

"You're sure?"

"Yeah. Jackson was taller . . . is taller."

"So he hired someone to do it," I said.

"You think he paid someone to beat me up?"

"Maybe he paid someone to scare you. The thing is people who take money to scare others don't have a lot of tactics in their inventories."

"I didn't think he'd want to hurt me," she said in a small voice.

"He might not. Maybe the guy who beat up Joanie was supposed to pummel whoever happened to be with you."

"Poor Joanie. It's all my fault."

"You didn't send someone to beat her up."

"But I slept with Jackson. Something told me I shouldn't, and we kept doing it. Look what happened."

"You can't blame yourself," I said. "Jackson is the one who's done all this."

Melinda gave me a resigned nod and looked at her coffee mug. "It's empty," she said after a moment.

I thought it wasn't the only empty thing at the table but kept it to myself.

I PONDERED MELINDA'S HISTORY AS I DROVE HOME. SHE'D entered into a sexual relationship with her stepbrother. Before Jackson, she grew up as the daughter of a wealthy, influential man. Boys would have tried to impress her with gifts her family wouldn't get her. I wondered if the association of a gift as a payment for gratification got imprinted onto her mind early in her teen years. I remained convinced Melinda possessed the smarts and moxie to do a complete career change, but she also carried a lot of baggage. She couldn't be a smiling secretary overnight.

I parked my car, went inside, and plucked a cold IPA from the fridge. Melinda became Ruby because of a bad family situation. Part of it was her own doing, but she couldn't control the way her parents reacted. Her father tossing his wife and stepson out struck me as the typical overreaction men of privilege and power display. They're so used to bows of servitude and obsequious nods they lash out and fly to an extreme when something disrupts life on Bucolic Avenue. What would the neighbors have thought about Melinda and Jackson's ongoing tryst? I knew it weighed on Vincent Davenport's mind when he made his decision. It was easier to explain his wife moved out than the truth behind her abrupt departure. I wondered how he explained Melinda's "disappearance" to the caviar crowd in his neighborhood? The foundation served as a good cover at least.

All this pondering didn't lead me any closer to solving anything, but it did drain my IPA. I tossed the bottle into the recycling bin and figured I would call it a night. Looking at my results would only make me stay up and obsess about them. I could do more for Samantha and her memory after a night's rest. I started to head upstairs when my doorbell rang. Fast knocking immediately followed.

I fetched the nearest handgun I had, which happened to be the .45 and endured the persistent rapping until I got to the door. I looked out the peephole to see Shade on my doorstep. One of these days, I would have to take myself out of the phone book. "I know you're in there, man!" I heard him say. I rolled my eyes, tucked the .45 into the back of my jeans, and opened the door.

"What do you want, Shade?"

"Where is she?"

"Where's who?"

"Ruby, you asshole. Where you stashing her?"

"I don't know where she is," I said.

"Look, man, I know—"

"She's spooked. This stalker thing has really shaken her. I told her to hide. I don't know where she is, and I don't want to know."

He considered what I said. His eyes narrowed in concentration. He looked around as if expecting someone to be following him. His left hand clenched and unclenched as if on its own. "Why do I think you're lying?" he said.

"Why do you think I care?" I said.

Shade surged forward and tried to push past me. I shoved him back. He tried again. I hit him with a quick left in the solar plexus. The breath left his lungs in a big gasp. I grabbed the front of his shirt and pulled him forward, slamming his head into the door jamb. The pimp staggered backward and stumbled, landing on his butt on my steps. A line of blood ran down his forehead. I took out the .45 and let him see it. "Go home," I said.

Shade shook his head. "He's dead."

"Who?"

"Jacko. He's dead, man. Shot." Shade's voice threatened tears. I doubted he cared much for Jacko's well-being.

"When?"

"Earlier tonight."

"Were you with him?" I said.

"I was nearby." He paused. "I'm scared, man. I don't know what to do."

"Run."

"Run?"

"Run," I reiterated. "Far and fast. If you want to survive, it's your best choice."

He stood as if it would fortify his flagging courage. "I ain't never run in my life."

"Of course not. You had Jacko." Shade bowed his head. "It's your best course of action."

"Can you help me?" he said.

"I'm stretched pretty thin already. You shouldn't need my help to leave the city."

"What am I gonna do with my girls?"

"You know a guy named Romeo?" I said. "He's . . . in your profession."

"Heard of him."

"Tell him you talked to me. Give him the short version of what happened."

"Then what?"

"Then do what he suggests," I said, getting annoyed. "Especially if it involves running."

It took the frightened pimp a few minutes to parse it with what happened earlier, but he finally nodded. "OK," he said. "OK. That's what I'll do. Thanks, man."

"Don't mention it . . . except to Romeo."

Shade wiped blood from his forehead and walked away. I closed and locked my door. Later, I slept with the .45 on my nightstand.

I woke up a few minutes before nine and hit the mean streets of Federal Hill for my run around the park. After last night's visit from Melinda's disenfranchised pimp, I wore the .38 under my jacket. I ran about four miles. Pounding the pavement gives me time to think. I pondered why I'd tossed Samantha's case aside to help Melinda. Samantha was my sister. Shouldn't she be more important? Melinda enjoyed the advantage of still being alive. I could help her in a practical sense. Finding Samantha's murderer was about revenge.

I stopped in mid-stride. For the first time, I realized I pursued Samantha's murderer not for her memory but for my own sense of justice and payback. I worked the case for me, not for her. This kind of mid-exercise epiphany might unnerve a lot of folks. I shrugged and finished my last lap. Regardless of the reason, I would find her killer. She would have her justice, and so would I. In the meantime, this was my chance to help someone else in dire need.

After finishing my run, I went back to my house and showered. Freshly dressed, I came downstairs and made a simple breakfast of turkey bacon and a toasted wheat bagel. When I finished eating, I walked into my office and looked at my screen. All my searches finished long ago. They dumped their results into a text file. I opened it.

A local ISP processed current email traffic by someone using the handle of Romirbo. It must be the same guy. He was still alive, which meant I hadn't missed my chance to kill him. I jotted the email address down. I would find Romirbo. Melinda needed me more, which conveniently gave me time to plot the timely demise of my sister's killer.

* * *

A COUPLE HOURS LATER, I walked into *Il Buon Cibo*. It's not the most famous restaurant in Little Italy—Sabatino's has a stranglehold on the title—but as its name suggests, it's always served damned good food. Through my parents, I knew the owner Tony Rizzo for most of my life. Tony is perhaps better known as Baltimore's organized crime boss. I figured it out long before my parents did, and I've remained tight with him while they've distanced themselves. They could at least come in for the food.

I walked to Tony's table by the fireplace. His goons were used to me by now; they didn't even go through the trouble of glowering anymore. Tony looked up and smiled at me. His face looked tired. Over the last year and a half, the man probably lost a good eighty pounds. He'd amassed a few to lose, but I thought he took the weight loss a little too far. Bitching about his doctors became a popular pastime for Tony. "C.T., it's good to see you," he said. We shook hands and I sat. "You hungry?"

"A little."

"Good. I want you to try something. We're starting to offer whole gluten-free pasta. These fucking health nuts keep asking for it." Tony snapped his fingers and a young waiter nearly tripped over himself to answer the summons. "Tim, bring my friend a plate of our fake pasta . . . with whatever kind of sauce he wants."

"Marinara is fine," I said. I didn't want to try the gluten-free pasta—from prior experience, I thought it possessed the taste and consistency of boiled cardboard—but I also didn't want to refuse Tony.

Tim nodded and scurried away. Tony looked at me. "What brings you by? I know you don't need a free meal."

"You remember Samantha."

"Of course I do," Tony said with a smile. "Great girl. Damn shame she died so young."

"My parents recently told me she didn't die of a heart defect." Tony frowned. In his line of work, he probably knew what I was about to say. "Someone killed her."

"Jesus." Tony's voice dropped to a whisper. He regulated his voice automatically depending on the subject. "Long time to carry a lie."

"Thirteen years," I said. "They told me they did it to protect me."

"You *were* sixteen at the time."

I shook my head. "Even if they needed to protect me from it then, they've had plenty of time to tell me since."

"True," Tony acknowledged. "I guess they have their reasons."

"Did they ever tell you?"

"Me? No." Tony gave a quick shake of his head. "Something so big, you don't tell many people, if anyone."

"I guess," I said.

"What are you going to do about this?"

"I've been looking for her killer since I got the news."

"And?"

"I'm pretty sure I found him."

Tony leaned forward. "You gonna take him out?"

"Damn right," I said.

As quickly as he'd leaned forward in his chair, Tony leaned back. He studied me. "You've killed people before," he said after a few seconds of thought.

"Professional hazard," I said.

"But always in defense of your own life."

"Once someone else's."

"There's a big difference between killing someone because you need to and doing it because you want to. If it's you or them, fuck 'em. Everybody gets it. But killing someone because you want to is different. It's crossing a line for a lot of people. And once you cross it, you can't come back."

"I've thought about it," I said.

"Could you live with it?"

"I'm pretty sure I could."

Tony said, "You're gonna have to be sure, C.T. Damn sure. You can't go back. You can't undo it."

"Are you trying to talk me out of it, Tony?"

"No. You're a big boy. Decide for yourself. I'll just tell you this. Everybody compromises. With ourselves . . . with other people. We all do it. We compromise because those are the choices we can live with."

"Could you do it?"

"Sure," he said, "but I'm not you."

"I'm going to find him, Tony. When I do, I'm going to kill him . . . exactly like he killed my sister." This earned me a glance from one of the goons.

"I hope you do," Tony said.

Tim returned with my food. He asked me if I wanted a drink. I requested an unsweetened iced tea, and he reappeared with it before I finished peppering my pasta. Despite being gluten-free, it looked like regular spaghetti. It carried the darker color of wheat pasta. Maybe this was an ironic touch. I snagged some onto my fork. It nearly spilled over the large plate, and the sauce avoided the tablecloth only through surface tension and my utensil skills. There were perks to eating at the owner's table. "What do you think?" said Tony.

"It's . . . not bad," I said. "Better than a lot of similar stuff out there."

"Gluten-free shit," Tony grumbled.

"Why not go with spaghetti squash? No gluten, and it's low-carb."

"Another fucking health nut." Tony looked at me and laughed.

"It's not easy looking this good," I said.

After I forced myself to eat some more pasta, I asked Tony about something else. "I think I'm going to do something most likely unwise."

"We still talking about Samantha's killer?" he said.

"No, this is something different . . . another case I picked up." I paused for a swig of tea. "I think I'm going to threaten Vincent Davenport."

"Are you serious?" Tony looked at me like I brought the car back after curfew and neglected to fill it with gas. "Why would you?"

I told him a condensed version of Melinda's past, present, and whatever future I tried to preserve. "He has to know she's alive," I concluded.

Tony considered it all and nodded. "I'll buy it. He's rich and smart. He could find anything out. Why are you going to threaten him, though?"

"Maybe I'll just unsettle him."

"Still not smart. He's a powerful man, C.T."

"Someone is making Melinda's life hell. Her step-brother is the easy culprit because he's stalking her. But what if dear old dad found out his long-lost daughter is a whore on the cheap streets of Baltimore? One of her coworkers caught a bad beating, and her pimp's bodyguard got killed last night."

"Could be the step-brother." Tony shuddered.

"It could be, but he recently got out of rehab. Vincent Davenport would certainly have the reach to get a hooker beaten and a lummox shot."

"Be careful, will you? Don't just walk into the man's office and accuse him of all this crazy shit. He could make your life hell."

"I know. I'll be as tactful as I can."

"Christ, you're really in trouble," said Tony.

"I'll be all right. My parents know plenty of people like Davenport. I can talk to him."

Tony smirked. "I'm not sure anyone your parents know is quite like Vincent."

"You're on a first-name basis with him," I said.

"You think I don't know every important person in this city?"

"I'm sure you do."

"Just be careful," Tony said again. "You can't avenge your sister if you get in over your head with Vincent."

"I know. Do you and he get along?"

"Not really."

"Why not?"

"Because he's an asshole," Tony said.

"Should be a fun meeting, then," I said.

D&S Bakery's production facility sat on the border of Little Italy and Fells Point. I would call it Fells Point, but when one can throw a sizable stone to an excellent Italian restaurant, one's stomach mucks up the calculus. To solve this pesky location problem, Vincent Davenport located his corporate offices in Canton. On the drive to it, I realized some people would erroneously label the site as Highlandtown, which would piss off any older Cantonites in earshot. Ah, the neighborhood peculiarities of Baltimore.

I parked in a numbered spot on the lot and walked in through the front door. An imposing security fellow scanned me as I entered. I walked up to a reception desk, where a perky young woman welcomed me to the building with a ready, pre-made smile. "Can I help you, sir?"

"Yes," I said, "I'm here to see Mr. Davenport."

Her smile twisted into a look of surprise, but to her credit, she tried to maintain the cheerful visage. "Do you have an appointment?"

"No."

"I'm sorry, but Mr. Davenport's schedule requires him to only see people who have made appointments."

"You can call his office, I presume."

"Sir, if you don't—"

"It was a yes or no question," I said.

Her smile had vanished now. Alas. "Yes."

"Good. Please call his office. Tell him someone is here to see him. When your counterpart upstairs scoffs and asks why, tell her it's about Melinda and fraud."

She mouthed the last three words as she frowned and picked up the phone. The security guard tried to stare me down. I shrugged at him and returned my attention to the receptionist, who was much easier on the eyes. She sported a sharp navy business suit with a white shirt buttoned to the nape of her neck. She wore her hair up, held in place by two large pins, a canister of hairspray, and good fortune. Her brown eyes glanced at me as she called upstairs.

"Hi, it's Megan . . . I have a man here to see Mr. Davenport .

. . no, he doesn't . . . yes, I told him. He said it's about Melinda and fraud . . . sure, I'll hold." She put her hand over the receiver. "I'm on hold," she said, as if I hadn't heard everything. I gave her a quick smile. She took her hand away from the receiver. "Yes . . . he did? Are you sure? OK, I'll send him up."

"You can go up, sir," she said, still frowning in surprise.

"I had a feeling," I said.

"I'll have someone from security take you."

"I'm pretty sure I can find my way to the elevator."

"Unless Mr. Davenport knows you," she said, "you travel with security."

"Is there a pat-down involved? Can I request you if there is?"

Megan flashed a small smile, and her cheeks reddened. "There's no pat-down," she said. She picked up the phone again and dialed a three-digit extension. "Can you send someone to escort a visitor to Mr. Davenport's office? Thanks." She hung up. "Someone will be down in a minute to take you to see Mr. Davenport."

"Thanks," I said.

She went back to her work. The phone rang a couple times. The security guy kept glaring at me, even as one of his compatriots stepped off the elevator and walked toward Megan's desk to collect me. He looked like he'd just finished abusing tackling dummies in defensive lineman drills. I felt glad there would be no pat-down—and doubly glad this fellow would not be administering it.

CHAPTER 21

THE MOUNTAIN AND I RODE THE SWIFTLY-RISING EXPRESS elevator. He didn't say anything to me, and I returned the silence. He sized me up but never searched me. I'd prepared for the possibility by not bringing a gun into the building. The odds of needing one during a conversation with one of the business leaders of Baltimore were remote. The elevator dinged for the top floor, and the doors slid open. The security guard gestured with a wave of his tree-trunk arm. I stepped off into a hallway inlaid with marble. The paintings on the walls conveyed sophistication and expensive tastes.

I walked through an open double doorway at the end of the corridor. Some ancient Belize mahogany behemoth gave its life for the doorway, which was, of course, inlaid with gold and decorated in the refined tackiness preferred by rich assholes the world over. On the other side, two women sat behind large desks of the same wood facing each other. Maybe the second secretary existed to feed her boss' ego.

"Good afternoon, sir," the closer woman said. She looked to be in her forties and dressed like a 1950s schoolmarm. I wondered if she would rap me across the knuckles and give me detention for not making an appointment. Her coworker, more my age, focused on her computer.

"Good afternoon," I said.

"Mr. Davenport will see you in a moment." She gave me a well-practiced and artificial yet pleasant smile. The opulence of the penthouse must have covered the multitude of sins with respect to the secretaries' warmth. Who would notice a fake facial expression while looking at ugly miniature statues and tchotchkes carved from bricks of solid gold?

"Thank you," I said, giving her a smile injected with as much sincerity as I could muster. I sat in a comfortable guest chair between the desks and the closed ornate door past them. If the waiting area looked like it did, I couldn't wait to see the decorations in Vincent Davenport's office. My mind flashed to *Indiana Jones and the Last Crusade*, when Indy and the female explorer are looking for the Holy Grail. All the cups they passed on would be on shelves in Davenport's office. Anything less would disappoint me.

The phone on the older lady's desk buzzed. She picked it up, said a quick, "Yes, sir," and cradled it again. "Mr. Davenport will see you now," she called to me. As if triggered by her voice, the massive door opened. I nodded my thanks and walked through.

I felt disappointed. Vincent Davenport's office could sleep a family of sixty, and windows dominated three sides. The square footage rivaled my house and probably won. Davenport sat behind a desk in the far corner, larger and darker than the ones at which his secretaries perched. A mahogany conference table occupied the near corner, surrounded by six chairs each costing more than all the equipment in my office. A large TV and bookcases took up the areas of the walls not covered in glass. Most of the floor was open space. An executive could get in some mean putting practice up here. I noticed Davenport kept a putter in the corner opposite his desk. Despite the encouragement of my father and grandfather, I'd never cared much for golf. Once I discovered lacrosse, hitting a stationary ball every few minutes never held any excitement for me.

"Mr. Ferguson," Davenport said as I approached. He gestured toward the burgundy leather chairs in front of his desk. I would have gladly used them in my office. With the prices of everything in here, bread must be a racket.

"Mr. Davenport," I said, taking a seat opposite him.

"The last time I saw you was at the fundraiser."

"Yes."

"Your girlfriend said you might be able to ply your trade and help my foundation reunite missing children with their families."

"She did," I acknowledged.

"Do you think my foundation does good work?" he said.

"I do."

Davenport nodded as if he already knew the answer and my vocalizing it was perfunctory. "Imagine my surprise, then, when I hear that you came to talk to me about Melinda and fraud." His eyes narrowed. "Those are two subjects I take very seriously."

"I thought you might."

"What exactly did you mean when you told my receptionist those were your reasons for visiting today?" he said.

"Exactly what I told her."

"Melinda was my daughter."

"She still is," I pointed out.

"Still is?" I studied Davenport for a change of expression but couldn't pick one up. Like father, like daughter. "You know she's alive," he said.

"Yes. Just like you do."

Now I got a reaction. Davenport glared at me over the tops

of his glasses. I met his stare and didn't blink. The hell with his boardroom bully bullshit. After about twenty seconds, he needed to blink and look away. Victory.

"You think I know where she is?" he said after a moment.

"She told me you threw her out, and I believe her. She's also your daughter, and you're obviously a well-connected man. I'm sure keeping track of her is pretty easy."

"And what is it my daughter does, pray tell?"

"You know what she does," I said. "I'd wager you also know where."

"You would?"

"Strangely enough, she's been . . . on the job for five years and never been arrested. Either she's luckier than everyone else in her profession, or you're making sure she doesn't get rousted."

"She told you I threw her out of the house?" he demanded

"Yes."

Davenport steepled his fingers under his chin. "Did she happen to mention why?"

"Yes."

"Considering the nature of her transgression and my justification for kicking the lot of them out, why would I exert any influence to keep her out of trouble? Assuming I know what she's doing with herself, I mean."

"Because you can," I said.

"Because I can?"

"Why do you have this ridiculous office? Why do your guest chairs cost more than most cars driving by? Why do you have some of the godawful decorations you do?"

"Because I can, according to you."

I smiled. "Exactly. You don't need it. Everyone knows you're a very successful businessman. Most people know of your foundation. The only explanation for the excess is you do it because you can."

"I can afford decorations," Davenport said.

"In the same way, you can afford influence to keep your daughter out of jail. I'm sure you have plenty to go around."

He nodded. "I do. I do, indeed." Davenport removed his glasses and fixed me with an inscrutable look. "I could call the commissioner and have your license revoked."

"My license is issued by the state."

"It could still get done."

I shrugged. "It wouldn't change the fact what I'm saying is right."

"Mr. Ferguson, I like your parents." I wondered when he would bring them up. "They're nice people, and they do their part, in their own little way. You see, folks like your parents latch onto an artist and fund an exhibit at a museum so they can call themselves patrons of the arts. People like me built the museum."

"'Of more worth is one honest man to society and in the sight of God, than all the crowned ruffians that ever lived,'" I said.

"The Bible?"

"Thomas Paine."

"You don't think I'm an honest man?" said Davenport

"I think my parents are honest people, and Thomas Paine would call you a crowned ruffian. Yours happens to be this building. Power and influence are great, right up until you run into someone you can't intimidate with them."

"I could bury you," Davenport said through clenched teeth.

"My family has long been friends with Tony Rizzo," I said. The implied threat made Davenport frown. "I could bury you, too."

Davenport glowered at me, glanced down, and released a

long, deep breath. "What did you come here for, Mr. Ferguson?"

"Melinda is being stalked. The stalker has so far beaten up one of her coworkers and shot her pimp's bodyguard."

"I'm glad she has you to protect her, then."

"You obviously know where she is," I said. "I wondered if you also have any insight as to who's been stalking her."

"I wouldn't know."

I wasn't sure I believed him but he wouldn't tell me anything more. "Jackson?"

"My former stepson?" Again, I couldn't pick up any surprise. I didn't know if Davenport played things close to the vest or as yet remained unaware of Jackson's machinations. Hell, what if he put Jackson McMurray up to it? The kid's rehab facility cost more than some universities. Someone signed the check.

"The same."

"He is no longer within my influence," Davenport said.

"I find it hard to believe," I said.

"Be that as it may, what I said is true. Now, what was this fraud you mentioned when you got here?"

"You started your foundation because Melinda was another tragic case of a girl who ran away from home. We both know it's not what happened."

"And now you mean to expose me? To damage my foundation?"

I pondered it for a second. "Probably not."

"Probably not?"

"Your foundation does good work. It's a grim situation, and I think you help a lot of families, whatever answer they find. I don't want to undermine the mission."

"But?" he said.

"It depends on you, and if Jackson McMurray really is out of your reach."

"You want me to stop him?"

"I think it will be better for him than if I do it," I said.

"What makes you think I maintain any contact with Jackson after . . . after what he did to my daughter?"

"A hunch."

"A hunch," Davenport said with a sneer. "Useful in your line of work, I suppose, but not very effective today."

"Kind of like your ability to intimidate," I said.

Davenport started to say something, stopped, and composed himself. "I will consider what you've said. Good day, Mr. Ferguson."

"Good day, Mr. Davenport."

I got up and left the office. The Mountain didn't come back up, so I got to be a big boy and ride the elevator down all by myself. No one gave me a lollipop at the bottom. I soldiered on and drove home, wondering if my chat with Davenport accomplished anything. I hoped he would talk to Jackson McMurray. Either way, I'd done a lot for Melinda.

Now I needed to do something for Samantha.

CHAPTER 22

I had Samantha's murderer's email address.

My results provided more information, but they started with the basics. I thought about sending him an email. What is there to say to the man who killed your sister? Before I sent any message, I registered an anonymous email account and made sure to bounce my traffic off every proxy server I could think of. Might as well make the whole thing impossible to trace back to me if he got spooked. I turned over a bunch of ideas for what to say in my head before deciding on brevity above all else.

I know what you did thirteen years ago, almost to the day. It doesn't matter how I found out. If you want to keep this part of your past quiet, you'll meet me, and we can talk terms. Otherwise, I go to the police. You have 72 hours to reply.

After sending the email, I considered my next move. I wanted to meet this bastard and kill him. I didn't know how much Samantha suffered, though I hoped not at all. Anthony

Tyler—Rondel and Romirbo's real name—would suffer before he died. He would learn he could not kill young, trusting women and get away with it. I looked forward to teaching him the lesson.

Tyler would reply. He couldn't take the chance I was some random crackpot. I might actually know the truth about him and go to the cops. He couldn't risk it. He would have to answer me, and then I would have him. His address was in the Eastern Shore area of Maryland. I'd make him come to Baltimore, where he met and killed my sister. I scoured a map of the city, looking for some places where I could torture and kill a man in peace.

I had a few spots in mind. As I turned them over in my head, I made sure to clean my .45.

* * *

I DIDN'T GET a reply from Tyler the same day. Gloria came by later. She asked how things transpired. "I've helped Melinda as much as I can for now," I said. "I'm waiting on Samantha's killer to get back to me."

"You reached out to him?" she said, frowning in surprise.

"I need to draw him in and get him here."

"So you can kill him."

"Yes."

Gloria shook her head. "You're not a killer."

"I have been before."

"That was different," she said. "You told me about those times. That's not the same as killing someone in cold blood."

I thought about telling Gloria how much her advice resembled the words of the local organized crime boss but thought better of it. "He murdered my sister in cold blood," I said. "He has to pay for it."

Gloria smiled gently, like a teacher who's finally reached a distant student. "And he will. You always make people pay for what they've done."

"Then my streak will remain intact."

The gentle smile remained. "I love you, and I know the man I love isn't a murderer. You'll prove me right when it matters." Gloria kissed me and walked upstairs. I stayed in the living room ruminating on what she said.

* * *

I CAME DOWN to find several new emails waiting for me in the morning. Most of them were spam. Did I want to help a Nigerian prince get money out of his home country? No, in fact, I did not. How were people still falling for this? I skimmed my spam folder every morning in case something important wound up there, but my attention focused on one message in my inbox.

Anthony Tyler sent a reply. I barely thought about what it might say before I opened it.

I DON'T KNOW what your talking about but I might be willing to listen. I did alot years ago.

WHAT DID IT MEAN, other than Tyler possessed a shaky command of basic spelling? Did his reference to doing a lot mean he killed other people? If so, I would be ridding the world of a plague which didn't need to darken it anymore. I resolved to delve into Anthony Tyler's background and see the kind of man I was dealing with. First, I replied to his message.

• • •

I'M PRETTY sure you know what I'm talking about. If you forgot, you're even worse than I imagined. Let's chat on IRC.

I ADDED some info about a chat room I would create for this purpose. While I waited for him to read the new message, craft another poorly-worded response, and figure out what IRC was, I made breakfast. Nothing fancy—I didn't want to wait long. Toast, a couple hard-boiled eggs, and some coffee filled me up but left my curiosity for Anthony Tyler unsated. When I walked back into my office, he'd joined the IRC chat room and sent a message.

USER ROMIRBO JOINED the chat room.
    Romirbo> u there?

I LOOKED at the screen for a few seconds, cracked my knuckles, and typed.

CharlieFoxtrot> I am.
Romirbo> wtf are u talking about
CharlieFoxtrot> Thirteen years ago. Patterson Park.
Romirbo> what about it
CharlieFoxtrot> You murdered a girl.
Romirbo> u got no proof
CharlieFoxtrot> Nice denial. And here I am, talking to you. I must have some proof, genius.
Romirbo> what do u want
CharlieFoxtrot> To discuss terms.

Romirbo> or u go 2 the cops

CharlieFoxtrot> Something along those lines.

Romirbo> ok lets talk

CharlieFoxtrot> Not here. Not over email, either. You're going to come to me.

Romirbo> where do u live

CharlieFoxtrot> Baltimore.

Romirbo> wtf thats like 3 hours away

CharlieFoxtrot> OK. I'll go to the police, then.

Romirbo> no

Romirbo> wait

Romirbo> cmon man u there

CharlieFoxtrot> I'm still here.

Romirbo> can we meet in the middle

CharlieFoxtrot> This isn't a negotiation. This is me telling you we're going to meet somewhere, and you agreeing because you have no choice.

Romirbo> u dont gotta be an ass about it

CharlieFoxtrot> I'm just making sure you know your role.

Romirbo> where u want 2 meet

CharlieFoxtrot> How well do you know Baltimore?

Romirbo> ok i guess

CharlieFoxtrot> Meet me in a bar called The Strand. It's downtown.

Romirbo> ill find it. when

CharlieFoxtrot> Tomorrow night, midnight. I want to make it easy for you to spot me, so I'll be dressed in black jeans with a white shirt and black tie.

Romirbo> u plan ur clothes lol

CharlieFoxtrot> If you want to laugh, we can scuttle these plans, and I'll just take what I have to the State Police.

Romirbo> no sorry

Romirbo> ill be there
CharlieFoxtrot> Looking forward to it.

CONNECTION TERMINATED BY USER CHARLIEFOXTROT

WHAT AN ASSHOLE. I would definitely be looking forward to it. Waiting until tomorrow gave me plenty of time to refine my plan, commit it to memory, and dig into Anthony Tyler's background. I closed IRC and email and got to work.

* * *

TYLER EARNED HIMSELF A CRIMINAL RECORD. None of it painted him as a killer, let alone a serial killer, but his history showed ample bad behavior, especially involving women. One arrest for sexual assault got pled down to a misdemeanor and allowed him to avoid the sex offender registry. A couple of other battery charges stuck, and he did time for one of them. He lived on the Eastern Shore for years. I called there to see if the locals devised any theories about him.

After a spot of phone tag, I got connected to a Sergeant Palmgren in the Salisbury PD. I introduced myself as Detective Ferguson. So far, all true.

"Who you with?" he said.

My small streak of truth-telling died a swift death. "Baltimore PD," I said.

"Ferguson?"

I strove to avoid providing a first name. "Yes. Common spelling."

"What can I do for you, Detective?"

"We're looking into Anthony Tyler. He's from around your

way. Right now, he's just a person of interest, but we might like him for a couple things with some more evidence." I hoped I sounded convincing. Years of watching cop shows—and time spent around Rich and the BPD taught me the lingo—or at least, what I thought to be the lingo.

"Tyler? You can just look him up."

"Already did. I was hoping for more insight than I can find in his file."

"You probably already guessed he's an asshole."

"We decide on asshole status pretty quick in the big city," I said.

Palmgren chuckled. "Well, Tyler certainly earns the title when it comes to women."

"I noticed. Any idea why? You talk to him?"

"Me? Questioned him a few times. Kind of a mousy fella. Not small, just . . . not much of a presence, I guess. Kinda fades into the background . . . or at least wants to. We had a shrink thinks Tyler has mommy issues."

"He hated his mother?" I said.

"That or he wanted to fuck her," said Palmgren. "Hell, maybe both, I don't know. I'm not a shrink. Either way, he takes whatever it is out on women."

"You think he could be a killer?"

"You like him for murder?"

"Maybe," I admitted.

"Some guys, you know they're killers right away. Something in the eyes." Palmgren paused to sigh. "Not Tyler. He doesn't have a killer's eyes. There's . . . something going on there. I'm not sure what. If you made me pick, I'd say he's capable of murder, yeah."

"Is he smart enough to get away with it?"

"Maybe. He's mousy, like I said, but he's crafty."

"So how come he's been busted three times?"

"I wasn't involved in all of them," Palmgren said. "The first one was before I came onboard. I do know from talking to some folks the bastard was harder to catch the second and third times. Smaller crimes, so maybe we didn't look quite as hard. But if he wanted to cuff a couple of girls around to audition for something bigger. . . ." Palmgren didn't finish the sentence. He didn't need to.

"What about sexual assault?"

"Tougher. I think he could do it. When a shrink says a guy has mommy issues, there's a good bet the guy is going to try and stick it in some women."

I winced. I knew Palmgren was talking shop with someone he thought to be a fellow detective, but I didn't like hearing what happened to my sister referred to so crassly. Palmgren filled in my gap in the conversation. "Sounds like you want him for something pretty fucked up."

"He's looking better for it all the time," I said.

"Well, you need any help with Tyler, let me know."

"I think we can handle him . . . but thanks."

"He up in Baltimore?"

"I . . . have a CI who says he will be."

"Good. I'll look forward to hearing about his arrest."

"Oh, I'm sure it'll make the news," I said.

* * *

WHILE COMBING through the slagheap of Anthony Tyler's life, I discovered a couple ex-girlfriends. Neither brought any charges against him, which was not to say he didn't mistreat them. The first woman hung up on me as soon as I mentioned Tyler's name. I couldn't blame her. The second, Connie Sweet, stayed on the line. "Whatever I can do to help bring that son of a bitch down," she said when I told her who I was—for real this time—and why I called.

"It's an older case, but I think Tony sexually assaulted and killed a girl in Baltimore about thirteen years ago," I said. Getting those words out proved a struggle.

"Jesus," she said amid a sudden, hissing breath.

"Did you see anything when you were with him to make you think he could do such a thing?"

Connie paused. I heard her sigh a couple times. Finally, she said, "I don't know. I was with him about twelve years ago, I guess, so it'd be after . . . after that poor girl died. Tony was . . . I don't know . . . a little strange. He was nice enough at first, but then he became abusive."

"Physically?"

"No," she said to my surprise. "He was just really good at manipulating me, making me feel like crap, you know? He had a way with stuff like that."

"How long were you with him?"

"Almost a year, unfortunately. Asshole just about ruined my self-esteem. Took me a couple years to really pick myself up."

"I'm sorry you went through it," I said.

"Well, he was a son of a bitch."

"Did he ever mention being in Baltimore?"

"We went to Baltimore a few times," Connie Swect said. "He seemed to like it there. The Eastern Shore was quieter, especially then."

"Any areas of Baltimore he favored?"

"He liked going to . . . some park somewhere."

"Patterson Park?" I asked.

"Yeah. Yeah, that's it. Patterson Park. He said he liked to walk around it. We stayed downtown but always spent some time there. I didn't much care for it, but Tony loved it."

"Thank you, Connie. You've helped me a lot."

"Please take that son of a bitch down and put him away."

"I plan to." I was sure my definition of "away" differed from Connie's, but I didn't care, and I got the feeling she wouldn't care overmuch either.

CHAPTER 23

I dug further into Anthony Tyler but didn't unearth much. Detective Palmgren and Connie Sweet confirmed what I already knew and suspected. The world would be no poorer for Tyler's loss. I turned my plan over in my head a few times. It was a damn good one. I'd likely be arrested for carrying it out, but between a claim of self-defense, a great lawyer, and a jury's sympathy over Samantha's murder, I didn't worry about doing any time. If forced to give up my PI career, I could live with it. Samantha's memory was worth it.

My phone rang a few minutes later, snapping me from my reverie. "Hello?" I said.

"I think he's on to me again." It was Melinda.

"Jackson?"

"Who else?"

"I thought you were staying with Joey."

"I have been, but I can't stay there all the time."

"Have you . . . gone back to work?"

"No." She paused. "I've been talking to some of the girls I worked with, though. Been near a lot of the same old haunts. I guess he picked me up again that way."

I shook my head. The exact thing I warned her not to do. "You think he knows where you're staying?"

"No. I've been careful."

I could have provided her a testimonial of Jackson's driving skills, but I figured it wouldn't do much good. "I'm still working my other case, too. In fact, I'm pretty close to wrapping it up. What would you like me to do?"

"Come meet me?"

Why did I know it was what she'd ask? Without trying to audition for the role, I got the part as Melinda's knight in armor. Anthony Tyler's blood would take the shine off it, but I could tolerate the result. I sighed. "Where are you now?"

"I went to a public place so he couldn't track me so easily. I'm at Papa Nick's."

"Do you see him?"

"He's not inside," she said. "I'm trying not to be obvious and look for his car outside."

"OK," I said. "Stay where you are. I'll come to you."

"I'll be waiting."

THE LAST TIME I picked Melinda up at a restaurant, she exited via the kitchen and got into my waiting car. I hate repeating myself. Besides, the logistics of Papa Nick's didn't lend themselves to the screeching-tires-in-the-alley plan. I drove around the building. The kitchen opened out on the side of the building. I could have spirited her away there, but it would be no better than the front door. Instead, I parked the Audi as close as I could. Jackson McMurray's silver Mercedes sat a few spots away. With the darkened windows, I couldn't even tell if he still lurked inside. I walked into the restaurant.

I saw Melinda at the bar as soon as I walked in. She nursed

a drink and looked around nervously until she saw me. Her eyes fixed on me, and she smiled as I walked to her and sat on the adjacent barstool. "Not every silver Benz is Jackson's, you know," I said.

"Ones that follow me here and make a show of driving around probably are," she said.

"Let's get you out of here." She gulped down the rest of her drink, and we made our way toward the door. I walked through it first. She grabbed my hand. I let her. We walked toward my car. The driver's side door of the Benz opened. A man I presumed to be Jackson McMurray stepped out. He looked about my height, a little heavier, but still in decent shape. His face still retained some good looks but a difficult lifestyle ravaged it. Beside me, my client sucked in a large breath of air.

"Melinda," he said, standing at his car.

I unlocked the doors of the Audi, and we stood at the car. "Get in," I told her. She did.

"You the detective?" Jackson said.

"I'm someone who's protecting her from you," I said.

"She doesn't need protection from me."

"She thinks she does."

"Maybe you're putting the idea into her head," he said, glaring at me.

"And maybe it was whoever you hired to beat up her friend and shoot her pimp."

Jackson stepped away from his car and walked deliberately toward me. "You putting those ideas into her head, too?" He stopped within arm's reach of me.

"Get back in your car and go home," I said. "Leave Melinda alone."

"You don't tell me what to do."

"Does Vincent Davenport?"

Jackson scowled. He shook his head and feinted turning

away, telegraphing the punch he threw. I blocked it, hit him with a quick jab in the solar plexus, and followed it with two more punches to his stomach. He doubled over, and I elbowed him in the face. Jackson stumbled backward into the car parked next to the Audi. A few people milled about the lot. We would attract attention before long if we hadn't already. I grabbed Jackson's arm and put him in a wristlock. "Get back in your car and go home," I said again. "Leave Melinda alone. I strongly advise you to listen to me."

Jackson grunted before he answered. "What if I don't?"

"I don't have time for you. I'm working on something much more important than your sister or you." I tightened the hold on his lower arm and watched Jackson wince. "Get back in the car and go away, or I break your arm."

It took Jackson a few seconds of staring up at me to realize I meant business. He nodded. I released the wristlock. He cast a brief glance at Melinda, got into the Mercedes, and drove away. I got into the Audi and started it. "Did you hurt him?" Melinda said.

"No more than necessary." We wheeled out of the parking lot.

"I wish he would just stop."

"Like I told you earlier, I'm really close to finishing something else, something really important. I'll tell Rollins what's going on. If you need anyone for the next day or two, you're going to have to call him."

"You're leaving me?"

"I figured out who your stalker is, Melinda," I said. "The only way I can make him leave you alone is to kill him. I'm not going to do it, and I don't think you want me to. You have to work things out with your father and eventually with Jackson." I looked at her, and she nodded. "My other case involves my family. I guess we both have some things to work on."

"Am I going to be OK?" Melinda said after a few minutes of silence.

"Eventually," I said. "I offered to help you get a real job earlier. I meant it. You have a life to get back on track."

She nodded. "I wonder if my family will be a part of it."

"Family is often a mystery," I said.

* * *

When I got home, I called Rollins and filled him in on what happened. "He tried to punch you?" Rollins said.

"He was unsuccessful," I said.

"I think I can handle him. I'll keep an eye on the girl. Where is she?" I gave him Joey's name and address. "He's your fat Italian friend?"

"His reputation precedes him as much as his stomach," I said.

"You close to putting your other case to bed?"

"I should wrap it up soon."

"You sure you're OK with it?"

"With my plan to kill my sister's killer, you mean?" I said.

"Yes."

"I've never fancied myself a killer. The only person I've shot who didn't pose a direct threat to me was the Chinese guy about to shoot you. I've thought about it." I paused. "I can do it."

"You trying to convince me or yourself?"

"I know what you're trying to do," I said. "On a different day, I might even appreciate it. You're going to take care of Melinda tonight?"

"I got her."

"Good. I'll check in with you tomorrow." I hung up. I stared at Anthony Tyler's picture on my monitor. If I possessed more time, I would print it out, take it to a shooting range, and satisfy myself with making his head the bull's-eye. Tonight, I would get the real thing.

* * *

I STAYED in and cooked dinner. If I ended up getting arrested for shooting Anthony Tyler, and if an arrest led to me spending time in prison, I wanted to fix my last free meal for a while. Going out somewhere very nice and expensive would have been easy. I hadn't spent so much time cooking in college for nothing. I thought about what I wanted, made a quick trip to the market, and prepared everything fresh. My stuffed peppers finished baking. I already steamed the spinach and made whole wheat garlic bread in the toaster oven.

The garlic bread made me think of Tony Rizzo. A free meal at *Il Buon Cibo* would have been appropriate, too, considering my plans for the night. What better company when venturing out to kill someone than the local mob boss? As much as I liked Tony's restaurant and enjoyed our chats, I decided to stay home and keep to myself. The fewer distractions—at least after I finished my delicious homemade meal—the better.

Speaking of distractions, my doorbell rang as I loaded the dishwasher. I grabbed my .45 on the way to the door. Rich stood on the front steps. I sighed and considered not letting him in. "I know you're in there," he said. "I can hear your existential angst."

I opened the door. "My angst is not existential," I said.

"Whatever. Can I come in?"

I stepped aside. "What's going on?"

"Just dropping by to see how you are."

"How I am?"

"We're worried about you, C.T."

"We?" I said.

"Your parents. Me. Gloria. Pretty much everyone who knows you."

"I'm fine."

Rich strode into the living room and sat in my recliner. "Bullshit," he said. "You're figuring out who killed your sister."

"I already have," I said. "It's more than you or anyone else in your precious system ever did for her."

"What the hell are you trying to say?"

"You knew she didn't die of natural causes. How long have you been a cop? How long have you passed on chances to do something about her case?"

"I can't just comb through cold case files until I find something interesting," Rich protested. He took a deep breath. If this were a cartoon, steam would have poured from his ears. "She was your sister. I get it. She was my cousin, too. I loved her." Emotion edged into his voice. "You think I didn't want to do something for her? For all of us?"

I sat on the couch and took a calming breath. "Then why didn't you?"

"No," Rich said, shaking his head. "I'm not telling you."

"Why not?" He shook his head. I leaned forward and stared at him. "You were in Afghanistan. Now you're a detective in Baltimore. Fear isn't the reason. You're not as fast and loose with rules as I am, but you'll flout them when you need to. I'm sure you'd also disobey an order if you felt it right."

"Stop."

I didn't. "What's left? Samantha was your family. You've said she was the sister you never had. She treated you like her older brother. I think my parents did, too." I started to say something else but stopped. Rich looked at me and shook his head. I ignored it. "Family's it, isn't it?"

"What do you mean?"

"My parents asked you not to look into it," I said.

Rich tried to scoff. "Why would they?" I wasn't buying it.

"You tell me."

He sat in silence. So did I. We stared at each other for a minute. "Fine," Rich said, long after the silence grew uncomfortable. "They asked me not to look into Samantha's murder."

"Why?"

"They had their reasons."

"Why?" I said, this time louder.

"Maybe you should ask them."

"Why, goddammit?"

"Because they didn't want to lose you, too!" Rich closed his eyes and shook his head once, admonishing himself for telling me this. "They didn't want to lose you, too."

"Why would they?"

"Because you'd get wind of what was happening. They knew you'd find a way to figure it out. They were already keeping one secret from you and—"

"So were you," I said through clenched teeth.

"Fine, we all were. Keeping the secret was hard enough on all of us. Your parents were worried you'd obsess then exactly like you're doing now, try and take on Samantha's murderer, and get yourself killed."

"It's not going to happen, Rich."

"But you're planning to confront her killer?" he said.

"Would you do any less in my situation?"

He leaned back in the recliner and waved a dismissive hand. "It doesn't matter what I would do."

"But it does," I said. "You're a lot more like me than you care to admit. You'd do the same thing in my place."

Rich stewed in silence before finally saying, "So?"

"So don't try to talk me out of it . . . and don't couch it with my parents' ridiculous concerns."

"They're worried about you. I think they have a right to be."

"I guess they do, but they have no cause for it. I'll be fine."

"Just don't do anything stupid," Rich said.

"Like kill the bastard who murdered my sister?"

"Yeah. Or get yourself killed in the process."

"I can take care of myself," I told him.

"Graveyards are full of people who could take care of themselves, C.T."

"I promise not to be one more headstone, then. Go sit with my parents and drink gourmet cocoa while you all wring your hands and worry."

Rich stood. "At least I tried to talk you out of it."

"I'm not sure you did," I said.

"Talk you out of it?"

"Try."

Rich smirked. "I'm going to tell them I did," he said.

"Your secret is safe with me," I said.

* * *

AFTER RICH LEFT, I poured myself a glass of port. If tonight were to be my last night of freedom, I wanted to enjoy a good dessert wine. These are the kinds of things you can't control when you leave other people in charge of your last supper. I swirled the fortified wine around in its small glass and watched tiny maroon rivulets stream down the side. It made me think of blood. Anthony Tyler's blood.

Maybe my blood.

Gloria left me alone for most of the day. I wanted it, and on some level, so did she. She went out for dinner with a couple of her girlfriends and went upstairs when she saw me in the office staring at Tyler's picture. Now she came down. "You have more of that port?" she said.

"How'd you know what I was drinking?"

She sat down beside me on the couch and kissed me. "You really think I don't know a *vidro para vinho do porto* when I see one?" Her Portugese for "port glass" sounded perfect.

"I should know better than to doubt your upper crust upbringing." I fetched another and filled it for Gloria. She curled up next to me on the couch and sipped her wine.

"So tonight's the night," she said.

"Tonight's the night."

Gloria's head nuzzled my neck and shoulder. "You sure you know what you're doing?"

"Positive," I said.

I felt her looking at me, so I tried to give Gloria a reassuring face. Her brown eyes stared into mine. I have never found brown eyes interesting, but Gloria's had a depth to them others lacked. A darker hue erupted from the center, ringed by a narrow band of tan. I never before encountered eyes like hers in any color and would always find them captivating. "You'd better be right," she warned.

"I am."

"What if you get caught?"

"Then I'll probably be arrested," I said.

Gloria released a delicate sigh. "Then what?"

"Then I hire an expensive lawyer like James Snyder and play on the distinct possibility at least one person on the jury understands my actions."

"You seem pretty confident of that."

"Revenge is a basic emotion. Everyone understands it."

"But there's a chance you could go to jail," said Gloria.

"Are you saying you wouldn't pop in for conjugal visits?"

Gloria smiled. "I'm saying I don't want you to throw your

career away. You do a lot of good work for a lot of people who need it. There's real value there."

"I'm not going to throw my career away. If I used what I know and what I can do to find Samantha's killer and then didn't act on it . . . then I'd be throwing it away."

She patted my leg, leaving her hand resting on my thigh. "That's what I love about you."

"My way with words?" I said.

"No, silly. Your conviction. No matter how amoral you seem, you have a code about you, and you stick to it. That's admirable."

"'I only know what is moral is what you feel good after, and what is immoral is what you feel bad after.'"

"Who said that?"

"Hemingway," I said. "Shitty writer, but he got off some good quotes."

"You think you'll feel good after you kill this man?"

I thought about it. "Good? I don't know. I've never felt *good* after I've shot someone. It's simply something I've needed to do. I think I'll feel . . . fulfilled."

"Does Hemingway have a quote for that?"

"Probably," I said, "but I've already reached my Hemingway quota for the day."

Gloria lapsed into silence. So did I. We each took occasional sips of our port. Her head rested on my shoulder, and I'd slipped my arm around her. A while ago, I noticed Gloria and I had become comfortable not saying anything. Some couples have to try and fill silence with drivel. Not long after I had this realization, Gloria told me she loved me. I kissed her forehead.

"When are you heading out?" she said.

"A couple hours."

"In history class, I learned that a knight who had a lady's favor would get a proper sendoff before going into battle."

"Am I a knight?" I said.

"Am I a lady?"

I smiled. "You don't need to be on your best ladylike behavior tonight."

"Deal," said Gloria.

CHAPTER 24

The Strand pulled a good crowd regardless of the night. Many bars and clubs make their money on the weekends and attract more tumbleweeds than customers during the week. The Strand did not suffer this fate. Unfortunately, most of the crowd it attracted were hipsters and women predisposed to liking them. For obvious reasons, I usually kept my distance.

Tonight, though, I would use the Strand and its usual crowd to my advantage. I told Anthony Tyler I would wear a white shirt with a black tie over black pants. He would presume few people would be so dressed, thus enabling his quarry to stand out. In reality, I would be clad in the perfect camouflage, Tyler would be confused, and I would get the drop on him before I led him away to his execution.

I chose a long-sleeved button-down shirt without a tie, a nice pair of khakis, a pair of moderately worn Ferragamo shoes, and a jacket heavy enough to conceal the .45 at my side. If this were going to be my last night of freedom for a while, I at least wanted to go to jail in snazzy threads. Gloria came downstairs and wrapped me in a bearhug. "Please be careful," she said, her voice muffled by my shoulder.

"I always am," I said.

"You don't normally go out to shoot someone you've never met." Gloria frowned and a pout played on her lips.

"I'll be careful." I gave Gloria my best reassuring smile. It didn't help—probably needed some work. "This asshole will never see me coming."

"Promise me. Promise me you'll be OK, and that I'll see you again."

"I promise." I tried the reassuring grin again, this time with the wattage turned down by a quarter. Gloria's pout morphed into a small smile.

"I love you," she said, giving me one more kiss.

"I love you, too. Don't wait up." I walked out the door and headed for the Strand.

* * *

I MADE sure I arrived early. The hipster count disappointed me by their sheer presence but reaffirmed my predictive powers. Tyler would be too busy looking at the drones to see the real threat. A half-hour remained, so I walked to the bar. The stools were about half full with a few stragglers standing around. I tried not to listen to the conversations. The crowd of guys was younger than me, probably just past college age. I hoped I didn't sound like them when I'd finished my fourth year. I ordered an IPA, paid cash for it, and tried to tune out the frat house conversations going on around me.

A couple of attractive girls sidled up to the bar beside me. The blonde wore a dress short enough to qualify as a shirt. I didn't object. It showed off her shapely legs and almost allowed me to read the tag on her panties. Her redheaded friend opted for tight jeans and a shirt with a neckline revealing the top halves of her breasts. A pair of hipsters on the other side tried to strike up a conversation. The girls looked at each other and rolled their eyes. I smiled. The blonde noticed and smiled in return.

She tried to strike up a conversation, but the fumes coming from her mouth almost took me from zero to drunk in record time. Soon enough, her friend collected her to take her home. I moved to an unoccupied table. A minute after they left, Anthony Tyler walked in. He looked like his driver's license photo, though his hair grew a little thinner and stringier in the intervening time. He wore a Salisbury State hoodie over a dingy pair of jeans. The girls who appraised him when he paused inside the door turned away and snickered. He'd probably gotten this reaction a lot over the years. Maybe it was why he hated women so much.

Maybe it drove him to violate and kill my sister.

From my table, I watched Tyler amble to the bar. He looked around at the crowd. There were at least five guys dressed like I told him I would be. He kept glancing among them, trying to figure out which one learned the truth about him. Of course, he didn't have the guts to approach any of them. Tyler ordered a cheap domestic draft from the bartender, paid cash, and sipped his lousy beer while he surveyed the room.

I became aware of the gun at my side, almost like it threatened to burn a hole through my jacket. If Tyler saw me, he looked right past me, scanning the hipster drones. He didn't want to be here and had only come under the threat of having his past exposed. It meant he'd be good for a beer or two before he left. I felt a palpable urge to pull out the .45 and empty the clip into him right here. There would be a bar full of witnesses, but I would have a good reason and a better lawyer. Most cases only required the latter.

I downed the rest of my IPA. Tyler still sipped his beer. He looked at the girls, though none paid him any mind. I wondered what sinister thoughts tossed around inside his head. Did he ogle my sister the same way he now looked at these girls? Had he come here hoping to find another girl to lure away if his accuser didn't show? I stood and walked to the bar. My heart didn't race, but I felt every beat as I stalked my sister's killer. He stared at some girls on the other side of the bar. I walked close to him. My hand went under my jacket. I leaned in to conceal the fact I drew a gun. Temptation gnawed at me. I pressed the barrel into his back. My heartbeat reverberated in my chest and ears. Tyler sat up straight and started to turn.

"Don't," I said in a quiet voice.

"OK," said Tyler.

"We're taking a walk."

"Don't want to talk here?"

"Not really," I said. "In a minute, you're going to get up and leave. I'll tell you where to go. If you try to run or yell for help, I'll shoot you. You're not smarter or faster than I am. We clear?"

"Yeah."

I nudged him in the back with the .45, then put it away. "Let's exit stage front." Tyler got up and headed for the door. I stayed two steps behind him. He pushed the door open. "Go to your right," I said. "Turn down the first alley you see." He did as instructed. Streetlights didn't illuminate the way back here. Baltimore had alleys upon alleys in a network behind the houses in its old neighborhoods. They formed a maze if you weren't familiar with them. I'd spent the time to acquaint myself with these. The occasional back porchlight and ambient glow of the city would be enough for me.

"Take a left," I said as we approached another turn.

"Where are we going?" Tyler said.

"Would you rather talk about what you did in public?"

"No, I just—"

"Then shut up and keep walking." I yearned to gun him

down now and be done with it. Shooting him in the back would be fine. The result would be the same. But I'd picked a spot, and this wasn't it. "Take a right."

After a couple more turns, we reached my chosen location. Five houses surrounded this area where two alleys crossed. I did my research. One was unoccupied. Two of the owners worked nights. One was deaf. One loved the nightlife. None would be able to hear us. The lights from their porches and a nearby garage mixed with the moon to illuminate the scene about to the level of dusk. "Right here," I said. Tyler stopped and turned around. He looked me up and down and frowned.

"You weren't dressed like you said you'd be."

"No."

"What do you want?"

"Do you even know her name?" I said.

"Whose name?"

"The girl you murdered in Patterson Park thirteen years ago. Do you even know her name?"

"You got any proof?" he said.

"Enough."

"For a jury?"

I smiled at his naïveté. I ignored rules but never the consequences, while I was amazed most scofflaws expected everyone to extend them every legality. "I didn't promise you a jury trial."

Tyler's eyes went wide. Color drained from his face. "Why did you bring me here?" he said in a small voice. He must have known the answer.

"Do you know her name?" I said again.

"I never do."

"So you have experience killing innocent girls."

"Not what I meant," he said.

"I don't care what else you've done. I only care about one innocent girl. Patterson Park, thirteen years ago."

Tyler nodded. "I remember her. She was into peace and all that shit. It's how I found her."

"And then you met her."

"In a small group at first," he said, a distant look coming onto his face. "Then we left together."

"You walked into Patterson Park." My pulse quickened. I heard my own breathing, and it sounded like I'd just run three miles.

"Yeah." The bastard had the audacity to smile at the memory. "The girl was a real fighter."

"What was her name?" I said through clenched teeth.

"Shit . . . I don't remember."

I pointed the .45 at Tyler. I wasn't even aware I drew it. "Her name was Samantha Elizabeth Ferguson, and she was my sister."

"Jesus Christ."

"He's not going to help you now," I said.

"I . . . I didn't know."

"No, you didn't care. Wastes of flesh like you never do."

"What . . . what are you going to do?"

"I'm going to kill you, right here in this alley. I'm going to empty this clip into you and watch your blood run toward that drain down there."

"You're cold, man," he had the balls to say. "This ain't fair."

"You killed my sister! Let's not talk about cold or fair. On your knees."

"What?" Tyler shook his head. "I ain't kneeling." He rushed me. I didn't want to shoot him yet. My left arm blocked his simple punches. Tyler reached for the gun. I hit him in the gut with a left. There wasn't room to put a lot into it, but it backed him off a bit. I followed with another punch, then kneed him in the groin.

He stayed bent over and staggered a few steps to his rear. I kicked him in his left knee, not so hard as to break it, but enough to make it buckle. Tyler grunted as his leg went out from under him. He wound up on all fours. I stared down at him.

"Much better," I said. I put the .45 in front of his face. My pulse thudded in my ears. The man who murdered my sister was at my mercy, and I didn't feel merciful. I saw Samantha's face. I remembered her senior prom, how much time she spent getting ready, and how beautiful she looked. I remembered making fun of her date when he came to pick her up. I flashed forward to her graduation and how proud we all felt of her. Her valedictory speech played in the back of my head. I looked away from Tyler. When I looked back, my vision blurred from the tears welling in my eyes. Tyler appeared distorted, like I saw him underwater, but I still held my pistol in line with his face. He shook his head in a last bit of desperation.

"C.T., don't do it!" I heard from behind me.

How the hell did Rich find me? I ignored him and kept the gun leveled at Tyler.

"Don't do it," Rich said again. His voice sounded closer this time. "You know she wouldn't want this."

I thought of Samantha, of the many social causes she embraced. A few of her friends were snooty. They came from money and didn't care about other people. Samantha was never like them. My parents' sense of charity rubbed off on her. She volunteered with programs helping less fortunate people. She worked in a soup kitchen every Thanksgiving. After 9/11, she supported a peaceful resolution to whatever conflict the country faced. Samantha spent years trying to help others and make the world a little bit brighter for people trapped in darkness.

She was a much better person than me.

Rich was right; she wouldn't want this. Samantha's social justice agenda allowed no room for the death penalty and certainly not for execution without trial. We didn't always agree on the issues, but she made her case well, and I always respected her opinion. Where was the justice, social or otherwise, for Samantha without me? Her case got resigned to the scrap heap, her killer free for thirteen years to torment more women and more families. Samantha needed justice. Those other families needed justice.

I needed justice.

"I mean it, C.T.," Rich said. "This isn't the way."

"He killed her, Rich," I said, my voice cracking. "He did it. You have to believe me."

"I believe you. I do. But I can't let you do this."

"It's what he deserves."

"But it's not what *she* deserves," he said.

Rich's voice grew closer. His years of Army and police training meant his gun was drawn and pointed at me. I didn't think he could bring himself to shoot me unless I posed a direct threat to him. If I were going to shoot, it needed to be now. Tyler still looked up at me, shaking his head and pleading with me. My finger itched. I had to pull the trigger now.

But I couldn't do it. I couldn't shake the image of Samantha looking at me not only with sadness but also with disappointment. It hurt a lot more. Rich was right; she wouldn't want this. She wouldn't want someone executed for murder, even her own, and she wouldn't want her baby brother carrying it around on his conscience. Tears ran down my face. Samantha's disappointed stare dominated my vision. I looked up and yelled in inarticulate rage, yelled until my throat grew raw, and I ran out of breath. I raised the gun and smashed Tyler in the side of the head with it. He pitched over in a heap. I tossed the gun down and crumpled into a crouch. Rich's footsteps approached from behind me. He put his hand on my shoulder.

I stood, turned, and sagged into him, sobbing onto his shoulder as he put his arms around me. When I was all cried out, I pulled back and wavered on my feet. Rich grabbed my forearm to steady me. I got my balance and nodded at him. He let go. I picked up the .45 and put it back into its holster. "How did you find me?" I said when I had recovered the ability to talk.

"I went to your house. Gloria let me in. When I unlocked your computer, I saw your map of the alleys." Rich knew my password. After getting arrested in Hong Kong and spending nineteen days in a Chinese prison, I set up certain protocols here. My father often called me paranoid. Maybe he was right.

"But how did you know I was doing this tonight?" I said.

"Apparently, I called a Sergeant Palmgren a couple days ago." Rich arched his eyebrows. "When I didn't remember our conversation, he filled me in on the details."

"To be fair, we do sound a bit alike on the phone."

Rich shook his head. "I'm glad he was working late. Otherwise, I wouldn't have come looking for you."

"I don't know I needed you. Samantha might have talked me out of it."

"I'm glad someone did," Rich said.

"What happens to this asshole now?" I said, inclining my head toward the unconscious Tyler. A small trickle of blood ran from his head where I hit him with the butt of the pistol.

"He'll go to jail. We'll submit evidence. He'll get a lawyer. The usual."

"You think he'll go away?"

"I think so," Rich said. "We can gather the evidence you got on your own to make a good case."

"Good. I hope he dies in jail."

"He's going to file a complaint about this, though."

"So?" I said.

"So your treatment of him isn't going to go over well."

"'What I must do concerns me, not what people think.'"

"Who said it?"

"Emerson."

"Look," Rich said, "I'm not trying to pile on, but if he files a complaint, we'll have to look into it."

"And you might get asked about it."

"I might."

"And you wouldn't lie about it," I said. Rich shook his head. "Fair enough."

"It's going to look bad for you. I know you play it fast and loose, but this is different. They might want your license for this one, C.T."

I took out my PI badge and ID. I looked at them one final time before tossing the billfold to Rich. "So give it to them." I turned and walked away.

CHAPTER 25

"You did *what*?" Gloria said after I arrived home.

"It's nice to see you, too," I said.

She cracked a smile. "Of course I'm glad to see you. Relieved is probably a better word. But . . . what did you do?"

"Let him live, but Rich is right. Tyler will file a complaint against me."

"He's a killer."

"Killers still have the right to file a grievance if someone mistreats them," I said.

"And you mistreated him."

"In the eyes of the law, sure. I led him to a public place under false pretenses, put a gun in his back, assaulted him, nearly shot him, and ended up pistol-whipping him. I think the prick deserved more, but the law's going to see it as mistreatment."

Gloria frowned. "And you could lose your license for it?"

I sat on the sofa. Gloria sat beside me, grabbed my hand, and squeezed it. "It's possible," I said.

Gloria let out a slow, deep breath. "What will you do?"

"There will be a hearing. I'll plead my case."

"I mean if they take your license away."

I shrugged. "I'll do something else. I haven't thought about it."

"You're good at what you do," she said. "It's important. You help a lot of people."

"Maybe I can find some other way to help. The thing is, if solving my sister's murder and seeing her killer rot in jail costs me my license, it was worth it."

"And you'd do it again."

"All day, every day," I said. "Maybe even twice on Sunday."

Gloria squeezed my hand again. "I love that about you. You're so sure that what you're doing is right, and you're willing to risk so much for it."

"Some might bundle those under the banner of stubbornness."

She grinned. "They might. I think it's a good thing, though."

"It's served me well over the years."

"You ready for bed?" she said. "It's been a long night."

"Lead the way," I said.

She did.

* * *

My phone ringing and vibrating on the nightstand roused me from my sleep. A quick glance showed me it was 3:51, and caller ID told me it was Rollins. This couldn't be good. "Hello?" I said, trying to summon a voice sounding somewhat awake.

"Someone found her," Rollins said.

My sleep-addled brain struggled to catch up. *Her* could be no other than Melinda—or Ruby—or whatever I should call her. Someone found her. She'd been staying with Joey, I remembered. I frowned. "What happened? Was she at Joey's?"

"Yeah. Someone got them both."

I swallowed hard. After dealing with Samantha's killer, I couldn't bury Joey, too. "Are they alive?"

"Both in the hospital. Your friend has a concussion and looks like he's gone a few rounds with one Wladimir Klitschko."

"What about Melinda?"

"At least as bad."

"Where are you?"

"At the hospital with them," he said. "University."

"I'll be there," I said.

I MET Rollins in the waiting area outside the emergency room. He led me down a hallway. Office doors lined each side. Rollins opened one and walked inside. We each sat in a chair. He closed the door. "What happened?" I said.

"I got there toward the end," said Rollins. "Saw a car I didn't recognize. A couple lights were on later than I'd expect, so I went to the front door. I heard some commotion inside, heard a scream, so I went in." I didn't bother to ask if the door had been locked. Small details wouldn't stop Rollins. "Whoever was there must have heard me and took off through the back of the house."

"You get a look at him?"

Rollins shook his head. "He wore a mask. Kind of a short guy, broad and powerful."

The description didn't fit Jackson McMurray. I wondered if this guy was the same one who beat up Joanie in the alley. "You got the tag number on the car, though."

A glare served as my only answer. "I thought about chasing

him, but Joey and the girl were barely conscious and looked bad, so I called for an ambulance."

"The cops come?"

"Yeah."

"You talk to them?" I said.

"No. When I heard sirens, I went back to my car, then followed the ambulance when it left."

I nodded. "You have the tag number?" He recited it from memory. I entered it as a note on my phone. "Any word on Joey and Ruby?"

"I'm sure they'll be admitted," he said. "Stay at least overnight for observation and all."

"All right. I'll hang out here and talk to them once they're in rooms."

"You need any help with whoever owns the car, you let me know."

I smiled. "Oh, I'll take care of him."

* * *

AND I INTENDED to after checking on Joey and Melinda. She said she wanted to give up the life and do something else. I hoped she got the chance to do it. I felt bad for her, but I'd known Joey much longer and doing a favor for me was the reason he'd been hurt, so I stopped to see him first. He, however, was out cold when I popped in, so I visited Melinda. She happened to be awake.

"How are you feeling?" I said, sitting in the chair by her bed.

She looked at me through weary eyes. Weary not just from the last few hours but the last few years. Her face was a mass of bruises, contusions, and puffiness. Someone beat her and enjoyed it. "Like shit," she said in a small voice.

I needed to be vigilant for hospital workers. Visiting hours didn't start for quite a while yet. Inquisitive nurses or staff would allow a few minutes if you flashed a badge and offered your best this-is-a-serious-investigation look. Of course, I tossed my badge and ID to Rich in the alley last night. Oh well—if pressed, I would think of something. "Melinda, who did this to you?"

"I don't know."

"I heard he wore a mask." She nodded. "The body type doesn't sound right for Jackson."

"It's not."

"But he has friends. Someone beat up Joanie a while back. Maybe it was the same man."

Melinda thought about it. She pondered it so long I thought she'd drifted asleep. "I think it might have been," she said after a couple minutes. "It was a mask both times. A black one with red around the eye holes."

"Could be the latest in maskwear. Blue eye holes are *so* last year."

She smiled and winced for it. I noticed a couple of teeth missing when she did. I clenched and unclenched my fist. Whoever this guy was, I would make sure he lost even more teeth if I needed a wrench to extract them. "Body type was the same both times. A little shorter than you, and thicker."

"Thick like muscle or like fat?"

She shrugged. At the risk of thinking indelicate thoughts, I figured Melinda saw the difference over the years. "Some of both, I guess."

I nodded. "Don't worry about him. I'll find him."

"Be careful, C.T." Melinda reached out and gave my hand a feeble squeeze.

"I'll be OK," I said, flashing a reassuring smile. "You should worry about the other guy."

"I'm not going to worry about him."

"There you go," I said.

* * *

I SAT at Joey's bed for a few minutes until he came to. He looked around dazed, and his swollen eyes struggled to focus on me. Joey's face looked like Melinda's but a little worse. He didn't have a square inch of skin not bruised, discolored, or lacerated. The bastard who beat Melinda and enjoyed it relished it equally as much with Joey. I hated this prick more and more every minute.

"Sorry, C.T.," Joey whispered.

"Don't be," I said. "You have nothing to be sorry for."

"I tried to fight him off. He got us when we were asleep."

I hoped not together, but I bit that question down. "You did your best, Joey. I shouldn't have put you in such a tough spot."

"I don't know how the asshole found her."

"Maybe I'll ask him before I kick his teeth in."

Joey shook his head. "He's tough, C.T. I know you want to get him, but be careful."

"Careful is my middle name," I said.

"The hell it is."

"It's better than my first name."

"So it is," Joey said with a chuckle.

"I heard the guy wore a mask."

"Yeah. White guy. Five-ten or so. Squat and compact."

"Looks like he enjoys his work," I said.

"Bastard. I mighta had a chance awake."

"I'll take care of him."

"How are you going to find who it was?" said Joey.

"Rollins got a plate number."

"Coulda been a stolen car."

I shrugged. "Could have been his car, too."

"Excuse me, sir," a voice called from the door. A redheaded nurse gave me her best thousand-yard stare. "Visiting hours don't start until nine."

"It's nine-o'clock somewhere," I said.

"Somewhere past England, yes."

I liked this nurse. "Can I have another minute with my brother before you give me the boot?"

She looked at her watch. "I'll be back by in under five minutes. You need to be gone by then."

"Yes, ma'am." The honorific earned me a quick glare as she walked away.

"I like her," Joey said.

"Moving on from prostitute to nurse so quickly?"

"Love is fickle," said Joey.

* * *

I TEXTED Rich as I left the hospital. To my surprise, he called back a couple minutes later. "You sound awake," I said.

"Because I am," Rich said. "What's up?"

"I have a tag number I'd like you to run."

"You can't do it?"

"It's easier if you do it."

Rich didn't say anything for a few seconds. "Are you OK? You've had a pretty trying night. Maybe you should get some rest and not worry about this tag number."

"I appreciate your concern, Rich. What I need is to keep working."

"Without your license?"

I sighed. "The tag number I asked you to run probably belongs to a guy who's beaten the crap out of two girls, plus Joey. I don't need a license to deal with this."

"All right," he said, "I'll run it. I'm just concerned about you. This whole thing with Samantha and your parents, the alley . . . it's a lot for anyone."

"I'm fine, Rich. Tell my parents you asked about me when you talk to them."

"They're worried about you, too."

"Did you tell them I caught the bastard who murdered their daughter?"

"I figured it was your place," Rich said.

He was right. "I'll talk to them at some point."

"You should."

"Send me a text with the tag info," I said to refocus the conversation on what mattered.

"I will. Get some rest. You've had a long day, and you can expect a summons soon."

"The sack of shit filed a complaint?" I focused on the road as I drove home. The weird hours I'd been keeping were catching up with me.

"Of course he did."

"I'll take my chances," I said.

"You'll probably have to take them soon," Rich said. "Things like this tend to go to hearings quickly."

"Should I be concerned?"

"They could take away your license for something like that, C.T. It's serious."

"I solved my sister's murder," I said. "Her killer will rot in jail. If it costs me my license, I'll gladly pay the price."

"Fine, fine. I'm just worried about you."

"So you've said. Send me the DMV info when you can."

"I will," Rich said.

I hung up. I appreciated Rich's concern, but I didn't want to dwell on it. License or not, I wanted to stay focused on the other case I had signed up for.

* * *

Rich texted me the registration and driver's license data a few minutes later. It wasn't a rental or stolen. Peter Kormos was 35 and listed his measurements at five-ten and 200 pounds. The dumb bastard took his own car to Joey's.

I did some research on Kormos. He owned a house in Rosedale and worked enough part-time jobs to keep it. The money he made beating up women no doubt helped, too. Kormos kept his work schedule on his Google calendar. He left some menial job at 1:00 AM and was due back in at noon for a nine-hour shift later today. I looked at the clock. I needed some sleep and would have a chance to get about five hours before I wanted to be at Kormos' house.

Maybe I could even write him an excuse note for work.

* * *

Before ten o'clock, I polished off a breakfast sandwich and coffee en route to Rosedale. I got to the house a few minutes after ten. He lived on a quiet cul-de-sac of about a dozen homes. Kormos' registered vehicle and one other sat on the street. If this were an old west town, I would have expected a few tumbleweeds to blow down the street. I got out of my car, checked for both tumbleweeds and nosy neighbors, and walked up to Kormos' house.

His storm door wasn't locked when I opened it. I didn't hear a dog bark. On the other side of the door were a regular lock and deadbolt both looking shopworn. I got them open in just over a minute. No neighbors took any notice of me as far as I could tell. I opened the front door slowly, looked around, and saw no one. I let myself in, closed up quietly behind myself, and padded into the house.

Kormos needed a maid. I'd seen neater dormitories during my college years. Detritus littered the living room. The stack of empty food cartons could have been used to fashion a new piece of furniture, and it probably would have looked better than what Kormos displayed. I'd planned to sit and wait for the asshole to come downstairs, but I didn't know if I wanted to experience the furniture up close. I settled for the kitchen table. It wasn't a federal disaster area in there, and I enjoyed the added benefit Kormos wouldn't see me —or the .45 sitting on the table—until he walked in.

A few minutes passed, and I heard no activity in the house. I nosed around in the fridge, grabbed a can of Coke Zero, and sat back at the kitchen table. As soon as I did, I heard an alarm buzz upstairs. Feet hit the floor a moment later, then footsteps came down the stairs. I would get Kormos before he had his morning coffee or shower. Cool.

He trudged into the kitchen and stopped. He glanced at me, then looked at the .45. I could almost see his tired brain spinning, trying to devise a way out of this. The hamster was working overtime. After a moment of standing and staring, Kormos said, "Who the hell are you?"

"Sit down."

"Who the hell are you?"

"I'm a man with a .45 on your table," I said, "and I don't care if I have to shoot you before I leave. Now sit."

He parked onto the stool opposite me, sulking. Kormos wore a tank top and sweatpants. I could see most of his 200-pound frame was muscle. His biceps definitely had a couple inches on mine. If we got into a posing contest, I would be in trouble. "OK, I'm sitting," he said.

"Why did you do it?" I said.

"Do what?"

"Beat up a hooker and the guy protecting her?"

"Who says I did?"

I inclined my head toward the gun. "My friend Sig Sauer told me."

Kormos' eyes flickered between the pistol and me. "OK, so I did it. What's the big deal about a whore and a fat fuck?"

"Who put you up to it?"

"Why's someone gotta put me up to it?"

"I've spent ten minutes in this sty you call a house, and I can tell you don't do anything without a lot of motivation."

"You think you know me?" Kormos frowned and balled his fists.

"Was it Jackson McMurray?" I said.

Recognition flashed across his eyes as I mentioned Jackson's name. "He's got nothing to do with it."

"You're a liar."

"Yeah?" Kormos said, leaning forward. "If you were gonna shoot me, you woulda already. What are you gonna do about it?"

Kormos was right—I wouldn't shoot him unless I needed to. I glanced down at the can of Coke Zero. I hadn't opened it yet. Kormos leaned in closer and tried to fix me with a menacing stare. I felt un-menaced. My eyes moved toward the gun. His followed.

I grabbed the soda can and clobbered him in the face with it.

Kormos spilled out of the stool onto the dingy linoleum kitchen floor. I put the .45 back into its holster and snapped the thumb release closed. Kormos shook off the cobwebs and struggled to sit up.

I clobbered him with the soda can again. When his head rebounded off the floor, I let him have it a third time. Then a fourth and a fifth. The bottoms of Coke cans were remarkably durable. The whole thing was dented all to hell but never exploded.

These would not be my proudest moments ever in a fight. Kormos would have represented a good challenge. The reality was I still felt drained after the Tyler confrontation, and this bastard beat the tar out of Joey and Melinda. He didn't deserve a fair fight, and he wasn't going to get one.

Kormos stirred on the floor but didn't try to sit or stand. I peered down at him. Blood covered his mouth. His cheekbones looked like he had run into a wall until the wall grew tired of him. I saw several of his teeth scattered on the linoleum. It would do. I crouched near him, close enough for him to see and hear me, but far enough away so he couldn't grab me. He raised his head. "Who are you?" Kormos whispered as blood sputtered on his lips.

"Someone who likes the whore and the fat fuck."

"What do . . . you want?"

"To teach you a lesson. Have you learned it yet?" Kormos nodded. "Good. Next, I'll have to teach your buddy Jackson a lesson, too." I unsnapped the Sig and showed it to him up close. His eyes went wide and followed the muzzle as I made a show of moving it around. "If I ever have cause to visit you again. . . ."

"You won't."

"I'd better not."

I put the .45 away, picked up the dented and bloodied can of Coke Zero, and gave Kormos one more shot for good measure. Then I left.

CHAPTER 26

AFTER LEAVING KORMOS' HOUSE, I WENT HOME. THIS HAD been a tiring night and morning. I took a quick shower and managed to get back into bed before eleven. I spent a few minutes reliving the encounter with Anthony Tyler. As I anticipated our meeting in my head, I expected him to fight back more. I looked forward to inflicting serious injury before I shot him. In the end, I did neither. I could live with it.

I harbored no particular objection to shooting people if the situation called for it. When I first arranged this job with my parents, I expected to do most of my work at a keyboard. I did some from my chair, but most of my cases required my boots to hit the streets of Baltimore and for me to interact with other people. Many of them proved unsavory. Some attempted to hurt me. A few tried to kill me. Shooting someone who's threatening your life is an easy decision. It took me a while to accept it, but I knew it was true. Shooting Tyler in cold blood, no matter what he did thirteen years ago, would have been different. My conscience—such as it was—couldn't carry the burden. It took thoughts of my sister for me to realize this fact.

I lay awake a while longer. Several days went by since I'd talked to my parents. Even then, I only spoke to to my father.

Yes, they'd lied to me. Yes, I thought their rationale was flimsy. Ultimately, they'd suffered more than I did. Rich had no doubt updated them by now. I would need to speak to them again at some point. They shouldn't hear their daughter's murderer was at long last arrested from Rich, even if he slapped the cuffs on Tyler.

Sometime soon, I would call them. I thought about that conversation as sleep finally came for me.

* * *

I woke up close to one in the afternoon. I couldn't remember the last time I rose so late without the influence of alcohol, a woman, or both the prior night. I strolled downstairs to find Gloria stretched out and reading on the couch. She smiled at me as I walked into the kitchen. "No kiss for your girlfriend?" she said.

"I never kiss before coffee," I said.

"You've done a lot more than kiss before coffee."

"Not after the night I put in."

Her smile faded, replaced with a frown of concern. "What happened?"

I told her about what transpired after I came back from the alleys and Anthony Tyler. "Jesus," she said. "Sounds like a trying night."

"I hope I never have one like it again." I brewed a half-pot of coffee. The smell of the percolating beverage washed over me. I waited for the sweet release of caffeine.

"What are you going to do today?" said Gloria.

"Eat some breakfast. Or lunch, at this point. Visit Joey and Melinda again. And I want to find Jackson McMurray and stop all this."

"What if he won't listen?"

"I'll take Rollins with me," I said. "Between the two of us, I'm sure we can get him to see reason."

"I like your odds," Gloria said.

I fumbled around in the fridge, looking for something to make for brunch. Options were not in abundance. I'd burned through most of my groceries. I ended up whipping an omelet together and ate it with coffee and toast. When I finished, my phone rang. I didn't recognize the number. "C.T. Ferguson?" a stern voice said.

"Speaking."

"This is Captain Dobbs with the Maryland State Police."

"What can I do for you, Captain?"

"There's going to be a hearing for your PI license." He sounded very matter-of-fact, almost like he were reading off of a cue card.

"When?" I said.

"Tomorrow morning, Baltimore Police Headquarters, oh-nine-hundred. Do you need to reschedule?"

"No, I'll be there. Do I need a lawyer?"

Dobbs paused. "Up to you."

"Do people normally bring lawyers in these situations?"

"We don't have these situations often," he said.

I could tell Dobbs wasn't going to be any help. Oh, well. I decided against a lawyer right then and there. I didn't know how much value James Snyder would add. I would take my chances. "Fine," I said. "I'll be there."

"Have a good day," Dobbs said and hung up.

"You, too, you cheery bastard," I said to the empty line.

"What's going on?" Gloria asked from the kitchen doorway. I told her about the hearing and my decision on counsel. "You sure you don't want to take James with you?"

I shrugged. "I did what Tyler is accusing me of. If it costs me my license, so be it."

Gloria sashayed over and kissed me. "I'll go with you. At least you'll have a cheering section."

"Can you dress up like a cheerleader?"

"We'll save that for after the hearing," Gloria said with a sly grin.

* * *

I DROPPED in to see Joey. He was half sitting up in bed, still looking like he'd gone ten rounds with a jackhammer. A tray of food sat on the table over his bed. Joey picked at it. I'd never seen him attack food so slowly. It could have been the nature of hospital fare, or it could have been the effects of his beating the night before.

"If you ate like this when I took you out, my food budget would be cut in half," I said as I walked into the room.

Joey smiled weakly. He could open one of his eyes wide enough to see, at least. The other remained mostly shut inside the mass of swelling and discoloration surrounding it. "Don't get your hopes up," he said. "When they let me out of here, I'm going to eat like a prince."

"On my dime."

"I think my regal status just got upgraded."

"How are you?" I said.

"Feeling a little better. Still foggy, but they tell me it'll clear. I avoided permanent injury, at least."

"I found the guy who did this to you and Melinda."

"Yeah?" he said, his tone perking up.

"He's going to need some facial surgery and dental work."

"Good. Fuck him and the horse he rode over me with."

I stayed for the rest of Joey's meal. As far as I could tell, he ate a beef-like substance covered in something approximating brown gravy. The carrots and corn looked mildly appetizing but—being vegetables—went largely ignored by Joey. We chatted for a little while, and then I went down the hall to see Melinda.

Like Joey, she picked at her meal. Melinda flashed a small smile when she saw me. I doubted she could manage more. Bruises still dotted her face. I wondered how long it would be before she looked like the very pretty woman she was before Kormos battered her.

"How are you?" she said in a small voice.

"Interested in how you're doing," I said.

"I'll survive. I hope to be out of here in a few days."

"Glad to hear it. I found the bastard who did this to you."

"And?"

"He's going to be eating through a straw for a while."

"Good," Melinda said, fire flashing in her eyes.

"He's one of Jackson's friends," I said. "He's the same guy who beat up Joanie in the alley."

She sighed and sagged back onto the bed. "So Jackson sent him after me."

"Looks like it."

"What are you going to do now?"

"Have a chat with your former step-brother."

"I know him, C.T. He can be obsessive. I'm not sure he's going to back down easily."

I shrugged. "I think I'll be able to persuade him."

"Please be careful."

"I will. I'm going to look for him when I leave. If he's not at his house, do you know where he would be?"

Melinda shook her head. "We haven't been close in years. I wouldn't know anymore."

I nodded. "I'm going to find him. I want to follow him and see where he goes. Rollins and I will talk to him soon."

"Remember your promise."

"I will," I said.

Melinda exhaled a mirthless laugh. "How messed up is it that I don't want him dead?"

"Families are interesting things," I said.

* * *

GPS TRACKERS ARE WONDERFUL INVENTIONS. With the device I put on Jackson McMurray's car, I could find him down to about two meters. My map showed him in Fallston, though several blocks from his own residence. The house was nestled in a hoity-toity community called Todd Lakes. The homes were even more pretentious than the name. Each sat on a generous plot of land and featured more rooms than a European palace. Brick covered most exteriors, and columns running up the façades were a common feature. Just for a Roman gladiatorial touch, I supposed. These homes went for five times what I paid for mine and could swallow it whole a dozen times over, but I would still take my place over some sprawling monstrosity in a development called Todd Lakes. I remembered what George Carlin said about guys named Todd. The same rules applied to prissy communities.

I followed the road and saw Jackson's silver Benz parked at the top of a winding driveway. Perhaps his mere Mercedes did not meet the price-tag requirements to enter the four-car garage. Bentleys or above. I pulled to the curb and looked at the house. Two stories, brick front, overlook balcony, ridiculous square footage. It was the kind requiring at least two servants, one of whom would be polishing the marble of the first floor on a continuous loop. A mailbox at the end of the driveway displayed a name in large block letters.

Davenport.

I closed my eyes and sighed. Why would Vincent Davenport be in league with the man who did such terrible things to his daughter? Families were interesting things indeed. I moved to the other side of the street and down a bit from the Davenport estate. I could see the residence and the garage. There didn't look to be a lot going on, and I wasn't equipped for a stakeout. I didn't want to leave and run the risk of something happening, so I called Rollins. He agreed to meet me and to bring the necessary supplies.

He joined me about forty minutes later with a bag of drinks and snacks. Rollins parked his truck a ways down the street and joined me in the Audi. "So he's staying with the girl's father?" said Rollins.

"Yep," I said.

"Some weird shit."

"Their family dynamics just keep getting stranger."

I drank some Gatorade and munched on honey roasted peanuts from a large bag. A few minutes later, neighborhood security cruised to a stop alongside us in a four-door sedan no one in Todd Lakes would let their dogs be seen in. Two fairly imposing men in the front seat scrutinized Rollins and me. The driver was Hispanic. The guy doing the heavier scrutinizing was white and portly. "Can we help you fellas?" he said. Normally, I would hold up my PI badge, make a pithy remark, and all would be well. Without the badge, my remarks would be less pithy.

Beside me, Rollins pulled out a badge and held it up. "Just doing our jobs."

The security guy squinted at the badge and nodded, apparently satisfied. They drove off without further comment.

"Real badge?" I said.

"Sure," Rollins replied.

"How did you get it?"

"Military Police. No one ever looks closely enough to tell."

"You were an MP?"

"For a while, toward the end of my time."

"Shouldn't you have turned it in?" I said.

"Oops."

We watched the house for a while. Afternoon rolled into evening, and dusk descended. Rollins fidgeted in the passenger's seat. "I want to check out their place and the terrain," he said. "I get the feeling we'll be coming back here to finish this mess."

He got out of the car, padded across the street, and made his way across Vincent Davenport's grounds. For such a large house, the lack of a fence surprised me. Then again, with Todd Lakes' crack security patrol, who really needed a fence? Rollins kept low and ran past the side, then disappeared up a hill behind it. About a half-hour later, he came back, appearing alongside the home as if he'd been there all along. He ran back down to the Audi and got in, barely breathing hard.

"Good terrain," he said. "The back of the house is a lot of windows. The hill goes on for a while. Good vantage point down to them, anywhere from 500 to about 1000 meters."

"So you want to take a sniper rifle up the hill?" I said.

"You're better dealing with the family than I am."

"Sounds like we need to make a plan, then," I said.

So we did.

CHAPTER 27

BEFORE ROLLINS AND I COULD GO BACK THE NEXT NIGHT, my hearing beckoned. I woke up early, showered, had breakfast, and pondered my suit options. I own quite a few. Despite the space they consume in my closet, I rarely wear them. Each added to a nice collection, and I like having choices. Gloria stirred on the bed behind me. I considered asking her, but her soft snoring changed my mind. My goal is always to cut a sharp image in a suit, but I didn't want to look too good. I wanted to go for "well dressed but not too opulent or self-important." I opted for basic Brooks Brothers navy.

Gloria remained asleep when I needed to leave, so I let her rest. I made it to BPD Headquarters without hitting a lot of traffic, parked, and walked inside. My hearing was in a meeting room on the floor below where bigwigs like Captain Leon Sharpe maintained offices. I got off the elevator and lingered in the area. A secretary found me after a few minutes and encouraged me to wait in a nearby leather chair. I accepted.

The chamber door swung open a few minutes later. My panel already sat in there. I couldn't take it as a good sign. A state police official I'd never seen before told me they'd be ready for me in five minutes. Six minutes later, he came back and invited me inside. The room could only hold a smallish meeting, or with some conversion, a hearing like this one. Three tables pushed together at the front formed a bench for my panel. I occupied one table as did the person playing the role of the prosecution, who happened to be the trooper who summoned me inside.

My panel comprised three people: an unknown man and a woman, both clad in state police dress uniforms, and Leon Sharpe. At least I would get one vote in my favor. Maybe the state folks put Leon on the panel so it wouldn't be a shutout. I walked to my table, trying to ooze the right amount of confidence with every step, and sat in a low-backed leather chair.

The woman, sitting in the center of the panel, called the meeting to order by banging a gavel. It was an actual gavel, too, not a crab mallet, which is a popular stand-in for non-official proceedings and fantasy football leagues. These folks were making this as formal as possible. I never really considered the possibility I would lose my license. I knew I would be OK with it if it happened—finding Samantha's killer was worth the price —but for the first time, I saw it as likely rather than a distant possibility.

"I'm Major Tompkins," she said, looking at me. "This is Captain Hardy, and you know Captain Leon Sharpe of the Baltimore Police." I nodded. "The man presenting the case against you is First Sergeant Brooks. Do you have any questions before we begin?"

"No, ma'am," I said.

"I will remind you, Mr. Ferguson, that this hearing is to determine whether you should continue to hold a private investigator's license in the state of Maryland. This is not a trial. I am not a judge, and you are not under oath. However, we expect you to be honest with us. Do you understand?"

"I do," I said.

"Let's begin, then. Sergeant?"

Brooks stood up, smoothed his shirt, and cleared his throat. "Major, Captains, I'm here today to present evidence C.T. Ferguson should lose the privilege of his private investigator license." I disagreed having the license constituted a privilege but figured an objection would be tacky. Brooks wrung his hands, shoved them into his pockets, and continued. "Mr. Ferguson flouted the law and violated Anthony Tyler's civil rights when he detained, threatened, assaulted, and nearly killed him in an alley. Mr. Ferguson planned these actions in advance." Sharpe peered directly at me. I gave a small shrug with one shoulder.

"I will now move on to questions. Mr. Ferguson, did you lure Anthony Tyler into a Baltimore alley?"

"Yes."

"Under what pretense?"

"I told him to meet me, or I would tell the police what he did thirteen years ago."

"And what did he do thirteen years ago."

"He killed my sister." I watched the panel for reactions and got none. Not encouraging. "And maybe other people, as well."

"And you can prove he killed your sister?"

"Enough to make him come to Baltimore."

"Why not go to the police?" said Brooks

"Because you did such a bang-up job catching him thirteen years ago." Major Tompkins cleared her throat. "She was my sister. I wanted to take care of it."

"Did you intend to kill Anthony Tyler?"

"Is he dead?" I said.

"Answer the question, sir."

I took a deep breath and thought about my answer. "At first, yes. In the end, I realized I couldn't do it."

"Why not?"

"Because my sister would have hated it. She fought against things like violence and killing." I paused and collected myself as I felt my eyes start to well up. "I couldn't fight for her and dishonor her memory at the same time."

"But you still detained Mr. Tyler and assaulted him."

"I caught a killer," I pointed out. "A killer no police agency in the state even knew about."

"And you think results are more important than process?" Brooks said.

"You tell me. All prosecutors in the state talk about their conviction rate. Every politician wants to be 'tough on crime,' whatever the hell it means. Lieutenants and captains like to see certain numbers when it comes to closed cases. Yeah, I think results trump the process, and I think most people in your field agree with me. Even if they wouldn't go on the record and say it."

"What do you think should happen to Mr. Tyler?"

"He should go on trial," I said.

"Nothing else?"

"I hope he's found guilty. I just wish the death penalty were still an option."

"Do you think you've avenged your sister's death?" Brooks said.

I hadn't expected the question. "Yes," I said after a moment.

"Is revenge part of your job?"

"Revenge is part of justice. It's part of your job, too."

"No, it isn't."

I simply smiled. "OK."

"Your cousin stopped you, didn't he?"

"He was there," I said "He didn't stop me, though."

"So you're saying if Detective Ferguson hadn't arrived when he did, you would not have killed Mr. Tyler."

"Yes, it's what I'm saying. He didn't stop me. I stopped myself."

"Why?" Brooks pressed. "How?"

"Like I told you, I couldn't fight for my sister's memory and dishonor it at the same time."

Brooks looked at Major Tompkins. "Ma'am, I have nothing more."

"Very well, Sergeant," said Tompkins, "thank you. Mr. Ferguson, would you like to say or present anything."

I stood and buttoned the top button of my suit. It felt like a courtroom move, and this wasn't a courtroom. I kept it buttoned but walked to the front of my table and leaned against it. "I only have one question," I said. "What would you have done?"

"To whom are you addressing that, Mr. Ferguson?" Captain Hardy said. His voice, perhaps aided by his grammar, sounded professorial. He looked old enough to have learned diagramming sentences in grade school.

"Any of you. All of you. I don't care. I just want to know. If you found out after thirteen years your sister didn't die of natural causes, and you tracked down her killer, what would you do?"

"You didn't know she was murdered?" Sharpe said.

"Not until recently," I said.

They were all silent for a moment, looking at each other with varying degrees of meaning. "I'm still waiting for an answer," I said.

"I would call the police," Tompkins said.

"Bullshit," I said.

Sharpe smirked. Tompkins started to reply but stopped. After a moment of studious frowning, Hardy said, "Mr. Ferguson, I don't see the point of your question. We are not on trial here."

"Captain, unless the nature of this hearing has changed since I got here, neither am I."

This sent them back into silence for more meaningful looks and shrugs. After a minute or two, they all leaned close and whispered in such low voices they must have struggled to hear each other. "I think we have all we need, Mr. Ferguson," Tompkins said. "We will contact you—"

"Major, I still want an answer to my question," I said. "An honest answer."

She pursed her lips and looked at me. "What I would do doesn't have any bearing on what you did."

"So you'd do exactly what I did."

"I didn't say that!"

"Not in so many words," I said.

"This hearing is concluded." Tompkins frowned and banged the gavel. She glared at me. "We will contact you with a decision in a few days."

"Thank you," I said after a moment of searching for an appropriate response.

I walked out of the meeting room with no idea how the hearing might conclude. Most of the questions fell in line with what I expected. I thought I acquitted myself well, but I always think I do. The facts in the case weighed against me: I'd done everything they said I did. What I needed to rely on was the fact most people's actions would have mirrored mine in the same circumstances. Even if I couldn't get Major Tompkins to admit it, I knew she would have done the same thing.

But would it be enough to save my license?

CHAPTER 28

I WENT HOME AND CHANGED OUT OF MY SUIT AND BACK TO more practical attire. Gloria sat in the kitchen eating brunch, which consisted of a bowl of cereal and two eggs whose status lay somewhere on the "fried" spectrum. It wasn't much of a brunch, but it reflected Gloria's ability in the kitchen. One of these months, I needed to teach her some of the basics. She smiled at me as I walked behind her chair, rubbed her shoulders, and kissed her. "How did it go?" she said.

"Hard to say," I said. "I expected most of the questions."

"What do you think will happen?"

"I think it'll come down to whether they feel they would have done the same thing in my place."

"You think they would?"

I shrugged. "I think most people would. Revenge is a motive as old as time. Leon Sharpe was on my panel. I think he would have done what I did, except he would have torn Tyler to pieces with his bare hands."

Gloria shuddered and sipped her coffee. "Maybe he can put in a good word for you."

I poured myself another cup. The machine was still on and kept the java warm. Serendipity on a morning lacking it so far.

"I think he'll try. The other two people were state cops. I don't know what they'll decide."

"What if they. . . .?" she trailed off.

"Take my license away?" I said. "I'll burn a hypothetical bridge when I get to it. Maybe I'll go into business with Joey. Make him pay for the food for once."

"I'm serious." Gloria frowned at me.

"I know," I said. "So am I. I don't know what I would do, and I'm not going to lose sleep fretting about it. I have things I still need to do now."

Gloria came to me and put her arms around my chest. "I just don't want to see you stop making a difference for people."

"I'm sure I'd find a way."

"Your parents would probably make you."

I groaned. "I need to get ready to go. Rollins and I have some work to do."

"Is this the part where you tell me not to wait up?" said Gloria.

"I'm afraid so," I said.

* * *

ROLLINS and I sat in his truck to watch Jackson McMurray's house. My tracker told me Jackson had gone into Bel Air. I didn't know how he divided his time between his own place and Vincent Davenport's. I especially didn't know why Davenport would even let him live in the same ZIP code, and I didn't expect to figure it out. Jackson stood between Melinda and a life of not looking over her shoulder expecting a beating.

After about a half-hour, with the prodigal stepson still in Bel Air, Rollins got out to scout around. It was just before noon, and there were people home nearby, but I knew Rollins wouldn't care. He'd flash his illicit MP badge and make up a story. About fifteen minutes after he set out, Rollins hopped back into the truck.

"Pretty similar to the other house," he said. "Smaller windows at the back. It'll be easier for me to shoot into Davenport's."

"I hope they're considerate about your shooting," I said.

"Me, too."

The community patrol pulled up a moment later. Rollins got rid of them with a quick flash of his army shield and the same story as last night. Most people don't inspect badges when they see them. I've had people think I was a cop merely because I showed a piece of aluminum. While I bristled at the association, I would capitalize on it if it helped my cause. Rollins did the same thing.

"How long were you an MP?" I said.

"A little over a year."

"You didn't like it?"

He turned to look at me. "Why do you think I didn't?"

"Just your tone when you talk about it."

Rollins went back to looking at the house. "No, I didn't like it. Never wanted to do it."

"So why did you?" I said.

"Had a CO who didn't like me. Nobody in the military likes MPs, so he transferred me."

"Why didn't he like you?"

"Guess," said Rollins.

"Oh."

"Once the homophobe got shuffled somewhere else, I got moved back to my old unit. Never turned in the badge, though. My CO there knew I got a raw deal. Maybe it's why he forgot to ask me for it."

We waited a while longer. I sipped water, and Rollins drank iced tea. My tracker indicated Jackson left Bel Air and headed this way. "He's on the move," I said. "Looks like he's coming back home."

Rollins nodded and didn't say anything for a few minutes. Then he said, "What's gonna happen with the guy who killed your sister?"

"He'll go on trial."

"Maryland won't kill him."

I nodded. "I know."

"You gonna try?" he said.

"I used my chance."

"So he'll go on trial and the press will cover it, and at some point he'll ask the family to forgive him."

"Fuck him," I said.

"You probably can't drop the F-bomb in court."

"I'm not wired for absolution. If he wants it, let him talk to a priest. Everybody else in prison does."

A few minutes later, Jackson McMurray's silver Mercedes pulled into the driveway. Rollins and I slid down in our seats. Jackson got out carrying a small duffel bag. He went into the house and stayed there for about fifteen minutes. Then he came back, sans bag, got into his car, and drove away. I checked the GPS tracker. "He's headed toward Davenport's," I said. A minute later, the car stopped at the other house. How lazy did he need to be to drive such a short distance? "He's there. I guess we should see how long he stays."

"We'll come back tonight," Rollins said. "Doesn't matter whose place he's in."

* * *

ROLLINS and I broke off our boring surveillance for the best of reasons: lunch. We also wanted to return at night. "If you have to lie on a hill and shoot someone, you should wait until dark,"

Rollins told me. I figured either he came up with it himself or our mutual friend Colonel Stevens passed it on. Either way, it sounded like sage advice.

We didn't go far, opting for Josef's Country Inn. I expected Eastern European tough guys to seat us but settled for a cute hostess with a pretty smile. All in all, better than the alternative. Then I wondered if the Russian mob maintained restaurants to serve as obvious covers for their real business, like Tony Rizzo and *Il Buon Cibo*. They probably didn't. People loved Italian food. The Russians tendered borscht and vodka, and those weren't much competition.

The cute hostess gave way to a plain waitress who chewed gum and looked around at everything in the restaurant while she took our drink orders. Josef's offered a fabulous look at trees found anywhere in Maryland. The scenery couldn't be so interesting. She returned quickly enough with our drinks, and we asked for lunch: a burger for Rollins and something called Pleasantville Toast for me. It was seafood, dill sauce, and French bread . . . how could I go wrong?

"What do you think is going on with the old man?" Rollins said after the waitress left.

"What do you mean?"

"Why is he letting this asshole into his house?"

"I don't know," I said. "I guess he doesn't know what Jackson has done to Melinda and her . . . coworkers."

"What if he does?"

I pondered the possibility for a moment and shook my head. "Then I have no idea," I said. "Unless Jackson has some dirt on Davenport."

"What could he have?"

"No idea. Davenport's been in business a long time. A couple marriages broke up, including the one with Jackson's mother."

"It was because of what went on with their kids," Rollins said.

"Was it?" He shrugged. "It might not have been the only factor. Maybe it just gave Davenport a quick and easy way to get out of the marriage."

"Has he married since?"

"No. Maybe he learned his lesson. I guess he'd rather have a string of lovers."

"You're speculating," said Rollins.

"It's a big part of my job."

The waitress returned with our food. She set it down, didn't look at us as she asked if we needed anything else, and walked away when we replied in the negative. I would hate to see her deal with high-maintenance diners. Maybe I would need to bring Gloria here. She'd have this woman tied in knots by the appetizer round. I picked up my Pleasantville Toast. Dill sauce oozed out between the fresh seafood and the baked French bread. A mix of mild seafood and dill floated into my nostrils. I took a bite.

Josef, wherever he hailed from, knew how to make a sandwich.

While we ate, our waitress paid attention to us long enough to freshen our drinks. When she brought the check, Rollins picked it up. "I got you into this mess," he said. "Least I can do is pay for lunch."

"Damn right," I said.

"And shoot someone later, if the situation calls for it."

"At least they were courteous enough to be at the right house."

"Who said rich people were all assholes?" asked Rollins.

* * *

LATER, the tracker told me Jackson McMurray remained at Vincent Davenport's. Rollins and I put our plan in motion. He left for the back of the houses, a dark duffel bag over his shoulder. He'd dressed all in black and painted his face in the truck. Someone would have to trip over him to notice him, and even then, the odds were fifty-fifty. I gave him a few minutes, then put a tiny, flesh-colored Bluetooth earpiece into my ear. An equally small mike looked like a button on my collar. I called Rollins and he answered right away. "In position," he said.

"Breaker breaker, over," I said.

"You a truck driver now?"

"I might need to find a new job soon."

"Just leave the line open," Rollins said.

"I've done this before, you know." I walked up Vincent Davenport's driveway. Todd Lakes would lose some prestige points: my parents' driveway was longer. My mother would be thrilled to hear it.

"You've gone into a house with a sniper out back?" Rollins said.

"Does *Call of Duty* count?"

Rollins chuckled. "Just remember the layout. My best shot is at the sunroom . . . or whatever you rich folks call it."

"Sometimes, we call it a solarium to feel extra fancy," I whispered. I rang the doorbell. My watch showed a few minutes past eight. Dusk began yielding to the blackness of night. I looked up. Fallston gave me a much better look at the stars. All the ambient light in Baltimore made the sky too bright for stargazing. I recalled my fondness for astronomy as a child and identified constellations when the large door opened. A blonde woman of about forty looked back at me. Her furrowed brow lent her a frazzled appearance. "Yes?" she said, the solitary word betraying an Eastern European accent. Maybe she could work at Josef's if everything went pear-shaped for her boss.

"I'm here to see Mr. Davenport and Mr. McMurray," I said.

"They're not here." She closed her eyes for a second, probably chiding herself for leaking the fact Jackson had been there.

I knew he still was. "You're not telling me the truth."

She glanced quickly to her right, back inside the house, then regarded me again. Her blue eyes were hard. I wondered how long she'd worked for Vincent Davenport. Between her own country and Davenport family shenanigans, she must have seen a great many things. "I do not lie."

"You've probably had to lie for this family a lot. I can help you if you'll let me."

"And if I do not?"

"I'm coming in either way," I said.

The housekeeper stared at me for a moment. Then her expression softened a fraction, and she moved aside. I stepped into the front room. It reminded me of Davenport's office—tackiness and unnecessary shows of wealth, signifying nothing. The foyer had a vaulted ceiling and a marble floor transitioning to dark hardwood in the hallways. "Where are they?" I said.

"Sun room," she said, reproach coloring her accent, "where they usually are."

I knew its location based on Rollins' descriptions of the back of the house and the floor plan for Davenport's model I found online. "Nice diplomacy," Rollins said into my ear as I walked back. I saw a few pictures scattered throughout the house, mostly on walls but also on an occasional table whose purpose seemed to be holding photos. All were of Davenport, either by himself and trying to fill the empty spaces with self-importance or shaking hands with someone powerful. I saw pictures of mayors all the way back to Kurt Schmoke and governors to William Donald Schaefer. It reminded me how long Davenport spent as a power broker in Baltimore.

A minute later, I walked into the sunroom. Like Davenport's office, windows dominated its walls. I realized he tried to make his house resemble his office as much as possible. He would need as much therapy as Melinda when all of this wrapped up. Both men gaped at me as I strode into the room. Vincent Davenport scowled and stood. "What's the meaning of this?" he roared. "How did you get past Cosmina?"

"I'm not an asshole," I said. "It was such a new experience for her, she forgot to stop me."

"What do you think you're doing here?" he marched to me and stopped one step short.

"You had a chance to be honest with me in your office."

"I was honest with you, Mr. Ferguson."

"Then why is the man who arranged for your daughter to be beaten half to death here in this room?"

"You're saying Jackson had Melinda beaten?" he roared

I didn't reply. Did he know Melinda took a pounding?

Davenport stared at me. I stared back.

"Jackson?" he said after a moment. "What's the meaning of this?"

Jackson stood and looked at me. "I saw you in a parking lot," he said. "You tried to keep Melinda from me."

"One way to look at it," I said.

"She's not yours to hide away."

"She's not yours at all, Jackson. It's kind of the point."

"I still haven't heard what this is all about," said Davenport.

"The point is your boy Jackson paid to have Melinda and a good friend of mine beaten," I said.

"You said so already."

"And I'll keep saying it until it sinks in," I told him.

"She's not yours to hide away," Jackson said again, this time with an edge of desperation darkening his tone.

"I took care of your friend Kormos, by the way. He'll be all right after the bones in his face heal and he gets a lot of dental work."

"Mr. Ferguson, you should leave," Davenport said. He stared at me again.

I smiled at him. "At the risk of sounding like a child, Mr. Davenport . . . make me."

"The police can make you."

"I don't think Jackson would want you calling them."

"Don't listen to him, Dad," said Jackson.

"*Dad?*" I said, unable to contain my surprise. They both stared at me. "You aren't related anymore." I pointed at Jackson. "And hasn't he done enough damage to your actual flesh and blood?" They both kept gaping at me. "You two are fucked up."

"Melinda made her choices," Davenport said.

"You don't give up on family. I've . . . had to learn it myself."

"How touching."

"Check your phone, Mr. Davenport."

"What? Why?"

"Just do it. Close the stock reports and look at your texts."

"How did you get my private number?" he said as he retrieved a Blackberry from an endtable.

"You shouldn't insult your guests."

Davenport glowered at me again. It must have been an important boardroom tactic. Maybe his stare cowed union leaders. I ignored it. Davenport diddled with his phone. I knew he looked at the picture when the color drained from his face. "It's your daughter," I said. "You see what Jackson ordered his friend to do to her." Jackson muttered something. "Check your phone, too, asshole," I said.

He took an Android phone from another table. Jackson frowned a moment later. "There's what I did to Kormos. He hurt a friend of mine, too. He's lucky I stopped with his face."

"Fuck you," Jackson said.

"Eloquent."

"Jackson?" Davenport said. I heard small trembles in his voice. "Is this what happened?"

"You're going to listen to him?" Jackson said, pointing at me in the event of any confusion. "Him? Over me? I'm your son!"

"Stepson," I said.

"Shut up," Jackson said. "Just shut up!" He went back to the table holding his phone and opened a drawer. A second later, he held a pistol in his hand. My pulse quickened. I knew Rollins covered me from outside, but someone pointing a gun at me spiked the heart rate. The day it didn't, I needed to quit.

"Jackson, put that gun down," Davenport said.

"Yes, Jackson," I said. "Put the gun down, before someone gets shot." I said it more for Rollins' benefit than for Jackson's.

"You mean like you?" he said.

I heard a muffled report a microsecond before a large window at the back of the sunroom exploded. Jackson staggered forward from an impact I didn't see. The semiautomatic tumbled from his hand as he pitched forward. Davenport dropped into a crouch and looked around with panicked eyes. "What the hell?" he said.

Jackson lay on the floor, clutching his left buttock. Blood oozed from between his fingers. The gun, a new-looking nine-millimeter, lay about six inches from his fingers. I walked to it and kicked it away, sending it sliding across the hardwood into the darkness of the yawning doorway beyond. "No, Jackson," I said. "I mean like you."

"Mr. Ferguson?"

"I didn't come alone, Mr. Davenport. I couldn't predict how Jackson would react."

"Will he be all right?"

"I don't think he'll be able to sit down for a while, but he'll live."

"Did he really do what you say he did?" I nodded. Davenport closed his eyes and shook his head. "What do I do now?"

"Go see your daughter, Mr. Davenport. She hasn't given up on you, even though she should have."

"I don't deserve her devotion."

"You're right; you don't. But you have it nonetheless. Don't squander it."

I walked out of the sunroom and left them as they were.

CHAPTER 29

When I arrived home, Gloria was already asleep upstairs. She heard me as I entered the bedroom and sat up as if waking from a nightmare. Even in the dark, I made out confusion and concern on her face, then saw them washed away by relief as she realized I'd come home. She sprang up and wrapped me in a tight hug. "I was worried about you."

"Everything went according to plan," I said.

"Davenport?"

"I think he's going to see his daughter."

"Really?" she said

"She still loves him. It's more than he deserves."

"What about Jackson?"

"Rollins shot him right in the ass," I said.

Gloria laughed. "Sounds like everything is going to work out."

"I hope Davenport and Melinda can patch things up. They need each other. He's as bad as she is."

"I'm just glad you're home."

"Me, too," I said.

"Tired?"

"Extremely."

"Come to bed," Gloria said with a smile.

I did. We were both asleep within a minute.

* * *

WHILE I ATE BREAKFAST, my phone rang. It was Melinda. "My father came to see me," she said. I couldn't tell much from her tone.

"Did he?"

"He didn't say you put him up to it . . ."

"I didn't. He wondered if he should go. I told him you still wanted him to, and I told him it was more than he deserved."

"Well, he came."

"How did it go?" I said.

"It went OK. It was good to see him again . . . to talk to him." Melinda's tone perked up. "In some weird way, I think he needs me as much as I need him."

"I think you're right."

"Thanks, C.T."

"Where do you two go from here?" I said.

"I don't know. He invited me to move back in with him when I'm discharged."

"And?"

"I think I will," Melinda said. "It's better than the alternative. Then we'll see about starting over."

I downed a mouthful of coffee. "I'm sure it will be easier with him behind you."

"I think it will. Maybe we'll even give you the credit for all of it."

"All of it?" I said.

"I'm Vincent Davenport's long-lost daughter. Missing for

five years and all that. It's a big story. I'm sure Dad has people who are already spinning it for him. I'll see if I can work your name in."

"I hope the spin doctors let you."

"Me, too," said Melinda.

* * *

AFTER LUNCH, I got another phone call. This time, caller ID indicated it was Leon Sharpe or someone in his office. I wondered if the panel at my hearing reached a decision. Only one way to find out. "Hello, C.T.," he said when I picked up.

"Wow," I said, "not your secretary asking me to hold for you. This must be important."

"I wanted to call and tell you myself."

"Didn't want someone else to cut my professional head off?"

"If anyone is going to pull your license, it'll be me."

"How reassuring, but you'll have to get it from Rich."

"You can get it from him yourself," Sharpe said, "so long as you wait thirty days."

I paused. Sharpe hadn't called to tell me I was done, after all. "I'm suspended?"

"Technically, I'm supposed to get you to turn in your guns, too, but this is a dangerous city. Try not to shoot anyone else for the next month, will you?"

"I don't plan to," I said.

"Maybe you should take a vacation."

"Maybe I will. How much did you have to do with the decision?"

"I don't think anyone actually wanted to pull your license. Maybe they only needed a few minutes with me to realize it."

"Whatever you did," I said, "I appreciate it."

"Sounds like you've come to like your work. I didn't know if you'd come around."

"It took me a while."

"I'll deny I ever said this if someone asks me," Sharpe said, "but you do good work. I'm glad we have you on the job."

"Thanks, Leon."

"Don't mention it. Now get out of town and don't shoot anyone on your way." Then he hung up.

Thirty days. I wouldn't need to find something else to do, after all. I breathed a sigh of relief as I set my phone back on the table.

MY PARENTS HAVE OWNED a timeshare for years. They rarely use it because they'll end up going away with friends for two weeks and renting a palace. When wealthy, aging couples get together, only a palace will do. The result is my parents' time-share account accrues unused weeks. Because I know the password my mother uses for everything, I accessed their account with ease, transferred three unused weeks to myself, and traded them in for three weeks in Hawaii. Then I paid for the fourth week. Might as well be gone for thirty days.

"Pack your bags," I said to Gloria. "We're going on vacation."

"Really?" she said, her eyes widening and a hopeful smile dominating her face.

"Really. My parents never use their timeshare, so we're going to Hawaii for four weeks. We're staying at the Ko Olina Beach Club."

Gloria wrapped me in a hug and kissed me. "Our first vacation as a couple," she said.

I hadn't thought about it, but she was right. Now I had to hope Gloria didn't attach too much significance to this trip. I merely wanted to get out of town, not think about cases or my sister's murder for a few weeks, and have sex with my girlfriend in one of the most beautiful places on earth. No diamond ring would find its way into my luggage.

"I'll book the flights," she said. "I have a ton of miles from my tennis tournaments."

"Sounds good," I said.

The next day, we departed Dulles International Airport on a nonstop flight to Honolulu.

* * *

GLORIA and I spent most of our first two days in Ko Olina in bed, alternately sleeping off the six-hour time difference and tiring ourselves out. We'd become well acquainted with our large and quite nice hotel room. Even Gloria couldn't find fault with it. On our third day, we ventured out to the private sand of the Ko Olina Beach Club. Blue water splashed onto the white shore. The Hawaiian sun, about forty degrees warmer than Maryland this time of year, made for perfect bathing suit weather, and Gloria wore the perfect bikini. It would be a pity to stop gawking at her long enough to get into the water. Thankfully, Gloria got in, and I stayed on the beach, allowing me to stare at her as the water washed over her body.

As we lay out on our *chaise longues*, my phone rang. I'd gotten a few calls from strange numbers so far and ignored them all. This swell of publicity normally happens after I close a case. If Melinda name-dropped me to the press, my potential incoming business would be greater than normal. Regardless, it could wait a month. This time, however, my parents called. I answered it. "Coningsby, you've been awfully quiet of late," my mother said.

"There's been a lot going on," I said.

"Yes. Richard told us." She emphasized my cousin's name, no doubt in an attempt to make me feel bad. Being in paradise with a beautiful woman, however, is a great way to mitigate guilt.

"I figured he would."

I could hear my mother sniff and tsk over the phone. "I know we've experienced a trying few weeks, Coningsby. Let's have dinner soon. We can celebrate."

"Sounds nice, Mom," I said, "but I'm out of town."

"Oh. For how long?"

"Four weeks."

"Four weeks!"

"My license got suspended for what I did to the bastard who killed Samantha. I figured I might as well take Gloria and get out of town. So we got *way* out of town."

"Where are you?" she said.

"Hawaii."

"Well, you certainly went far. Are you staying someplace nice?"

"Have we met?" I said.

"Of course you are. Between you and Gloria, I can't imagine you're at anything less than a fine resort."

"You know us." I didn't tell her I cashed in their timeshare weeks. They'd probably never know.

"It sounds very nice."

Being in paradise with a beautiful woman goes a long way toward overcoming a troubled conscience, but it can't eradicate the feeling. A small pang gnawed at me. "Do you want to come out here?" I said, wincing as the words left my mouth.

"That sounds nice, Coningsby. Thank you for the offer. But you and Gloria enjoy your time away. We'll catch up when you get back."

"All right, Mom."

"Your father and I put some money into your account. I know you helped someone else too, dear, but this is the most important work you've done yet."

My nod was invisible to her half an ocean and a continent away. "It really is. Thanks, Mom."

"Enjoy yourself out there, Coningsby. And if you're going to propose, make sure you get down on one knee."

"Mom!"

"Goodbye, dear."

"'Bye."

Gloria walked to me, dripping water from her small, provocative two-piece as she approached. I watched with interest as drops ran down her neck and over her breasts. I couldn't wait to peel the suit from her later. "Who was on the phone?" she said as she grabbed a towel.

"My mother."

"Oh. What did she want?"

"Nothing we can't put off about four weeks," I said.

END of Novel #5

Dear reader,

I hope you enjoyed the book. It was definitely C.T.'s most personally challenging case so far—and my favorite to write.

C.T.'s next adventure sees him searching for a missing girl and taking on the Internet's worst predators in *A March from Innocence*.

· · ·

Thanks,
    Tom

THE END

Do you like free books? You can get the prequel novella to the C.T. Ferguson mystery series for free. This is unavailable for sale and is exclusive to my readers. Visit https://bit.ly/CTprequel to get your book!

If you enjoyed this novel, I hope you'll leave a review. Even a short writeup makes a difference. Reviews help independent authors get their books discovered by more readers and qualify for promotions. To leave a review, go to the book's sales page, select a star rating, and enter your comments. If you read this book on a tablet or phone, your reading app will likely prompt you to leave a review at the end.

The C.T. Ferguson Crime Novels:

1. The Reluctant Detective
2. The Unknown Devil
3. The Workers of Iniquity
4. Already Guilty
5. Daughters and Sons
6. A March from Innocence

7. Inside Cut
8. The Next Girl
9. In the Blood

While this is the suggested reading sequence, the books can be enjoyed in whatever order you happen upon them.

The John Tyler Thrillers

1. The Mechanic
2. White Lines (Summer 2021)

Connect with me:

For the many ways of finding and reaching me online, please visit https://tomfowlerwrites.com/contact. I'm always happy to talk to readers.

This is a work of fiction. Characters and places are either fictitious or used in a fictitious manner.

"Self-publishing" is something of a misnomer. This book would not have been possible without the contributions of many people.

- The cover design team at 100 Covers.
- My editor extraordinaire, Chase Nottingham.
- My wonderful advance reader team, the Fell Street Irregulars.

9 781953 603104